Wherever Our Journey Lead Us

Alec and Aliah's Story

By

SM Stryker

SM STRYKER

TO JOIN MY MAILING LIST AND TO RECEIVE A FREE COPY OF
WHISPERS IN THE WIND
PLEASE SIGN UP HERE.

WWW.SMSTRYKER.COM

CONTENTS

SM STRYKER

WHEREVER OUR JOURNEY LEADS US

TITLES BY SM STRYKER

-----~”*°•.♡.♡.♡.•°*”~-----

Falling into You
Beckett
Mitchell
Carson
Richard
The Locket
Whispers in The Wind
Then There Was You
For Better or For Worse
Wink
Wishes on Falling Stars
When You Loved Me — Coming Soon

SECOND CHANCE SERIES
-----~”*°•.♡.♡.♡.•°*”~-----

Beckett
Mitchell
Carson
Richard

THEN THERE WAS YOU SERIES
-----~”*°•.♡.♡.♡.•°*”~-----

Whispers in The Wind
Then There Was You
For Better or For Worse
Wherever the Journey Leads Us

WHEREVER OUR JOURNEY LEADS US

Dear Reader,

Just a quick note that the beginning of Wherever Our Journey Leads Us, runs concurrently with the end of For Better or For Worse, so some events you will see again but from another perspective. I hope you enjoy Alec and Aliah's story. If you haven't read the previous three books, no worries. You'll be able to follow this book fine without, although you will have a better understanding of some of the other characters if you read them in order.

SM STRYKER

It is the deepest pain that empowers you to grow into your most spiritual self. The pain you feel today is the strength you'll feel tomorrow. Push through it. There's a reason for every hardship. Nothing worthwhile ever came from easy times or simple lessons. Spiritual and soul growth comes from perseverance, belief, courage, and strength. Have faith in the journey. ~Vishwas🕉

PROLOGUE

Strength comes from love and forbearance ~ which helps you through the most difficult times ~ Strengthen and mold the fabric of your heart ~ softly ~ It will lift your spirit ~
~Vishwas ॐ

BEFORE

ALEC
1995

Feeling devastated, as though someone has kicked me in the gut. I'm finding it hard to breathe. My life as I've known it is gone, as I sit in an old beat up and oxidized plastic chair that looks as if it was recycled from the dump instead of holding mourners of a funeral home. Is this what we get because we had very little money, and I wanted them buried instead of cremated? We just buried my mom and dad, and I can't bring myself to leave, so I sit at the foot of their freshly dug gravesite in this rickety old plastic chair hoping it with withstand my weight. The noise of the freeway, just yards from where I sit, has me glancing up. My parents' plots are only feet from the parking lot. No headstones; nothing to signify just how special these two people were to me. This isn't where they should be for their final resting spot. But after pulling all the money out of my college fund, this is all I could afford. It's not as if the mortuary would give me a loan. I'm only seventeen, and my job at the restaurant sure as hell isn't going to pay the bill. I don't have a choice. This will have to do for now. But I swear to all things holy that I will do everything in my power to give them a place that's quiet and peaceful.

I told Connor, my best friend and neighbor, to take my sister home. I needed to be alone and think about the papers I received. I haven't told Natasha about them yet. She can barely cope with the deaths of our parents four days ago, let alone the idea that she's being taken away from us.

The stiff document neatly folded in the front pocket of my suit jacket is burning me. I don't want to read it again. Maybe if I don't look at the papers this whole thing will all go away. I'm afraid to believe what they say. When the man and woman approached me and handed me the legal documents at the funeral service earlier today and introduced themselves as my aunt and uncle, I was stunned and taken aback at their revelation. Mom and Dad said we didn't have family, but the document they gave me states otherwise.

The woman, Susan, is supposed to be my mother's sister; my aunt, and the man; David is her husband. Something doesn't feel right, but what am I supposed to do? What am I supposed to believe?

God, I'm seventeen; I don't know anything about legal shit.

My fingers tremble as I pull the papers out of my jacket, reading them over again.

DISTRICT COURT

MULTNOMAH COUNTRY, OREGON

In the Matter of the Guardianship of:
Connor Nash
Natasha Nash
A Protected Minor.

LETTERS OF GUARDIANSHIP

On the 4th day of April 1995, a Court Order was entered appointing Susan Welch and David Welch as Guardians of the above-named protected minors. The named Guardians, having duly qualified, are authorized to act and have authority to perform the duties of such Guardians as provided by law.

In testimony of which, I have this date signed these Letters and affixed the Seal of the Court.

Flipping the page, I continue to read.

OATH OF GUARDIAN

I Susan Welch, residing at: 235 Commons Place, Cleveland, Ohio 44110 whose mailing address is: 235 Commons Place, Cleveland, Ohio 44110 solemnly affirm that I will well and faithfully perform the duties of Guardian according to law. I affirm that any matters stated in any petition, document or court preceding are true of my own knowledge or if any matters are stated on information or belief, I believe them to be true.

I declare under penalty of perjury under the law of the State of Oregon that the foregoing is true and correct.

EXECUTED this 4th day of April 1995.

There is so much I don't understand. Two strangers' hand me legal papers and I'm supposed to just let them take my sister? I don't even have twenty-four hours with her. It's the goddamn weekend. Mr. and Mrs. Nash, Connor's parents, made an appointment with their lawyer to look over the papers, but I can't get in until Monday. By then, Nat will be gone.

God, I wish I knew what to do. The document states that I'm supposed to go too, but there's no way in hell that I'm leaving. Especially moving across the country. I'll be eighteen in twelve days, but Natasha... she's only fifteen. There has to be a way to keep them from taking her. Connor's parents have told Susan and David that they will gladly be her guardian, why take her from everything she knows? This is her home. All her friends are here. We are here, but they adamantly refused.

I keep staring at the date. Our parents died the evening of the fourth, so how could these people have been granted guardianship when they weren't dead yet? No court would be open that time of night. Would it? And how did anyone know that they had even died? It wasn't until after midnight on the fifth that the police knocked on our door telling us about the accident.

But again, why didn't we know we had an aunt and uncle? Why would our parents keep this from us? Why would they lie? There has to be a good reason.

CHAPTER 1

*It takes a lot of strength to push through hard times. Have faith.
Sometimes it's all you've got to keep you going. ~Vishwas* ॐ

ALEC

Bounding abruptly out of my chair in horrified, as it topples over at the words the lawyer tells me, words that will haunt me for the rest of my life. *"The papers are fake."*

My God, who were these people and what... Fuck. Nat. What are they planning on doing with her. My gut twists as I bolt to the bathroom, as I begin to wretch at the thought.

Rinsing the bitter taste of bile from my mouth, my hands propped on the countertop, I find my reflection in the mirror. Dark circles ring my red swollen eyes. The only color in my face is the blotchy red patches from my tears. Upon returning to Mr. Halsey's office, I pick up my fallen chair, noting the concern etched in everyone's faces. "I'm sorry." Shaking my head, I brush the falling tears from my cheek. "I just can't imagine what could be..." My stomach sinks at the thought of what's happening with Nat. I'm unable to finish my thought. Glancing around the room, I spot Mrs.

Nash, Connor's mother, dabbing tears from her eyes as Mr. Nash wraps his arm around her, drawing her close to his side. Connor looks just as bad as I do. After all, we are like brothers and even though he hasn't said anything, I know he has feelings for Nat, and she for him. I could see it in the way they looked at each other, but right now, I don't care, I just want Nat back.

The property search, Mr. Halsey conducted also proved to be false. My heart stutters in my chest, and I can't catch my breath, I'm going to be sick again. I might be a kid, but I've seen enough news to know what can happen to young girls. With no leads to where they were going, it will be nearly impossible to find her.

Feeling helpless, I ache to hear her voice, anything to know she's alright. Slipping my phone from my pocket, I'm hoping maybe she'll answer this time. I push her name on my phone and wait, anxiously to hear her voice. My stomach sinks when I hear the unfamiliar voice on the other end of the phone. *"Welcome to Verizon wireless, your call could not be completed as dialed. Please check the number and dial again."* No, there must be something wrong. I hit the little green circle again. *"Welcome to Verizon wireless, your call could not be completed as dialed..."* Pressing the red dot, I end the call. My eyes sting, as tears fall once again. "I should have gone with them. I shouldn't have let them take her. This is my fault," I cry out. "At least I could have protected her if I'd gone with her."

"We'll find her, Alec. I promise to God we'll find her. If it's the last thing I do, we'll never stop searching for her." Connor clasps my face forcing me to meet his gaze, showing me he's just as distraught and scared as I am.

Mr. Halsey called the police notifying them of a child kidnapping, but with no way to know where they were headed or if they were driving or flying. Not that it mattered. They could have rented another car and crossed any state lines by now. Our options are bleak.

I need a private investigator to find her. If they've taken her out of state, I don't want my only option to be the police; the thought terrifies me. I've tried to call the number they gave me, and it all makes sense now, the reason I kept getting the *out of service* notification.

Gripping at my hair, I yank at it in fear and frustration, I don't know what to do. Hell, I'm just a kid. I'm sure most adults wouldn't know what to do if their loved one was kidnapped. How could I be so stupid to just let them take her? Sighing, I know why, because when I told them no, they threatened to have me arrested for breaking a court order; they called it contempt of court, I think. I was concerned about getting arrested, it was about them taking her and losing contact with her. If I'm in jail, how could I help her. My mind plays a mental game of ping pong of what I should a, would a, could a done.

"I've called every official agency that works with lost or exploited children and even put her face on milk cartons and in the papers. And since they said they were leaving the state, we can get the FBI involved. The police and FBI will want to interview you later for your statement."

"Thank you, Mr. Halsey," I say, standing. I have no choice now; I have to become a man; the man of the family; a man who has to find the only family he has left.

I reach my hand out to him. He comes around his desk, clapping me on the shoulder. "I'm sure they'll do their best to bring her home."

Head down, I follow behind Mr. and Mrs. Nash, feeling like a lost puppy dog that's been kicked. I give Connor a side eye; he looks as glum as I feel. He brushes away a stray tear with the sleeve of his letterman's jacket.

The drive back to the house is a quiet one. I have so many questions and no one to answer them.

Needing money to hire a private investigator, I begin the tedious task of selling everything I have of value. The house and all the furnishings are up for sale. I'm only keeping a few personal items. Family photo albums, Mom's jewelry, and a safe that I found in a hidden crawlspace behind Mom and Dad's bed the day a consignment shop came in to pick up the furniture. It wasn't a large safe, but it took a lot of work to get it out from the tiny space it was hiding in. It had to have weighed close to a hundred pounds. It took the three of us and Mr. Nash's hydraulic lift to get it out. We moved it to Mr. Nash's garage for now. It has both a combination and a key lock. After gathering up all the keys I could find in the house, I set them on Connor's Dad's workbench next to the safe. Each time a key would slide into the lock my stomach would twist with hope and anticipation, then when it wouldn't turn, my hopes plummeted. Discouraged and frustrated, we went through all the keys not finding one that would open it.

I tried every combination I could think of for the code as well. Mom's birthday, Dad's, Nat's and mine, nothing worked. It became an obsession for the whole family. Even the manufacturer couldn't help us since we couldn't prove it belonged to my parents. I finally put it in storage with the rest of my things once I graduated from high school.

The private investigator I hired, came back with nothing. Nothing on Natasha and nothing on my so-called aunt and uncle. So far, he's been a waste of money.

After using my college funds to pay for my parents' funeral and their plots, I knew college was out of reach for me, but I also knew I needed an education if I was ever going to get enough money to find Nat. Prior to graduation, our high school sponsored a job fair. That's where I met a marine recruiter. To be honest, I hadn't ever given it a second thought because I grew up knowing I was going to go to college. It's funny how things can change in the blink of an eye. I'm literally homeless, penniless and my outlook on ever getting a well-paying job is looking grim.

Connor and I are checking out all the different companies represented at the job fair and what kind of education they require. That's when I knew there was only one option for me. I stopped so quickly in front of the recruiter Connor slammed into my back. "Oof, what the hell, Alec?"

I am not the only one having a difficult time with the loss of Natasha. Connor is taking it just as hard as I am. He's been my best friend since birth. Our families were close. I could see it in the way he looked at Nat. He cared for her, and maybe even more. Yeah, we were the three musketeers, but this was more. I genuinely believe he loved her. Of course, he never said anything to me, probably because he knew I would kill him for even thinking that way about her. But deep down, I knew he would protect her with his life, and this was gutting him.

It didn't take much for me to sign on the bottom line when they handed me the recruitment papers. I didn't need to talk it over with anyone because there was no one, but I was surprised when Connor signed up. He does have a family, and this is a huge decision that should be talked about with his family. "You go, I go," he said. "This is our best way to find her."

"Your parents are going to kill me. They're going to think I talked you into this." The last thing I want is to carry the burden of Connor's life on my shoulders. If anything happens to him, I'll never forgive myself.

"And what do you think I'm going to do if you get yourself shot at without a good wingman?" He slaps me on the back. "Besides, where else can I go to have someone pay for my food, housing, and clothing, not to mention, pay for my education?" He chuckles. "I'm a growing boy, I can't afford to feed myself," he chuckles.

CHAPTER 2

There are many paths that lead to one road. No one can give you faith and no one can choose for you what you believe. ~Vishwas ॐ

ALEC

We were told not to bring anything other than our civilian ID when we left for boot camp.

I'd been told the United States Marine Corps boot camp training is the longest and toughest of all the armed services. Not only are their physical requirements tougher, but all recruits are required to memorize a lot of information.

Our education began the moment we stepped out of the bus onto the yellow footprints. Thirteen weeks of the most challenging experience of our lives. Everyone had the opportunity to call their loved ones, letting them know we made it, that was one call I didn't have to make... I had no one. We were then searched for contraband and issued basic uniforms and toiletries. At that point, we had to surrender all our civilian possessions including our underwear.

After that when we were shaved... bald. Then more paperwork, medical and dental screenings, and numerous vaccinations. I was exhausted. I couldn't wait until I could close my eyes and sleep. But that wasn't to be. By the second night, I was wondering what I had gotten myself into and from the looks of it so was Connor—I guess I need to start calling him by his last name, now that we're in the military. Thank God, I kept in shape, because the physical fitness test was fucking hard. Muscles that I didn't even know I had, ached.

Then black Friday came, and I don't mean the fun shopping after Thanksgiving. That's when we met our drill instructors. I understand the experience in boot camp is to simulate the stress in combat and to provoke immediate responses to orders but, fuck me. They give you one "out" to come clean about drug use or other disqualifying conditions and from then on, you have no choice but to become a marine.

Thirteen weeks later, we're finally referred to as marines.

We have ten days off before having to report back for training, and I don't have a minute to spare. I didn't even have to say anything to Nash. We both knew we were driving to the address that was given to us. I've come to the conclusion the address isn't real I'm just hoping I can find something, anything, a breadcrumb is all I need. But of course, we find nothing but an empty lot.

Driving back, we both feel dejected.

CHAPTER 3

It's ok if you fall down and lose your spark. Just make sure that
when you get back up, you rise as the whole damn fire ~Vishwasॐ

ALIAH
1997

Standing in my doorway, I stare out at the street. The new
government laws will not allow me to leave my home without a
male relative. I have no one. When my father and mother found I
was with child, they left, ashamed of me. I dishonored my family.

The war is getting worse. I cannot go to school. I cannot go to
the market to gather food. I am a prisoner in my own home, I will
die without food and water. This is the reason my parents left. It
was their way of killing me without having to touch me. After
rationing out what little food I had left, I knew I only had one
choice to survive.

My belly grows with child and I am afraid I will not be able to
save myself to save my child.

When it is dark, I sneak out to find wasted food scraps, or go to the spring to get water. If I am caught, I will be punished, but I must try to save my baby.

I remember my Joe. He brought me food and water and taught me a little English. He was kind. He had pretty blue eyes and would come back day after day. He showed me how to love and put his baby in me. Then he was gone.

Now I am scared and alone.

CHAPTER 4

"The real you is found when your heart is broken yet it dares to fight back ~Taleeb

ALEC
2002

It's been a while since I've been back in the states. I feel like a vagabond, traveling from country to country, never staying in one place longer than the next. It's getting old, and I'm getting tired, but something is going on. I don't know what it is, but I feel it in my gut. I felt it right before Nash was shot by a sniper while we were on a peacekeeping mission. That just doesn't happen. Yes, if we were in a hot zone, but we weren't; it was a goddamn peace mission.

We were traveling to small villages bringing food and supplies to the impoverished villagers. The country has been in a drought leaving little food or water.

If there was any luck in this whole goddamn thing it's that the bullet hit his flak jacket. Connor was shot in the shoulder which was protected by his flak jacket. The force of the bullet broke his collarbone. It was another close call. There have been a lot of those over the years, and I don't mean from our missions. Cars would swerve out of nowhere barely missing us, muggings gone wrong when the attacker's gun would jam allowing us to catch them, and beat the shit out of them, and car accidents that didn't happen because of quick thinking and great driving skills; these are just a few coincidences we've found ourselves in.

Nash will be out for at least six weeks, so I decide to take leave for a couple of weeks myself. I know I need to go back, I'm just months away from retiring from the marines, but I just want a little down time.

Coming back to home stirs up all the memories of Natasha. I think about her every day and pray to God she's safe. Over the years, we've hired private investigator to find anything, but she's vanished, as have my aunt and uncle.

As usual, when I come home, I head over to the storage unit, my notepad, with all the different number combinations either I've tried or want to try, in hand.

The storage unit is small, but then again, I only had a few personal items that I wanted to keep.

Mom was a crafter. Smiling, I remember the spare room she made into her craft room, but God, she was talented. She made all sorts of artsy things selling them at the local bazaars for extra cash at Christmas.

One year she gave us Nat and I the most amazing scrap books. She gathered all our old photos she and Dad had taken of us as children along with others that I'd never seen before and personalized them for each of us. Almost all the pictures had the three of us in them. We were never apart.

Feeling a little nostalgic, I locate the box that has my book in it and pull it out. Then I flop into Dad's old leather recliner; it's the only piece of furniture I couldn't get rid of, it held too many memories.

Getting comfortable, I flip open the cover. Each page is filled with bittersweet memories. Reaching the end, I notice a message that I don't remember seeing before. But as a kid—let me rephrase that—as a teenage boy, only concerned about girls and sports, I was in my own little world. Scrap books didn't mean what they mean to me now.

Running my fingers over her perfect inscription, I reread it again.

There is only one place you can find the truth. *"Ask and it will be given to you; seek and you will find; knock and the door will be opened to you."* Matthew 7:7

My heart races as shivers cover my body. A memory flashes me back to my childhood, the family Bible, but I was so upset, I don't remember if I kept it. Jumping from the chair, I begin to ransack the boxes and hope to God, I kept it.

Opening one of the last boxes, I freeze as it stares up at me. A feeling of relief but anxiety spreads through me. Reverently, I lift it out of the box, swiping my hand over the dusty cover hoping to find some answers. Flipping through the pages, I don't see anything. No writing, no highlighting nothing. I'm back at square one.

Frustrated, I toss the bible back into the box, not understanding. Maybe that was just Mom's advice to me.

I'm done. I don't know what to do. As I turn to close the storage room door, a loud crash echoes throughout the unit. *Fuck!* Upon throwing the door back up, I see the old cardboard box that I'd tossed the Bible in has fallen, all its contents littering the floor. Damnit, that also held Mom's jewelry box, which is now lying shattered.

My heart aches at the thought of breaking something so precious, and I shake my head in shame. That's what I get for disrespecting the Bible that Mom cherished. Tears flood my eyes. I know how much that jewelry box meant to her. She was always so protective of it. I remember when Nat got into it when she was a small child. I don't think I ever saw my mother that mad before or since... Oh God!

I drop to my knees and cautiously pick up her scattered jewelry, careful not to step on any of it and hoping I don't miss any of it. Maybe I can glue it back together. Lifting the jewelry box, I notice one of the bottom drawers is loose and falling apart. Inspecting it, I notice an extra bottom to one of the drawers. I remove the false piece, exposing a metal key. My heart skips a beat, and my hand is shaking as I slowly reach for the key. The old dried tape is yellowed that has held it secure, hidden for years. It's been sixteen years and I finally found the key. I didn't even have to wonder. I knew what it's to. I feel it in my gut.

When it easily slides into the lock of the safe and turns, I exhale; hadn't realized I'd been holding my breath. Opening the door, I'm suddenly apprehensive. Thick files and a couple of journals fill the interior. Upon pulling them out, I open the first one and begin to scan them, gleaning information and processing it.

Oh my God. I think my parents were murdered. My heart thunders in my chest, battering hard against my ribs. I need to take these to someone, but to whom? This is so much worse than I had ever thought.

CHAPTER 5

ALEC
2002

Back on base, I'm getting ready to go in country for the last time. In a couple months I'll be out, and Nash and I can start the business we had talked about, a security company. After all, that's what we've been doing for the last seven years.

Nash is still pulling desk duty while his shoulder heals. I didn't tell him about the safe yet, not wanting to pull him into it if I don't have to, so instead I gave it to my commanding officer Major Bryant.

While I'm eating my chow in the mess hall, my phone chimes signaling an incoming email. It's a Google alert that's popped up on my screen, a picture in the Living Section of the New York Times. Not understanding why I would receive anything from the New York Times, I enlarge the page to get a better look at the photo. My fork clatters loudly as it drops to the floor.

Gasping to draw oxygen into my lungs, I begin to choke on my scrambled eggs. "Oh fuck," I mutter, studying the photo. Clicking

the link, I read the announcement. It has to be her, but the name...
That's not her last name. Why would she change it? Examining the
photo, I stare at her eyes, my eyes. I know it's been seven years, but
God. Although her smile looks a little forced, she's grown up into
a beautiful woman. Feelings rush over me, but I can't define them.
Yes, I'm excited that I think I finally found my baby sister, but
who's the old man she's marrying? And why the name change? Was
it to hide her from us?

ENGAGEMENT ANNOUNCEMENT
KINGSTON - WELCH
Truly a Cinderella Story
International Financier Louis Kingston III
is pleased to announce his impending
nuptials to Natasha Welch an Event Planner
The groom's father is International
Financier Louis Kingston II of Kingston
Investments and his mother Socialite Muffy
Kingston
The bride was raised by David and Susan
Welch.
The couple will wed at Bourne Mansion in
Long Island, New York
August 2, 2002

I do a search for all the event companies in New York. Dialing
each one, desperate to find her. Every time the phone rings, my

heart speeds with the possibility of finally knowing I have found her. Seven goddamn years of looking. Praying that she's been okay.

I've called a dozen or more agencies and my excitement of finding her is waning. God, I don't even know that she's living in New York, but I have to keep trying.

The phone rings again. "Elegant Beginnings, how may I help you?"

"Yes, Natasha Turn... I mean Natasha Welch please."

"Just one moment please."

This is it, I found her! Finally, after seven years of searching she's within my grasp. As I read the engagement announcement again, my chest tightens, emotion lodges in my throat. I thought I had more time, but I'm being shipped out soon. I wish I had Nash to talk to about this, but if I'd told him my plan, they might figure it out before I get the truth.

My train of thought flashes back when I hear the voice on the phone.

"Elegant Beginnings, this is Natasha, how can I help you?"

Thank God, I finally found her.

Her voice sounds so refined, cultured.

It was just a fluke that my Google alert on her popped up today with the notice of her recent engagement. I'd put every name in the alert that I could remember. I'm glad I had especially since the Google alert popped up with a different last name.

"Nat?" It's almost a whisper, still not believing it could be possible. I understand this is a shock for her, but why isn't she saying anything? "Nat, it's me... Alec."

"Alec? Is it really you?" Her voice is quiet, as if not understanding it's me on the line.

"Thank God. We've been searching for you for years."

I don't know how my aunt and uncle were able to get guardianship of Nat, what power do they have over her. She's and adult now. God, I didn't think I would ever see her again. She was gone, smoke in the wind, vanished. All the contact information we were given was bogus; fake numbers, phony addresses, everything. For all we knew, they sold her into the sex slave trade.

"Seven fucking years, you've waited seven fucking years and now you contact me?" Her voice is a low rumble. She's furious. "Go fuck yourself!"

I'm taken aback at her anger. "Hello? Nat?" What the fuck? She hung up on me. I never thought I would get this kind of reaction. She fucking hung up on me.

When I realized that the guardianship papers from Susan and David were fake, I panicked. I'm afraid I'll never be able to find her. I was cut off with no way to contact her. I started to look further into them and what they had to gain in taking Nat. God only knows what's happened to her these last seven years.

I don't have much time. Our team is leaving on a mission. Dialing her back, I need her to understand that I—hell, we never forgot about her.

"Elegant—"

"Nat, please don't hang up." My voice comes out in a rush. She needs to hear me out. I need her to understand. "Just give me one minute, please."

I could hear the anger in her voice, in the exasperated breath. "One minute, that's one minute more than you've fuckin' given me the last seven years."

"It's not what you think Nat. We've been trying to find you. It's a long story, which would take more time than I have. I'm going in country..."

Nat gasps. "What do you mean you're going in country?" Her voice cracks as her words come out slow and accentuated.

"I'm heading back to Afghanistan..."

Another audible gasp, but this time I hear her voice quiver. "My God, Alec! What are you doing there? Why?"

"Nat, I don't have much time to talk, I'm heading out, but I needed to talk to you before I leave. I'll be back in a couple months and we'll come and get you."

"Alec, I don't want to wait. I need you. I need to get out of here."

I know I don't have much time. I don't know what I'll do if I can't get to her in time. According to the engagement announcement, they're getting married in three months. That's quick for a society affair. What's the rush? "I promise, I'll be back to get you. I have to go Nat, I love you. Remember that. Always. Remember, I always keep my promises."

She's crying. *Fuck*, I don't know what she's been going through, but fucking hell, Nat doesn't cry. "I love you too, Alec. You better keep your promise, or I'll kill you myself."

Chuckling, she could always bring a smile to my face. "It's a deal. Bye sis."

"Bye Alec."

"Turner, Major Bryant's requesting to see you," I hear from outside my room. Grabbing my gear, I push through my door and wonder what he wants. Maybe he found something out.

Knocking on Major Bryant's door, I hear his low gruff voice on the other side. "Enter."

I open the door and salute my CO before stepping inside. "Sir." Grover is sitting across from Major Bryant. Grover doesn't acknowledge me. Major Bryant has a serious look on his face. More so than usual.

My eyes drop to the top of Major Bryant's desk, and I notice the thick file. Papers and photos are strewn all over his desktop, and my stomach sinks. I have to remind myself to breathe as I swallow the lump of emotions stuck in my throat, trying to keep from staring at the photos.

Major Bryant holds his hand out in invitation to sit. I sit next to Grover who's still looking straight ahead, as if I don't exist.

As I sit, I stare at all the photos that line his desk. My breath catches as I recognize several of the photos from my parents' accident; the car with yellow tarps covering the windows, a partial photo of Natasha that's covered by a photo of a man—the same man pictured in the engagement photo. Then there are the ones of

Nash and me at different ages after my parents' deaths. The last one I see is of a jewelry store. Susan and David are standing behind a jewelry case, and a young Natasha stands beside them. She looks at the camera, but there is no life in her eyes.

I slowly lift my stare to focus on Major Bryant. "What's this about, sir?"

"There's going to be a change in plans."

"A change, sir?"

"Yes. Grover was approached recently. It was quite disturbing."

I sit ramrod straight in my chair, not uttering a sound. My stomach twists and I fight back the bile that's forcing its way up my throat.

I don't know Grover personally, other than I've seen him around. He had recently been transferred to our platoon. Rumor has it, he's a rebellious wildcat, a hothead, and Major Bryant was to break him of his bad habits.

"Grover is going to be your eyes and ears." My eyes flash sideways to Grover. His eyes still not wavering. "He was recently approached, and he accepted an outside job."

"An outside job, sir? What kind of job?" The sound of my blood thrumming in my ears is all I can hear as the hair on my neck prickles, standing on end.

The major's eyes slowly lift to meet mine. His body straightens as I stare at him. His Adam's apple bobs as he swallows, this isn't good. "A dispatcher."

"A dispatcher?" My eyes flick from the major's to Grover's and back again. "I don't understand."

"Assassin. He was hire to take you out."

My heart is in my throat as each rapid thump pounds in my ears. I don't understand. My brows knit in confusion. Did I hear him correctly? And why if he accepted the job would Major Bryant allow him to be my backup?

"Sir, with all due respect, I don't understand." My voice is hushed, and I'm still not able to breathe. It feels as if a vacuum has sucked all the oxygen from my body, and I'm finding it had to concentrate on his words.

Major Bryant smiles at me, but it doesn't reach his eyes. What the fuck. Does he think this is a joke? "Yes, of course not. Grover is our wild card. His job *is* to be wild. Someone who isn't trustworthy. Someone who can be approached knowing his defiant reputation. Luckily, he *is* trustworthy. This is what he was trained for. Once you gave me your mother's papers, I made arrangements to have him transferred. His job is to be approached for missions like this. With Nash out of the picture, it was easier to slip him in. And shortly after his transfer he was approached. He came to us right after you went on leave. Unfortunately, there are some soldiers who go rogue, mercenaries, out for the almighty dollar. We can't catch them all, and unfortunately, one of them tried to take out Nash. Thank God the bastard was a poor shot."

Oh, fuck, Nash. I feel the blood drain from my face. I think I'm going to be sick. *Swallow, quick, swallow it down, just swallow it down.* My hands grip the armrests of the chair so hard my knuckles ache at the pressure.

Nervous, I keep raking my fingers through my hair, as Major Bryant fills us in on the new plan. "I have to say, I don't like it. You're asking me to lie, not only to Nash, but to my sister as well. I just found her again. You know how many years I've been looking for her, and now you want me to play dead? It will devastate her, not to mention Nash. This will gut him. He'll blame himself because he wasn't with me. He's always had my back." This will break Nat. I'm breaking my promise to her. She's already been through enough.

"It's the only way. You have to be a ghost. Besides, it shouldn't take us that long to complete this mission, and then you can go back and make it up to them."

All I can do is stare at the major. I wonder if he had to do the same thing; lie to his best friend and family, if he would be so unsympathetic. Still Grover hasn't said a word or acknowledged me. Running my hands down my face, I do the only thing I can. "Yes, sir."

CHAPTER 6

Sometimes life is about risking everything for a dream no one can see but you. ~Vishwas ॐ

ALEC

I've talked to Nat a couple times since being in country. I can't tell her the plan though. It needs to be real. It has to play out in order to sort through all the bad to get to the good. There's so much more to this than I can grasp.

Major Bryant has built a substantial dossier on Louis Kingman III. From drugs to weapons and more, and this is the man they arranged for my sister to marry. I'm still trying to figure out why. I didn't get the chance to go through all my mother's journals. I just knew that they had changed their identities to protect not only them but Nat and me too. But there's nothing that I could find on who they really were.

God, I wish Nash was here. Not that I don't trust the guys in my platoon, but I know without a doubt that Nash always had my back. But when he got hit by the sniper, I was never happier that it was only an AK 47, and, as the major stated, fortunately the assassin was a bad shot and only hit him in the shoulder. He'll be on desk duty while it heals. Unfortunately, that leaves me here not fully aware of Grover's abilities. Nash and I could read each other without speaking. Probably because we've known each other all our lives, and like Nat, Nash can't know anything either. God, I hate this.

Thank God my last mission is a humanitarian mission. I love meeting the villagers, especially the children. They've been dealt a horrible hand of cards, but I love putting a smile on their face even though it won't last long. I'm counting down the days to my exit interview. Ha, I guess that's not true any longer. After today, I become a spook.

Walking through the hot dusty streets of a little village in Afghanistan, rivulets of sweat stream down my back as we let our presence be known. The village children are playing in the bullet riddled streets as if the war going on around them is just a way of life.

They run up to greet us, knowing that most of us carry goodies in our pockets. Walking through the villages isn't something new. In fact, we do it quite often. Most times, like today, we're bringing supplies. This is an extremely poor village mostly occupied with women and children. There are a few elderly men who are too old to be a soldier. This is a way to get to support the families and for them to get to know us, to understand we're there to help and not hurt them. We want to put a personal feel to who we are. I often fill my pockets with bitesize candies or snack bars to hand out to the children. My heart goes out to them. They're the innocent ones in this political mess and the ones who are often caught in the middle of this shitstorm. I couldn't imagine growing up in a place fearing for my life. No child should have to grow up in fear, never experiencing what it's like to be really free.

The streets are littered with junked, corroded cars. Some are burnt out; others are just damaged and rusted. The buildings are riddled and scared with bullet holes, evidence of the war that continues in this poor country.

Dust coats my sweaty skin and fills my nose. I can't wait to get back to base and take a shower to wash the grime off me.

There is something about today, that makes the hairs on the back of my neck prickle. Maybe it's the mission. My mission is different from that of the other guys. I just hope it goes as planned.

Nothing appears out of place; it's just a gut feeling, and in this job, I always listen to my gut.

Grover is my battle buddy. He's a pretty cool guy. After our meeting several weeks back with Major Bryant, we've spent a lot of time together learning to trust each other and to have each other's backs. He looks younger than he is, as though he should still be in high school. His skin is tanned from the desert sun, and his light brown hair is highlighted with golden streaks from the sun, as if he were just off the beaches of Hawaii, but it's his baby face that makes him look so young. He's the one who tipped me off about the hit on my life, and for that I'm extremely grateful.

Playing tag with the children, I'm tackled to the ground as we playfully wrestle and they try to sneak candy out of my pocket. Out of the corner of me eye I notice a little girl sitting alone on the stoop of her door. She's not like all the other children who are laughing and playing around us, looking for the sweet treats in our pockets. She sits there watching and observing us. She's young, maybe four or five. She's barefoot and filthy. Our eyes meet. Hers are a striking sapphire blue. She quickly drops her gaze.

A young woman, who I imagine is her mother peeks out from around the doorway watching us as the children laugh and play in the streets. She's exquisite. Long black wavy hair and a face of an angel, but there is a sadness in her caramel eyes.

I approach them, walking slowly over to the front of the building. Holding out my hand, offering the candy sitting on my palm, looking at the beautiful woman, silently asking for permission to give them to the little girl. The woman nods, then pulls her scarf across her face only leaving her incredible cognac colored eyes exposed, as if to hide her beauty behind it.

Kneeling, I keep my distance from the child, holding my hand out to her as though to a frightened animal. Her big blue eyes are full of fear as she peers up to her mother for permission. Smart girl. I hope she always keeps that fear. Her mother says something and the little girl glances into my face then down at my open hand. She cautiously reaches her hand to mine. I hold my breath, afraid that any movement will spook her. She quickly snatches one of the little bars, holding it in both hands. Her eyes light up like she's won the best prize ever.

Taking one of the bars, I silently hold it up and show her how to open the little package. When she finally gets her wrapper open and sees the surprise inside, her eyes sparkle with excitement, she smiles up at me. Hell, I just won the fucking lottery.

BANG!

A loud explosion has the ground shaking as debris falls from the sky. The guys are yelling, children are crying as women are screaming.

As if on autopilot, I grab the little girl, pushing her and her mother into the house throwing myself over the top of them, shielding them from the subsequent blasts and debris.

Several more blasts reverberate through the village causing the stone and mud building we're in to crumble down around us. Rocks and debris clatter to the ground bouncing off my back, head, and legs. Using one hand to try to protect my head. I'm using the other to hold myself up, keeping my body from crushing the little girl and her mother lying under me.

Something big hits the back of my head. My ears begin to ring. It's a deafening silence. The feeling of an ice pick being shoved through them comes to mind.

My head is pounding, and something trickles down the back of my head and down the side of my face. Reaching my hand to the tender spot, knowing the warm tacky wet substance is blood and intuitively know that I have a laceration on my scalp, but how bad, I'm unsure.

Sounds begin to echo in my ears as if am in a tunnel. The smell of charred flesh and hot metal permeate my senses as the sounds of screams and cries haunt my ears. I try to move, but I can't. I can't breathe.

Reaching for my dog tags as if they're my lucky talisman, I find nothing. they're not there. My thoughts flash to how I'll be recognized. How will they identify me if I don't get out of this? I'll just be another unknown soldier.

WHEREVER OUR JOURNEY LEADS US

This wasn't the way the plan, was supposed to go. Maybe they found out I was on to them.

Air, I need air.

My head begins to spin. My eyes grow heavy, and I can't hold them open.

This is it.

My body shivers. I'm so cold.

This isn't what was supposed to happen.

I'm so sorry I broke my promise. I love you, Nat.

My body goes limp as darkness surrounds me.

CHAPTER 7

ALIAH

I cautiously watch the man approach my Neelam. The smile on his face as he plays with the village children warms my heart. But men are all the same. They only want to use my body for their pleasure and now I have no choice but to use my body to feed my Neelam. It is the only way. Some bring coins, others food. I use the coins for the medicine to keep me from having another child. I prefer the food since it is still not legal for me to go out without a male relative.

The man holds sweets in his hand, but he looks at me as if asking me for permission. Men don't ask woman anything, they just take. They take what is not theirs. They take from my body.

The man slowly kneels in front of Neelam. His eyes are the same color as Neelam's. He doesn't approach her; he lets her come to him. She glances up at me needing reassurance I am alright with her taking from this strange beautiful man. This is good. I always want her to trust me, come to me with her safety. He is still like a statue, his hand stretched out, holding the treat in his palm.

She cautiously takes the sweet from his hand. He pulls another one out of his pocket showing my child how to open it. He is teaching her. Men don't teach girls. This is something I have never experienced with the men here. Opening her little present, her eyes light with excitement as she places her treat into her mouth. Her eyes light as her lips curl into a beautiful smile, something I haven't seen her do in a long time. There isn't very much here to smile over.

A panicked scream escapes my mouth at the sound of a loud explosion. Before I can reach my baby, the man with the pretty blue eyes the color of lapis, has my baby in his arms and he has tackled me to the ground, shielding us from harm. Stones fall from the ceiling, but the man protects us. He stares down into my eyes making sure I am not hurt, his eye not leaving mine.

Suddenly a big rock falls on top of him. A moan rumbles in his chest. Blood rolls down the side of his face and his eyes cannot see me any longer. They roll back into his head, collapsing on top of us. I don't know if the man is dead, but I need to help him. He saved me and Neelam. It is my duty to help him.

Neelam is crying. She is scared. She has not seen the ravage I have seen in our village. Rolling the large man off us, I first making sure my baby is not hurt.

Standing, I go to the door to see if any of his men are still here or even alive. Although this war has been going on for years, it has never been outside my door like this in a long time. Bodies are everywhere, I have to help them. They came here to help us, bringing us food and water. Ripping a strip of fabric from the bottom of my dress, I kneel by my man, instructing Neelam to hold the rag to his head and not to come outside. She is young and innocent, and it is not needed for her to see the carnage.

There are only a few elderly men in our village. Most were taken to fight in the war. Women are wailing for their children who have been either hurt or killed.

Outside, I gather some of the weapons, putting them in my house. I fear for my daughter and need a way to protect her. I am afraid of what they will do to us if they find out her father is not Afghan.

The stench in the air is one that I cannot describe. My stomach roils, and I think I am going to get sick, but I have to be strong, I need to help.

Ripping more of my skirt, I tie it tight around a man's leg. He doesn't have a foot any longer and I hope I am doing the right thing, but there is so much blood it's the only thing I think of to keep it from pouring out of his wound. I use the water they have in the bottles hanging from their belts to wipe the blood off their faces. Wetting the fabric again, I place it over his mouth letting him suck the moisture from the cloth. Some of them are already dead. Others wander around as if lost. Taking their hands, I bring them to an old automobile that has been sitting in the street. I am hoping they will be protected there.

I don't know how long I am outside helping when a couple of big vehicles pull up. They have big red crosses on them. I stand by and watch as they put needles into the arms of all the hurt children and men. I need one for my man. I try to get their attention, but they are too busy, so I take a couple and put them inside my house checking on my man. He is still sleeping, but the bleeding has stopped.

Going back outside I carefully watch the doctors work. Learning what I need to do. Standing over the man with no foot, they put him on a bed and start to carry him to the vehicle. He grabs my hand startling me. Looking at the man he says. "Thank you." I nod my head at him as they continue to walk. His hand finally slipping from mine.

A doctor calls to me, waving me to come to him. He has one of the bags of liquid in the arm of a man and another in a little boy—Nadia's boy. She lives in the house across from me. The man motions for me to hold the two bags in the air, and I comply. As the man starts to moan in pain, I watch the doctor pull out a small bottle. He sticks a needle into it then into the tube of liquid. Shortly after that, the man is quiet, his face relaxed. I need to get some of that for my man.

I try again to tell them about my man, but they don't understand me.

The doctors begin to carry all the injured and dead into one of their trucks. They take the injured villagers in another truck, so they continue to get medical help.

Luckily, I was able to get some medical supplies and water, sneaking it into my house.

Struggling, I drag the man hidden in my home into my bedroom, managing to get him onto my mattress that lays on the floor. After pouring water on a rag, I wipe the blood from his face, checking for injuries.

I wrap a piece of cloth tight around his arm like the doctor did for the others, feel for a blood vein, then stick the needle in, watching as the little bubbles flutter to the top of the bag of liquid.

Holding the bag in the air, I watch him sleep and when he starts to moan, I give him a little of the medicine that helped the other man's face relax. It doesn't take long for the two bags of liquid to be gone. Removing the needle, I wrap his arm with a rag to keep his blood from leaking out.

It has been a couple of days and my man still has not awakened and I am scared that I did something wrong. What if he does not wake up?

I try to sleep, but I am afraid the bad soldiers will come soon. They will capture my man if they find him here, and I am afraid of what they will do to me and Neelam.

Sneaking out at night after Neelam is asleep, I take my jugs and walk the long distance to fill them with water. My soldier man's skin is extremely hot, and I need to keep him cool. Placing a cool cloth over his forehead, I continue to replace the cool cloth until his skin is no longer warm.

Watching my man as he sleeps, I admire his long dark lashes that rest unmoving on his cheeks. He is a beautiful man. No one would suspect he is not Afghan if it were not for his pretty blue eyes.

He starts to move. Moaning as his hand reaches for his head. Placing my hand on his arm I try to quiet him. "Shh, you still."

CHAPTER 8

ALEC

My head is pounding, and my body is stiff and sore. I feel like someone beat the shit out of me. Where am I.

Think Alec, think.

The mission, the children. Oh fuck, the explosion. The little girl and her mother. Moans escape my lips as I try to move, but my body is in torment. I try opening my eyes, but the bright light is too much for me.

My head throbs my pulse pounds in my ears.

Pressing my fingers into my temples, I'm hoping the pressure will alleviate the hammering in my brain.

A cool cloth is placed across my forehead. I try to open my eyes again, but gentle fingers brush over my brow causing them to close. "Shh." The soft hand touches my shoulder. "You still." Her voice is velvet. It's the voice of an angel.

The ground is hard, and I need to move to get comfortable, but my stomach roils every time I move. I think I have a concussion. I try to open my eyes again. Raising a shaky hand to my face I try to block the bright light from the sun. My eyes find hers. Her eyes are the color of caramel. She's the woman in the door. "Shh, you still."

"Your daughter," I croak out, my voice rough and raspy but I need to make sure she's alright. A cough seizes me, shooting paroxysm of agony into my skull. It's dusty, and my mouth and lungs are laden with grit and sand. My mouth feels like the proverbial desert. I need water.

Placing her hand behind my shoulders, she helps me sit, pressing a cup to my lips. I swallow the warm liquid greedily. My head feels as if someone is taking a hammer to it. Pressing my hands to my temples again, I need to do something to stop the pounding, but nothing helps. Then I remember. Reaching into my pocket, I pull out a couple packets of pain reliever. Ripping them open, I toss them to the back of my throat swallowing more of the warm water.

"Your little girl?" I try to do my best pantomime. She smiles a beautiful angelic smile and points to a little girl dancing with her shadow in the corner of the room.

I tap my heart, nodding. "Good."

She whispers. "Thank you. Thank you."

Pointing at myself, I say my name. "Alec." Pointing again, I repeat myself. "Alec." Then I point at her. "You?"

"Aliah." She points to herself. Then I point to the little girl. Aliah smiles, and I know that child is her pride and joy. "Neelam."

I hear yelling outside. Terror and fear washes across Aliah's face. She holds her finger to her lips. Her daughter runs to her. Fear etched in her little pixie face.

Aliah picks the little girl up and points at me to follow her. Grabbing my hand, she begins to pull at me. Her voice scared; her words hushed. I try standing as the room begins to spin. My hand finds the wall as my vision goes black. A hand grabs my arm steadying me, keeping me from falling. Securing my balance, Aliah rushes me into another room. The house she lives in is nothing more than a mud house that looks as if it's been standing since the time of Christ.

Tapestries hang over the pocked walls, but I notice no real furniture. There are a couple of mattresses, but she has no running water or electricity. Lifting one of the tapestries, I see a hole in the wall; a hiding place.

The voice is getting closer. Someone has entered her home and he's yelling something. From her expression, he is yelling for her. She pushes me into the dark room. But what surprises me more is she hands me her daughter. What is she afraid of? Who is this man and why would he just barge into her home?

Is she married?

Is it her husband?

She holds her finger to her lips again. Her eyes are pleading. "Please, take."

I accept her daughter as she drops the tapestry. The room is dark, just a hint of light from the edges of the fabric shines in. It smells of musty dirt and earth. It's like a hidden passage, but why?

I hear a man yelling. He's angry. Then I hear the sharp sound of a slap, Aliah cries out as if he hit her. Now it sounds as if she's pleading. Oh my God! What is he doing to her? I hear her sobbing and him grunting. I quietly pushing the tapestry away. I see Aliah laying on the ground. Her cheek red and swollen, blood trickles from her nose. Her eyes find mine; a look of embarrassment and shame fill them. She begs me with her gaze not to do anything. The man, a soldier, is on top of her, raping her. Reaching for my side arm I find it missing. I can't do anything to help her. I don't have a weapon to protect her. The man lets out a loud groan and says something to her before I hear his heavy footsteps clomp away.

Minutes later she pulls open the fabric door, taking her daughter out of my hands and hugging her close to her as she continues to sob. The little girl, Neelam, wraps her arms around her mother's neck, holding her tight.

Walking back through the house, I look for any movement outside. Grabbing the bowl of water and the rag she had used on my me, I take it back to the room she's in. Setting the bowl down, I dip the rag into the water, wiping away the blood from her nose. Her daughter's head is cradled in the crook of her neck.

I stare into her sad gold eyes and realize that her daughter's father is probably not an Afghan.

She built the secret passage to protect her child.

Now I'm here and a danger to both her and her daughter. I need to figure out a way to protect them both.

My stomach growls bringing a smile to Aliah face. I'm starving and the protein bars in my jacket won't last long. Aliah walks into another room returning with clothes in her hand. She hands them to me. "Please."

Taking the clothes, my brows draw together as I examine them. The fabric is a tan cotton. There are a pair of baggy pants and a long shirt. I wonder who they belonged to. She repeats herself as she pushes me toward another room. "Please put. Market."

Glancing out a window, it dawns on me that I can't be seen in my uniform. With my dark hair, I could probably pass as an Afghan. I remove my uniform and put the traditional salwar kameez and sherwani on and then place my uniform in the secret room. When I come out of the room barefoot, Aliah smiles up at me. I glance down, and my lips curl as I notice how white my feet are. She hands me a pair of sandals.

Aliah covers both her and Neelam with scarves. She hands me a traditional cap that I put on before walking out the door.

I don't know what day it is, how long I was unconscious, but as I walk outside, the signs there was a bombing are minimal. This is surprising because with all the damage to Aliah's home, I would think the outside should be worse. I'm not sure why my unit didn't pick me up. I did notice the empty IV bags in the room I was in though. Did Aliah steal them to help me?

She walks behind me but uses her finger to push me in the direction of the market.

Keeping my head down, I try to mimic the other men in the market as Aliah picks through the produce and grains. She slips coins in my hand for me to pay. I get it. This is a man's world and I need to be careful.

On the way back to the house, she fills a jug up with water.

Aliah makes food when we get back to the house. It's good, the rice and lamb fill me up. I can tell this isn't a typical meal, though. I have a feeling they live off fruits and vegetables.

My head still throbs, but it's a lot better than what it's been. Lying down to sleep, it's a hot night and I'm just in my boxers. Beads of sweat coat my hot dusty skin. I'm just drifting off when I feel the mattress shift. Aliah slowly crawls in next to me, pulling the blanket over us. Her soft warm hand caresses my abdomen. She's naked. Her full breasts press to my back causing my boxers to tent. But then again, I was hard from the first moment I saw her. There's no doubt that she's a beautiful woman, and I felt an instant attraction to her even with the language barrier; my thick aching dick proved that.

As I roll to face her, the moonlight silhouettes the stunning angles of her face.

Her breasts press against my chest, her nipples hard and longing to be sucked as they press firmly into me. Goose bumps pepper my skin, and not due to the temperature. I fight the urge— no, the *need*—to run my hands down the curves of her body. To her perfect ass. I want to thrust into her making her forget everyone else; I want to taste those tempting lips. But I couldn't use her like that. She was just raped, and it wasn't a one-off situation. That was her way of getting food, and I wouldn't do that to her. I won't use her like other men have.

Her hand strokes down my hard length as a groan slips from my lips. Closing my eyes and taking a deep breath to gain my sanity. I catch her hand in mine, pulling it to my lips. "No."

"I make feel good."

"No." I shake my head, unaware whether she can see me. "You don't need to do that."

"But I need make feel good," she whispers. And I wonder if anyone has ever made her feel good.

"You rest. Sleep," I say, turning away from her.

Closing my eyes, I feel a shudder and hear her sniffle. "Aliah are you crying?"

"You no like me?"

I roll back over until I face her. Cupping her chin, I lift her face to look at her brushing the shimmering tears from her cheeks "Oh baby, yes, yes I like you. I wish you could understand me. I don't want you to feel like you have to. I want you to because you want to." I realize she doesn't understand me, but I have no other way to tell her. Stroking her hair, I kiss her forehead and pull her into me. God, the things this woman does to me. But why is she all alone? Where is her family and Neelam's father?

It won't be long before my guys will come back and get me, but could I leave her here? Do I want to leave her? She and Neelam would just add another complication to my whole fucked up life.

The next several days are filled with me teaching Aliah English. She learns quickly, and I can tell she's extremely intelligent. What is her level of education?

My head is feeling a lot better and only hurts if I turn move it too quickly.

Wearing the clothes Aliah gave me, I walk out to the spring to collect water. On the way back, I hear a scream that I recognize as Aliah's. I also hear Neelam crying out. The jug slips from my fingers as I sprint back to the house. I'm faced with a man in military clothing, Badges decorate his chest. I would say he's a high-ranking officer and he has Neelam by the throat. Muddy tears wash down her dirty cheeks leaving a trail in their wake. Her eyes are wide with fear as they flash between Aliah and me. This is when I wish I knew fluent Dari instead of only a few words.

His fingers press into her tender flesh. I step in front of Aliah. "Go," I say quietly. I see her shake her head out of my peripheral vision. "Please, Aliah, go." Aliah is sobbing as she reluctantly leaves the room. The man is yelling, shaking Neelam like a rag doll, her face begins to turn blue. Mere moments later, she's back behind me. "Aliah, you need to leave." I feel her put something to my back. My sidearm. "Thank fuck," I whisper. "Neelam, close your eyes."

The officer pulls a knife from his belt, raising it to her neck, there is no time left.

She looks up at me as I mimic closing my eyes. As soon as her eyes are closed, I take my sidearm from Aliah's hand and shoot. The man drops his hold on Neelam as his knife clatters to the floor. He falls backwards against the wall with a thud. Neelam runs into her mother's open arms.

Taking the blanket from the bed, I toss it over the body. My stomach falls because we now only have a limited time before someone comes looking for him not to mention the sound of the gunshot.

Pointing to my gun, Aliah takes me to the passageway. Inside I find several rifles and ammo. Smiling, I think I have a little kleptomaniac on my hands.

Taking the guns, I put them on the ground inside one of the rooms along with my gear. Then I drag the officer into the hiding place. He'll be difficult to find. Well, until he starts to decay which will be within a couple of days with the heat in there.

CHAPTER 9

ALIAH

"Your daughter?" he asks. His voice is hoarse. I help him sit, pressing a cup of water to his dry and cracked lips. He clenches his eyes tight, pressing his hands to his head. Pain creases his face, but I have nothing to help him. I gave him all the medicine that I stole from the truck with the red cross on it.

Suddenly, he feels in his coat, desperately searching, reaching into pockets pulling out two-little packages. Ripping them open he drops the contents in the palm of his hand; pills. Tossing them in his mouth, he takes the cup of water, swallowing them.

"Your little girl?" my soldier man says, but I do not understand. He gestures with his hands until I do. Smiling, I point to my baby girl dancing in the corner of the room.

He is asking about Neelam. The look on his face is one of caring and concern, but it relaxes when he sees her. His eyes light as the corners of his lips curl upward. I knew when he approached us the other day, that he had a kind heart, something the men in the army here do not have. The soldiers here are mean and bad. They want things of me that I do not want to give. I am scared that if they see Neelam, they will hurt or kill her.

He taps his chest, over his heart and nods his head. "Good." He is troubled for my child. I am no one to him, yet he cares about us. If he had not covered us with his body when the bombs went off, we might be dead like some of the villagers. What kind of stranger would do that for someone they do not even know?

"Thank you. Thank you," I say, bowing my head and closing my eyes, I place my hand on my chest and hope he understands just how much I appreciate what he did for us.

He points to his chest. "Alec." He taps his chest again and repeats the word. "I am Alec." Then he points to me. "You?"

Ah! That is his name. I point to myself like he pointed to his self. "Aliah. I am Aliah." Turning, I point at my baby, "Neelam."

He points to each of us and repeats our names.

My soldier man's name is Alec. I like it. It is a strong name.

Oh God, Oh God! I hear the soldiers. If they find an American here, they will kill us. I feel the blood drains from my face as my stomach twists with fear. My heart is thundering in my chest. Neelam runs to me, clinging tight to my legs. She realizes this is not good and that the men hurt me. I need to hide them. Alec begins to speak, but I hold my finger to my lips.

Picking Neelam up, I grab Alec's hand. He stumbles, catching his balance on the wall. I hold him from falling. When he is steady, I rush for the hidden passage, pulling him quickly behind me. Lifting one of the tapestries, I shove Alec through the door pushing my baby into his hands. "Please, take," I whisper. The yelling of the officer is getting closer. "Shh! I press my fingers to his warm lips pleading with my eyes before dropping the tapestry.

"Whore, I demand service. I should not have to come searching you out."

I try to apologize to the soldier, but before I can say anything, he strikes me with the back of his hand. I cry out in pain as the force of the hit knocks me back against the wall. Stars flash in my eyes.

"I should just kill you now. No one will miss a whore."

"No, please, it will not happen again." Pain radiate up my face and blood seeps into my mouth from my nose. Wiping my arm across my face, I try to remove the blood from my lips, but he pushes me hard to the ground, laughing. Lifting my skirts, he pulls out a knife, I am terrified, shaking with fear that his is going to follow through with his words and kill me. I cry out when he cuts my underwear off, nicking me as he does. Tears leak from my eyes as his knees shove my legs apart. He tries to thrust his flaccid dick into me, but my dry tissue makes it difficult. He wraps his hand around my throat, choking me. I fight for air; my fingers pull at his hand so I can gain a little air. He likes to hurt me; it makes him excited, hard. He rams into me, ripping me. I want to scream, but I have no air left to make any sound.

Finally, he lets loose of my throat, I drag air into my burning lungs. Closing my eyes, I try to find a happy place to hide in my mind, but his rancid breath keeps drawing me back.

I hear something and my eyes flash to the tapestry. Alec has pulled the tapestry away and is staring at what the soldier is doing to me. There is anger and fury in his eyes. He starts to step out of the room, but I beg with my eyes for him not too. The soldier is a high-ranking officer and if he finds out about Alec, we will all be killed, but they will take much pleasure hurting Neelam in front of me. The soldier sinks his teeth into my neck as he groans out in pleasure of release. Pain shoots down my body, but I hold in my cries. He tosses a coin on the ground, rights himself and leaves.

Straightening my skirts, I pick up the coin and quickly pad to the secret room. Pulling the fabric covering the passage aside, I take Neelam in my arms holding her tight to me as I cry. I live another day.

Alec slowly and cautiously walks through the house ahead of me, making sure no one else has entered without us knowing. He brings the bowl of water to me. This time he is caring for my wounds. Dipping the rag into the water, he carefully wipes the drying blood from my nose while Neelam cradles her head in the crook of my neck.

A groan from Alec's stomach has me smiling. He has not eaten for a long time, he must be extremely hungry. He was sleeping for a full day. Getting up, I walk to my father's room gathering some of his clothes. He took my mother and left me here. He knew the laws about women needing to be accompanied by a male family member, but he left me here anyway. Left me here to starve, knowing I would die with a baby in my belly. So, I have no problem letting my man use my father's salwar kameez and sherwani, the traditional dress of Afghan men. Upon returning to the room, I hand Alec the folded clothes. "Please."

Alec takes the clothes, tilting his head as he studies them.

"Please put. Market," I say.

He glances out a window, and I see when he realizes why he must wear the traditional salwar kameez and sherwani. With his dark hair, it will be a lot easier for him to pass as a family member. He places his clothes in my secret room. I smile when I see his bare feet. "What are you smiling at?" he asks. My eyes drop to his feet. He curls his toes, making me laugh. "What? You think my feet are funny?" He places one of his feet on top of the other as if to hide them, as though embarrassed by them, making me laugh. Running out of the room, I hear him holler more words I do not know. "What, they scare you so much you need to run and hide?" He speaks to me as if I understand. I just love seeing his feet naked and so white. "Oh, come on, they're not that bad."

Hiding behind the wall, I peek around it, just as Alec glances the other direction. Squealing, I begin running, but he grabs me by the waist, turning me toward him. Our eyes stare deeply into each other's. My eyes flick back and forth between his. They are such a beautiful blue. He's holding me tight to him. He's breathing heavy, panting. His hard chest presses against my aching breasts; my nipples brush uncomfortably against the fabric of my dress. His desire presses into my stomach, as my desire for him trickles down my thighs. "You are so beautiful, Aliah." His hand caresses my cheek as I lean into his palm. His thumb draws down over my dry lips as my tongue sweeps over them, licking his lingering thumb.

My eyes search his. What is happening here? His lips part as his tongue darts out and slides across his bottom lip leaving a shiny wake along its path. Our eyes never leave each other's. Slowly, he leans forward, lifting my chin slightly. His breath whispers across my lips as his lips brush over mine. I moan into his kiss. My heart explodes in my chest and it is hard for me to catch my breath. My stomach clenches with a feeling I have never felt before. I am breathless with need, with a desire I have longed for. Our lips speak in their own language. We are so captivated with our kiss I had not realized Neelam is pulling at my dress.

"Mommy, my tummy hurts."

Taking a shuttering breath, breaking our connection, I step back. I have not had the chance to sneak out at night to gather food scraps. But with Alec and the few coins that I have been given, I can now go to the market and maybe even buy some lamb.

I had dropped the sandals when Alec started to chase me. Picking them up, I hand them to him.

As he slips them on, I gather my coins and a scarf to hide my face at the market.

After covering both Neelam and myself with scarves, I hand Alec a cap. He puts it on before walking out the door. Recognizing my place, I walk behind Alec, pulling and pushing him slightly toward the direction of the market.

Keeping his head down, Alec pretends to be like the other men in the market. As I pick through the produce and grains, I give him the coins. It's as if we have known each other for a long time. We move in unison. His hand would slip back, and I would drop the coins in his palm. He might not be from my world, but he understands what his role is. I wonder if that is how it is in America.

I try to be cautious, not to draw attention to us.

On the way back to the house, I fill a jug up with water.

I was able to get a little bit of lamb, some rice, fruit, and vegetables. I make a special lamb and rice dish and hope Alec likes it. I should not be spending my extra coins, but it's important to me that Alec eats well. We haven't eaten this good in a long time. Mostly I dig through others unwanted items at night since I am not allowed outside without a male family member.

I can tell Alec is still in pain. He rubs his head a lot, and his eyes squint in the bright light. He lies down while I rest on another mattress with Neelam. Once she is asleep, I slowly move to Alec's bed, dropping my dress to the floor. Crawling up behind him, I pull the blanket over us. Alec is laying on his side He only has his undergarment on. The moonlight shines through the uncovered window. His body shimmers in the light. I watch as his naked chest rises and falls. I have never seen a man's naked chest before. The soldiers just lower their pants far enough to pull their manhood out. And Joe did almost the same. He was nice to me, but maybe he too only wanted my body to make himself feel good.

I want to touch Alec, trace my fingers across the ridges of his muscles. I want to lick his nipples. My stomach begins to tighten and flutter as I reach for his stomach. His skin flinches when I touch him. He is warm and soft, but also hard under the skin. My nipples tighten and begin to ache as I touch him. Slipping my hand under the elastic of his undergarment, I gasp at the feeling of his desire for me. It is hard yet pliable. It is hot and so silky soft. I am amazed how it pulses and throbs at the touch of my hand. Thick veins ridge his length as I caress him. He takes a deep breath before taking my hand and pulling it to his lips, kissing it. "No."

"I make feel good," I say in the little English I know.

"No," he shakes his head. "You don't need to do that."

"But I need make feel good," I whisper. Maybe I was wrong. Maybe he did not like my touch?

"You rest. Sleep," he says.

Turning away, I can't stop the emotions coursing through me. I let out a shuddering breath, trying to keep the unwanted tears from falling. "Aliah are you crying?"

"You no like me?"

He turns to me to look at me. Gently, he brushes the tears from my cheeks. "Oh baby, yes, yes I like you. I wish you could understand me." His words sound frustrated. "I don't want you to feel like you have to. I want you to because *you* want to." He kisses my head and strokes my hair, pulling me into him. I close my eyes and sleep soundly in his embrace.

Alec is teaching Neelam and me English. I am so excited to be able to learn again. I used to be knowledgeable in school when I was able to go, but that was a long time ago. Before my country changed.

I gave Alec some of my father's clothes to wear. Apart from his eye color, he can almost pass as an Afghan.

He leaves to go to the well to get water while I make some rice. All is quiet when my front door suddenly bursts open, startling me. A soldier yells for me, not the same soldier as before. This soldier has more medals; he is more powerful. I try to explain that I am married and that my husband is out getting water, but he will not listen to me. He grabs me by the hair yanking it. I let out a scream as he drags me to my mattress, throwing me down hard. Neelam runs into the room, pounding her small fists into the soldier's legs. He glares down at her, then grabs her around the throat. "You are the worst kind of whore," he snarls. "You bred with the infidels that are trying to take over our country. You are no better than a loose dog that needs to be put down."

"No, please, don't hurt her. She is an innocent child," I beg.

Suddenly Alec is behind me. He's panting. He steps in front of me. "Go," he says quietly.

But I shake my head, I cannot leave my baby, she is all I have. "Please Aliah, go."

Sobbing, I tell Neelam that I love her and that it will be alright.

The soldier laughs at me, shaking my baby like a lamb to be butchered. Her face is turning blue from his tight grip on her neck.

I have to trust Alec because I cannot do anything to help save her. So, I race to the secret passage and grab for one of my hidden weapons. Stumbling back to Alec, I stop behind him.

"Aliah, you need to leave."

In answer, I press his gun to his back.

"Thank fuck," he whispers.

With an evil smile spread across his face, the officer pulls a kukri from his belt, raising it to her neck.

"Neelam, close your eyes." Her eyes flash up to Alec. As soon as her eyes are closed, he takes his gun from my hand and shoots. The man crumples to the ground, dropping his hold on Neelam. She runs into my arms, her body shaking from fear.

Alec takes the blanket from the bed and tosses it over the crumpled body. Pointing to his gun, I take him to the passageway. Inside he finds all the guns that I have hidden in there.

Removing them, he lays them out on the floor. He works diligently, making sure there are bullets in them and placing them around the house as if he is getting ready for a war in here, while taking care to keep them out of Neelam's reach.

He then drags the officer into the passage.

CHAPTER 10

Our reaction to a situation literally has the power to change the situation itself. ~Vishwas ॐ

ALIAH

I startle awake the next morning to yelling and banging on my door. Alec is jumping into action making sure his weapons are ready.

The look on Alec's face as he spies out the window is not good. Soldiers are still pounding on the door. Picking Neelam up, he takes her to the back of the house. When he returns, he whispers while gesturing, "If they ask you to come to the door, tell them you are having sexual relations with your husband."

Nodding my understanding, I yell back at them. The soldiers will not stop until I show myself. Thinking quickly, I remove my clothes holding them up in front of me. Opening the door a crack, I peek through it at the soldiers. I try to convince them, but they want to come in and look around. Out from the bedroom, Alec yells in Dari, anger tinges his voice "Fuck me now!" He did a good job, and I almost laugh. I wonder if those are the only Dari words he knows. The soldiers believe us, and they turn to leave, but everyone around here is well aware that I am not married, and I am sure they will be back.

After slipping my dress back on, I run to where Alec is pulling the other mattresses into the room with Neelam. He motions for me to crawl behind them. Then holds his finger to his lips. He knows this is not over too. "Stay. No matter what, don't come out." He lifts his hands and shows me to stay.

It is not long before I hear men hollering. The villagers told them; the soldiers are back. This time they will not stop. I might not ever see my Alec again.

The sound of guns has me holding Neelam tight against me, whispering in her ear that we will be okay, that Alec will save us. Then it is quiet, the gunfire has stopped. I am scared. There were so many soldiers and only one Alec. I pray he is alright.

Suddenly the mattresses are pushed off us.

CHAPTER 11

ALEC

It's been a couple weeks since I woke up after the bombing, and I'm starting to wonder if my GPS is working. I know the plan was for me to *'die'*, but they don't have my body, right?

I'm jolted awake, when I hear yelling. *Shit*, soldiers, I thought I would have a little more time before they came looking for the officer stashed in the hideout.

I won't let them take hurt her. Getting the weapons, I double check that they're still loaded and ready for battle, because that's what this will be. I'm on my own and there is no one to help. Aliah needs to keep hidden so I don't have to worry about her or Neelam. I need the safe. I don't have a lot of ammo, so I'm going to have to be careful not to waste it.

Glancing out the window I can see about twenty-five soldiers going house to house searching. It won't be long before they're at the door. Taking Neelam to the back of the house, I lay her down against the wall and place the mattress on top of her telling her to stay still and not get out. "If they ask you to come to the door, tell them you are having sexual relations with your husband," I whisper making gestures to Aliah.

She nods in understanding.

It's not more than a minute when a soldier yells into the house. Aliah yells back at them, but the soldier insists she come to the door. Aliah quickly removes her clothes and holds them up in front of her as she peeks around the corner to the front door. She speaks to them, but by the tone of their voice they're still insisting on searching the house.

I yell the only words that spring to my mind. "Fuck me now!" I'm hoping that it sounded okay. I had repeated the angry words the soldier said to Aliah before he raped her. The soldier says something then leaves. But we're not out of the woods yet. And all it will take is one of her neighbors to say they heard a gunshot a couple of days ago and that Aliah isn't married, and we're screwed.

Pulling the other mattresses into the room with Neelam, I stack them against the wall and tell Aliah to crawl back behind it with her daughter. "You stay, no noise," I say bringing my finger to my lips hoping she'll understand. "Stay."

Sure, enough it wasn't more than five minutes until the soldier is back and yelling. When no one answers back, he hollers for the other soldiers. I can see them surrounding the house. Thank God I hid Aliah upstairs where they couldn't get to her unless they get around me. They enter the front door shouting. I wait for the perfect time. I'm primed at the front door and have a clear view of the two side windows.

Once they enter the house, they begin shooting.

I'm almost out of ammo leaving me with maybe twenty rounds. I've tried to only fire when needed, but with so many soldiers, that's not always possible. Pulling out my sidearm I only have about seven rounds left and three points of entry.

Two down, five left.

Sweet baby Jesus, I hear it. The cavalry. The whirl of the helo blades and the sounds of guns coming in blazing. The roar of the Humvee's races toward me and has me breathing again. Maybe we will get out of this alive.

Stepping to the door, I see Grover leading the charge. A large smile lights up his face. "Nice dress you have on, Turner. You have a funeral to get back to."

"Good seeing you too Grover. I was getting worried that you thought I really was dead."

"Seems someone snagged your tags and got brought back with us."

"Did you get the guy who pulled this off?"

"Yes, sir, and he's singing like a canary. Grab your gear, things are going to get hot here."

"I'm going to have two extras with me."

"Afraid I can't allow that, sir."

"They don't go, I don't go. She saved me, and I won't let them have her."

Grover is quiet for some time before agreeing. "Fine, you have thirty seconds to be out here."

Running back inside, I take the stairs two at a time to get my girls. As I round the corner into the room, Aliah is standing there, tears streaming down her face, a soldier holding a knife to her throat. Neelam is white as a ghost.

"Neelam," I hold out my hand to her. She shakes her head. "Neelam, come here." Aliah whispers something to her, and Neelam runs to me. "Go downstairs." I push her toward the steps. I show the officer my gun and slowly bend to set it on the floor as I try to think of my options. I could fake putting the gun down and shoot up at him, but I risk not only shooting her but him slitting her throat before he goes down. Blood trickles down her neck as the sharp blade presses hard against her delicate skin. There's an electricity in the air. "Close your eyes, baby." Setting my gun on the ground, I can see boots slipping up the stairs. I pause, but the officer's eyes never leave mine. He doesn't see it coming as Grover takes the shot. The knife cladders to the ground, and Aliah is in my arms before she has time to think. My lips are on hers as our fear turns to passion.

Grover slaps my shoulder. "I told you thirty seconds, and you're up here screwing around," he says, chuckling.

Breaking apart I take her by the hand, pulling her to the front door. She stops, jerking me to a stop. Neelam is already in the Humvee with a helmet on her tiny little head. Tilting her head, Aliah's brows furrow as if not understanding. "You're both coming home with me."

"Home?" she asks as she turns and look at her house.

"America, my home. Freedom."

Dropping my hand, she runs back into the house.

"Um, Turner, more soldiers are on the way, we have to leave now!" Grover growls.

"Just give her a second," I beg.

Aliah appears at the door, a small box in her hands. "Okay?" She gives me a quick nod as if asking if she could take what few belongings she has.

"Of course." She takes my hand and I take her belongings as she steps up into the Humvee.

We're moving before either of us has the chance to sit down. Neelam is sitting on Grover's lap. He pulls out a packet of M&M's and hands them to Neelam. She glances up at me as she rips the candies open. Once again, I see her eyes light up with excitement as she remembers how to open the little package. In that moment, I vow that I'll do everything in my power to put that look in her eyes forever.

CHAPTER 12

*Trust the timing of your life. Stay patient, stay calm, stay
determined, stay focused, & most of all trust your journey.*
~Vishwas ॐ

ALEC

The drive to the military base hidden deep in the desert is long and
exhausting. Neelam laid her head on Grover's lap. She looks so
comfortable with him. Nothing like the shy little girl hiding at the
front door that first day. She wouldn't even play with the children
in our village. When we arrive at the base, several soldiers try to
take Neelam and Aliah away. Anger grips me and I grip Aliah's
hand tighter. I won't let them take her from me.

We're escorted inside the tent and into the room Major Bryant
is in. He stands from behind his desk, his face red with anger.
"What the hell do you think you're doing? This isn't the time to
play house. She and her child will be transported back to where she
came from."

"I wouldn't have survived without her." I point at Aliah. "She
saved my life."

Bryant's voice becomes eerily quiet. His eyes keep flashing from me to Aliah's. "Listen, Turner, if this is because she gives good head or is a fantastic lay, and you promised her something for her services, I get it," his voice is so low I can hardly hear him. "We can quietly take her and her daughter into town and drop them off, so you don't have to worry. It's obvious this isn't her first time with a soldier; her child isn't Afghan."

The muscles in my jaw clench then release with rage and I want to hit him for what he's saying. My hands tighten into fists tingling from lack of circulation.

"With all due respect sir. I have never touched Aliah in that way, nor has she touched me, and I never promised her anything—"

"Good," Bryant cuts me off clapping his hands together. "That'll make things easier, she won't make a scene then." He begins to shuffle paper on his desk. "I'll get someone to drop her and her child off."

"No, sir. They *will* come with me back to America, or I won't finish this mission. I've put my time in, I don't have to re-enlist. I care deeply for not only this woman, but her child as well. As I said, she saved my life and risked not only hers but her daughter's life to do that."

Grover sticks his head into the office. "Excuse me sir. May I have a word?"

"What is it Grover? Can this wait?" Bryant's voice sounds even more irritated for being interrupted.

"No sir. This has to do with the woman and child."

"Oh? Good, then maybe we can get this all straighten out and get on with it."

"Yes sir."

"Enter and help me to shed some light on this preposterous idea of Turner's."

Grover pushes through the door which is really just a flap of fabric hiding us from others who pass by. As he walks though, he doesn't approach Major Bryant, but holds the flap open as several soldiers walk through. They are all from my platoon. Each one of them turn and smile at both Neelam and Aliah as they approach Major Bryant's desk. All them stand in a straight line in front of the desk, their hands clasped behind their backs.

I hadn't seen what happened to them, but several of them have bandages on their faces, or their arms or legs.

"Cook." Bryant acknowledges.

Glancing down at Aliah, her face is ghostly white as a tear slips from her eye. She's trembling in fear.

I step in front of Aliah, lifting her chin to see her eyes. Brushing away the residue of the tear. Addressing Major Bryant, I say. "Sir, you have to see that she's scared. She understands truly little English and with what she has been though, she probably doesn't trust a lot of men. Can you please at least bring in an interpreter for her, so she can understand?"

Bryant rolls his eyes, letting out a long sigh. "Yes of course. Grover, since you started this, go and find Kahl."

Within a few minutes a Kahl enters the room with Grover. As he enters, he looks at Aliah with kind eyes. He stands beside Aliah and whispers. "It is all right. I am here to explain what is being said." Then repeats it in English

Taking a deep breath, Aliah nods her acknowledgement.

Reynolds is next to speak. He has a cast on his arm and a couple small bandages on his face. Kahl quietly repeats in Dari. "As Cook stated before, this was a peacekeeping mission. None of us were prepared for any type of combat. Although we're trained for that, this strike wasn't gunfire, it was an explosion. The force of which threw me into the air, landing on top of an old vehicle breaking my arm and some ribs. I couldn't move. I could hardly breathe, but I was one of the lucky ones. Our whole team was down, and of course, being a peace mission, we didn't travel with medics.

"Most of the villagers ran and hid. Others mourned for their loved ones who were killed in the blast.

"The smell of death was all around me. My ears were ringing from the blast. Clenching my teeth, hoping it would stop the pain that shot through me, I struggled to breathe. My mouth crunched with dirt, sand, and God knows what else. The metallic copper taste of blood tinged my tongue and I truly hoped it was my blood that saturated my mouth. The smell of Sulphur, hot metal, and chard burning flesh, assaulted my nose." He pauses to collect himself, wiping his unbandaged arm across his face. "I was in a haze when I came to. The street was stained dark red with blood. Body parts littered every flat surface. Moans and cries filled the air, but it was still eerily silent. I didn't know if the cries were from our team or not. Hell, I'm not even sure where the blast came from. All

I knew was I couldn't move my arm and my head and ribs hurt like a son of a bitch.

"Then she came out and started to help." Reynolds turns and points at Aliah. His eyes smile at her. "She was all we had until the medics arrived. She quickly and without any hesitation or fear of being exposed to another blast was out in the street helping everyone she could. She used her skirts as dressings, compresses, and tourniquets. She gave me water to rinse the debris from my mouth and cleaned my wounds. When the medics came, she continued helping them in whatever they needed. But the most important thing she did, was to let us all know that we weren't alone." Reynolds turns again and smiles at her. "Speaking for myself, I was scared, I thought I was going to die out there, but she cared enough to help all of us. She let us know that there was someone there, holding our hands if that's what was needed. Thank you," he says before turning to look back at Bryant.

Each soldier told of his story. Aliah was a hero in everyone's eyes "They were scared, in pain and afraid they might not make it home. It was the least I could do for another human being." Aliah whispered. After all the soldiers finished speaking, they were dismissed, leaving me, Major Bryant, the interpreter, and Aliah.

Bryant once again clears his throat. As he speaks, the interpreter translates. Aliah eyes don't leave Major Bryant's as he speaks. "Turner, you're supposed to be dead. How do you expect you're going to explain this to anyone?"

"Sir, I have a place where she can live. I don't have any living family in the area. Aliah is smart. She will enroll in school and learn English. No one will be the wiser."

"They won't just bypass the rules for a civilian. There are rules and background checks, which takes time. Time you don't have."

"Not if she's my wife, sir."

Gasping, Aliah turns and stares at the interpreter. Then her eyes flash to the shocked look of Major Bryant and I almost bust out in a laugh. "Sir, I love her, and I think she loves me. I'll take full responsibility for her and her daughter. Please sir."

Tears fill her eyes as I brush a finger across her cheek.

Bryant closes his eyes, making a small gesture with his head. "I hope you know what you're doing son."

I can't control the smile that stretches across my face. Tears fill my eyes as I stare down at the woman that stole my heart. "I do sir. God, I do. Stepping in front of Aliah, the interpreter by her side, I take her hands in mine and stare deep into her exquisite caramel eyes. Her long dark lashes damp with tears. Her cheeks are stained with her tears, and I hope they're tears of joy.

"Aliah, I know we haven't known each other very long, but there's something about your soul that pulls me to you. I felt it from that first moment that I saw you standing in your doorway. I want to be with you forever. I want to be a father to Neelam as if she were my own child. Please say that you will marry me."

The interpreter glances up at me making sure I've finished before repeating my words.

Neelam's lips curl into a big smile as she looks up at her mother. She tugs at her mother's skirts. Tears slide down Aliah's cheeks as she nods her head. "Yes, my Alec, I would be pleased to be your wife. You are the only man who has treated me with respect and honor. I will obey and abide by your rules."

The smile falls from my face at Aliah's words. I don't want her to feel that she's owned. I'm not here to marry a slave, I want her to be equally bound.

Lines appear between Aliah's brows as fear crosses her face. Offering her a gentle smile, I run my finger between her brow, and say, "Aliah, we will be one. I'm not marrying you to control you or to enslave you. I'm marrying you because I love you and Neelam. You have your own mind. All I require from you is your love." I point between Aliah and myself as the interpreter relays my words.

Aliah throws her arms around my neck, pulling me into her. "Yes, yes, I love you my Alec."

CHAPTER 13

Now even the heavens are thankful that because of Love I have
become the giver of Light. ~Vishwas ૐ

ALIAH

I cannot believe that Alec wants to marry me. I have not only a
child from another man, but I have had to do bad things to feed
my child. I am not a good woman, I am a whore, a tool to please a
man. Is this why Alec wants me, to be his whore? I cannot believe
he is that way. He has never even tried to touch me, and the night
that I came to him, he told me no. I have never had a man look at
me the way Alec looks at me. I know he is different. No man, not
even my father has protected me the way Alec has.

Leaving the officer's office, Alec turns me to look at him.
Holding my shoulders, he asks, "Are you okay?"

"Yes, thank you." I say nodding. The interpreter by my side.

Leaning into me he presses his lips to my head. "Good." My
heart floods with the feelings I have for this man as tears once again
fill my eyes.

WHEREVER OUR JOURNEY LEADS US

As we walk back to Alec's tent, several women approach us, speaking so fast I cannot understand them. The man they had sent for has been following behind us. "Alec." One of the women speaks, the interpreter whispers in my ear what is being said. "We just heard, and we want to help. We thought we would take Aliah to our barracks and let her get cleaned up and then take her shopping, she'll need to get an outfit to get married in. We want her and you to know that you're not alone, and after all, it's a wedding. All little girls dream about the day they get married."

The look on Alec's face is... I am not sure, it changes from surprise and happiness, to concern, then he glances at me and I see the love. He smiles down at me and I feel my heart flutter and I know this is right. I am not saying it will be easy, but I will make it the best that I can.

The interpreter holds up a hand to stop the girls from speaking so fast so he can repeat what the women have said, and tears sting my eyes at their kind words and actions.

"Will you be okay?" Alec asks.

I am a little nervous, but Neelam is so excited, I do not want her to be unhappy. She jumps with excitement, a pleading look on her face. "Yes, alright."

Alec told me that we are to be married tomorrow and then fly to the United States the day after. I have been to many weddings before my parents left me, and they are several days long. Obviously it is different with American weddings since we will be getting married tomorrow and leaving the day after.

The women are almost as excited as Neelam. All of them are laughing and giggling. Neelam takes the hand of two of the women as they start to swing her as they walk. I have never seen her laugh and smile as much as she has since Alec came into our life.

The ladies lead us to a smaller tent. Inside are several beds that are made the same way, and at the end of each of them is a big black plastic storage box. The women invite us in, leaving us standing inside the door as they scatter about opening the trunks at the end of the little bed, each of them pulling different items out. Two of them have clothes of assorted colors of gray and blue. The other one has a plastic bucket thing.

"Come on, hun," one of them says. She has the prettiest smile. Her hair is very pale and pulled back tight against head, and she has green eyes that sparkle. She looks so exotic. We walk to another tent. The man who has been interpreting for me stands outside. I look to him for any type of help.

"It's a shower," he explains

"Shower?" I question, tilting my head not understanding.

"A bath?" He smiles down at me. "but the water comes from above your head. You don't sit in it, you stand."

Oh! I haven't had a bath, a true bath in years. Not since I was able to go to the river with my family. We step into the tent. There are walls everywhere. One of the women stands at the door relaying messages to the interpreter who relays messages back. Neelam and I step into a little room, removing our clothes as we are told.

"Aliah, there are two knobs in front of you." Kahl says from outside the tent's door. "The one on your left is hot, the other is cold. The water will come from just above your head. Stand out of the way and turn the knobs until the water is the right temperature."

The water changes temperature? I've always had to warm the water over the fire.

Looking up at the little metal pipe coming out of the wall. I pull Neelam to the side of the little room next to me then turn one of the handles. Suddenly, water shoots out of the pipe, and Neelam begins to giggle. I feel the water and it starts to get hot, really hot, so I turn the other handle, feeling it again. It feels so good, it is not cold like the river can be.

One of the women speaks as she hands me a bottle.

From outside, the words are translated by the interpreter. "When the water is warm, step under the cascade of water and get your hair wet. The bottle has shampoo—soap for your hair. Squeeze some into your hand, rub your hands together and put it on your hair."

Bringing my hands to my nose, I smell the liquid. It is pretty, sweet like flowers.

The woman says something else, then I hear from outside, "Keep your eyes closed, it will sting if it gets in them."

I step out of the water and run my hands down my hair, moving them as bubbles form and my hair becomes slippery. Neelam giggles. After rinsing the bubbles from my hair, I do the same thing to Neelam.

The woman hands me a slippery bar. "Soap," she calls it and mimics rubbing the bar over my skin then points to my body.

The warm water feels good as I wash the dirt from my body.

I step out of the little water room, into another where the floor is not wet. Sitting on the bench is a pair of pants and a couple of shirts. I have not ever experienced a shower before, but I cannot wait until I can have another one. I feel so good, and the bubbles that they told me to put my hair and Neelam's left a scent when I rinsed it out. It smells of the prettiest flowers.

When we are dressed and emerge from the little room, they have Neelam and I sit down, as they run a brush through our wet hair and braid it, so it does not tangle.

We walk through the tiny town; it is like a village that they live in. I am surprised that there are so many women walking about who have no man with them.

There are little shops that sell everything from food to clothing. Then I see it. The nikah dress I desire to be married in. It is beautiful. Lavish gold thread lace embellishes the neck, between my breasts, my waist, around my wrists, and bordering the bottom of the skirt. The front of the skirt stops just below my knees then sweeps long in the back to drag on the ground. The same elegant stitching is also embroidered at the ankles of my partug. The woman must notice the expression on my face when I see the beautiful wedding outfit, because they have me try it on. I have never had anything so beautiful. The women talk to the shop owner about what else is needed for a bride. He pulls out a headpiece. When I start to object, they buy it anyway along with a bright colorful outfit for Neelam.

We stay with the women in their tent to sleep, and for the first time I feel like I belong. Even though I don't understand everything they say, they have been so nice to both Neelam and me.

In the morning, Neelam and I are taken to the doctor. We have to get shots and they have to take some blood. Poor Neelam, the doctor was good with her, but it hurt me, so I know it hurt my baby too. At the end, he gave her a candy on a stick, and it was as if she forgot the whole thing.

I am glad I was allowed to grab my box. I gave my papers to the man who asked for them, and he gave me other special papers to keep with me.

Becky, one of the women who helped me the day before, stayed with me to get ready for my marriage. Through the interpreter, she explained what happens in an American wedding. She told me about vows and what they were. I wanted so badly to write the words that I feel for my Alec. Becky gives me paper and a pen and the translator helps me write them, then memorize them so I can say them to him without them being translated. As I say my vows to her, she clutches her chest as her eyes sparkle with tears. "Oh Aliah, your words are beautiful. They'll take Alec's breath away." She pulls me into a tight hug and whispers. "This is so romantic, a fairytale in the making."

"Thank you, Becky."

It is an hour before my wedding. Becky is here to help get Neelam dressed as well as me. My hair is so shinny. It is wavy after taking it out of the braids. My stomach twists; I am so nervous. I never thought I would be allowed to marry. I hope I will remember the words I want to say to Alec.

I think about what Becky and the other women did to help put this wedding together and wonder what it would be like to do this for others. Do they have such a thing in America? If not, maybe after I learn English, I can offer this as a service to others.

Quietly sitting, I think of my parents and wonder why they left me. Yes, I embarrassed them, but I was their only child. I couldn't imagine walking away from my Neelam. She is the only thing that made me want to live.

Thinking back to when I was a child and what I wanted for my wedding, I do not think I could have asked for more. Yes, there is no brides price, but there should not be. My parents left me to survive on my own with a baby. But I would never go back and change that. I am also marrying for love, not because some old man paid my parents. I also wonder what Alec is like as a lover. Other than Neelam's father, all the soldiers were mean and forced me to do things I did not want to do. It was not as though I wanted to be a whore. I did not have a choice. When they found out that I had no family, they took advantage of it and me. If I did not submit, they would hurt me more, threatening to kill me if I did not do as they demanded. Then what would happen to my baby.

Becky taps my shoulder. "Aliah? Are you alright?"

Nodding, I say, "Yes, yes. I am alright."

"Are you ready?"

Thinking of Alec, a smile spreads big across my face. Nodding again, I say, "Yes."

I pick up my skirt as we walk to the tent where we are to be married.

WHEREVER OUR JOURNEY LEADS US

Bumps of nervous excitement raise on my skin. My stomach flutters, and my heart beats rapidly in my chest. I cannot wait to see my Alec's face when he sees me in my dress.

CHAPTER 14

Your soul and my soul once sat together in the Beloved's womb, playing footsie. Your soul and my soul are very, very old friends.
~Vishwas ॐ

ALEC

The word of my nuptials traveled around the base like wildfire. Afterall, who would marry someone from a war-torn country only weeks after meeting?

Several of the female soldiers on base offered their help to Aliah. Knowing that she needed something special. "All little girls dream of their wedding," one of them said to me. They not only took her and Neelam to get a dress, they are also helping them get ready for our little ceremony while I went to find the chaplain and invited the guys from my platoon. I wish I had Nash here. God, I want to tell him my news, but I can't. After all, I'm supposed to be dead, not marrying the most amazing woman in the world. Holy hell, I'm going to be a daddy. I always thought Nash would be my best man, but since I don't have that option, I've asked Grover to stand up for me.

WHEREVER OUR JOURNEY LEADS US

I know this isn't what isn't the type of wedding Aliah dreamed of, but maybe one day we can renew our vows in a real wedding ceremony, so she can feel like a princess.

When I packed my dress blues, I never thought I would be dusting them off here in the desert. Pausing, I think of the look on Aliah's face when I asked her to marry me. Emotion lumps in my throat as I think of what she does to me and how I want to make her life better.

It's funny. I never thought I would get married, let alone so quickly, but there's something about Aliah that makes me want more. Some would say it's just lust I feel for her, but I've been with other women and none of them have ever made me feel the way Aliah makes me feel. I want to shout it out so everyone knows.

As I walk to the chapel, the butterflies in my stomach take flight. I can't wait to see Aliah. Even if she's in the same dingy dress. She beautiful no matter what she wears. I just can't wait to make her and Neelam mine. Afghan wedding traditions are totally different from ours, but we don't have the luxury of time. We leave in the morning for the States.

The chapel is filled to capacity as I stand in front of my fellow soldiers. I'm surprised all the seats are filled, as more soldiers stream through the door, trying to find a place to sit. They're here to see the woman who risked her and her daughter's life to help not only save me, but the other soldiers who were wounded that day. My small wedding has turned into a large event.

Three soldiers play their guitars as everyone takes a seat. The music changes and Neelam begins her walk down the aisle. She's garbed in a traditional dress. It's so colorful, it reminds me of a peacock with the bright colors and gold stitching. Her smile spreads wide across her face. My heart leaps in my chest with the love I feel for this child.

She bounces up to us, hugging my leg when she reaches me. She's not the same scared little girl I met a couple of weeks ago; she's blooming like a rose. Grover holds out his hand to her, which she gladly grabs. I hear the rustle of paper and see he's opened a package of M&M's. I silently laugh, shaking my head.

The music changes again, and I think my heart stops beating. My breath hitches, and I can't swallow around the emotion lodged in my throat. My God, Aliah is stunning. She's in a knee-length dress, which is shorter in the front and longer in the back like a train, slightly dragging the ground. The bottom of the outer green skirt is etched in an intricate wide gold design, which is replicated in the leggings or pants—whatever they are—that peek out from under her skirts, around her waist and neck. She has a beautiful gold choker around her lovely neck. Her long black hair shimmers in the light as a headpiece adorns her head. She's barefoot and God, if that isn't sexy as hell. Our eyes lock, and my heart tells me that I'll do anything, give anything, to make her happy.

Never in my life did I think I would get married. I never wanted to put anyone through the stress of having to leave. Hell, I wouldn't like it. But she's changed me. She's such a strong woman, I could only imagine what she's had to go through the last six years being an unwed mother.

She walks up to me as I hold out my hand to her. Lacy henna designs decorate her hands and fingers. I fight to control my desire for her that pushes tight against fly of my dress blues. Taking her hand in mine, I lean into her whispering. "You are so beautiful, Aliah." I press my hand over my heart.

The female soldiers did an amazing job. I am aware the base has a bazaar, but I didn't realize they carried traditional Afghan wedding dresses.

The chaplain clears his throat, and we turn our attention to him. The interpreter stands quietly next to him.

Looking up at the chaplain, he smiles kindly at us and if asking us if we are ready to start. I give a little nod as I glance over at my beautiful wife to be.

"Friends, thank you for being here on this important day. We've gathered together to celebrate the wonderful love between Alec and Aliah, by joining them in marriage."

He turns his attention to the two of us. "Alec, Aliah, your breathless tale is about to begin. If love is not all, then it is nothing. It's opposite – If love is all, then it is everything – it's going to be the basis for every aspect of your relationship. All you have to do is simply love one another, and that love shows through in everything you do, in good times and bad.

"Love isn't just a word; it's an action.

"Love isn't something you say, it's something you do.

"Love never dies.

"This new journey will be at times richly rewarding and extremely difficult, but, most importantly, it will be a journey you take together."

We turn to each other as I speak my truths to the amazing woman standing in front of me.

"Aliah, the feeling hit me the moment we made eye contact that day out on the street. It was so immediate and powerful—far deeper and inexplicably beyond any calculation of time and place." Warmth washes over me. "Aliah, I give you my heart, my promise, that I will walk with you, hand in hand, wherever our journey leads us. Living, learning, loving, together, forever. I promise to be here to wipe away tears of sadness, to elicit tears of joy, and to cry out to everyone who will listen how much I love you."

I know Aliah understands part of what I said, even without the interpreter. Tears well in her eyes as she listens to my words.

I, too, went to the bazaar. I wanted to find a ring for her. I will always strive to put a smile on her face and make her feel as special as she is. I found a beautiful white gold ring with an inlaid natural Afghan lapis. Delicate lace filigree decorates the side of the band and around the stone. Gold flecks dance through the beautiful blue stone.

She wasn't expecting a ring. Traditional Afghan marriages don't give rings. But when I pulled the ring out and slipped it on her finger, the tears she was holding back streamed down her face. She couldn't stop staring at it. So, I guess as an almost husband, I did something right.

I brush her tears away as she clears her throat.

"I call you 'My Alec' because you are my everything." Aliah's voice is barely a whisper as the chapel falls silent, each person there straining to hear her words. "You are my light, and you have shown me more love than I have ever known.

WHEREVER OUR JOURNEY LEADS US

"I say these vows not as promises but as privileges: I get to laugh with you and cry with you; care for you and share with you. I get to run with you and walk with you, build with you, and live with you."

For not being a marriage she was familiar with, she shared words that I also believe. We both are new to love, but we will travel this life together and learn with each other.

As we return our gazes to the chaplain, he continues.

"Aliah and Alec, you have expressed your love to one another through the commitment and promises you have just made. May your journey, wherever it leads you be a blessed one.

"Today, your kiss is a promise.

"Alec, you may kiss your bride."

My heart twists in my chest. Yes, we've kissed. But nothing like this, not in front of others. But I don't care. It's just her and me at this moment.

I run both of my hands up her cheeks, into her hair as I gaze down into her shimmering brown eyes, pulling her to me as I lean into her, taking her moist warm lips with mine. Our souls melding together as we become one.

CHAPTER 15

When you start loving it is only then you will start living. ~ Taleeb

ALEC

With all our paperwork approved, we settle back into our seats as we begin our long journey home. First to Germany, then to the states. It's going to be a long couple of days.

Neelam's eyes are wide with excitement as she stares out the window. Her nose is literally pressed against the glass. There's a roar of the engines as we're hurled down the runway. Aliah grips my had as the floor vibrates below our feet as we lift off and the landing gear is stowed with a thud. I remember she's never flown before.

Her hand is soft and petite but fits mine perfectly, and I hope she never stops coming to me as her protector. I will guard her and Neelam with all that I am.

I mentally begin to make a list of what I need to do once we return to the states. First, I have to find a place for us to live. That will be the hardest part. I can't put anything in my name. I'm dead after all. I'll need to find a home that isn't overseen by a management company. I need a place that won't run my credit and where I can pay with cash or money orders.

Before we left the base, I had the interpreter explain to Aliah my new mission and why I need to pretend to be dead.

Next, I'll need to find a school for Neelam, somewhere she can learn English. There is a local community college that Aliah can go to and learn as well. Then there's my funeral. God, I can't imagine the torment Nash and Natasha will go through. That is if Natasha even knows.

I need to get to the bottom of this, to find out who's behind the murder of our parents and why they took Nat. As a ghost that's the first thing I need to look into now that I found her and know where she's been living.

Of course, it was too late once we found out the court papers that our long-lost aunt and uncle supplied were fake. They were in such a hurry to get out of town, I should have known, I should have made them wait, but God, I wasn't even eighteen myself. Call it a sheltered life, but why would I suspect otherwise.

Walking through a grocery store, gathering a few supplies until we can find something more permanent than a hotel. I overhear a man on his phone. "I have no problem leaving early, but I need to rent my house before my wife and I can fly there." He pauses, listening to the person on the other end of the phone. "I understand, sir, but you haven't given us much time to get our effects in order. I don't have the luxury of time to go through the normal channels to rent our home." I follow him around the store like a madman stalker until he ends his call.

He pockets his phone and heaves a loud sigh.

I'm desperate to find a place to live and think what the hell would it hurt. So, I approach him. "Excuse me," I say, catching him off guard.

He turns, his eyes narrow and his head slants as he takes me in. "Are you speaking to me?"

"Yes, I'm sorry, I didn't mean to eavesdrop, but I overheard you say that you had a house you needed to rent?"

His eyes squint even smaller.

"Look," I continue, trying not to show *too* much desperation. "I just back from Afghanistan and need to find a place to live with my family. I'll be traveling and want my family to live in a smaller safe community."

The guy nods, his posture relaxes as a slight smile crosses his lips. "Sorry," he apologizes. "I didn't know what to think. They…" He points to his phone in his pocket as if that explains who "they" are. "…want us there in a week, not two months like we had originally agreed on and I'm not sure how we're going to pull it off." He reaches out his hand. "I'm Brody. My brother is in the army."

"Nice to meet you, Brody, I'm Alec. Marines. I understand this is a strange request, but if there is any way we could put this in my wife's name, I'd appreciate it. She's new to the country and I'm trying to help her build her credit. I can set up an auto deposit into your account and give you all my identification, I just can't have my credit pulled right now. It's a security thing with the marines."

"I think we can work something out." Thirty minutes later, we were at his home signing a lease agreement, and in a week, we will be moving into our new, fully furnished home.

CHAPTER 16

Sometimes life is about risking everything for a dream no one can see but you. ~Vishwas ॐ

ALEC

Goose bumps shiver across my skin as the sound of the bugle begins to play Taps. Even knowing this is *my* funeral and there is no one in the wooden box sitting in front of everyone under the tent, my stomach still roils. I've been to one to many funerals of my fallen friends to have any entertainment from the notes blasting from the horn.

It's funny, the air is still. No birds flying or singing and the squirrel that's been chirping for the last fifteen minutes is now silent as the tune plays in respect for all lost soldiers.

Standing back as if I'm paying my respects to another patron of the cemetery, I watch, scanning the grounds to see who shows up. Yeah, it's kind of morbid, but who wouldn't like to be a fly on the wall at their own funeral?

I could have had a formal military service in a military cemetery, but when my time *does* come, I want to be with the people who are the most important to me: my family.

Observing from a distance, I notice Nash in full blue dress bravos. It's a sweltering hot and muggy day; I can only imagine the sweat he has rolling down his back. It's bad enough in my jeans and T-shirt.

As stoic as his face is, I see the pain and sadness shadowed in his eyes and face. I know what I'm doing is hurting Nash, but I have to find out who's behind this. What I do know is that someone murdered Mom and Dad, but why? And why are they trying to kill me?

Mom and Dad; God, I miss them. That was the day my whole life changed. The day Susan and David, an aunt and uncle who I never knew about, and who were apparently as phony as those fake papers they shoved into my hands, took advantage of a naive kid and stole my sister away from me. Leaving me an orphan without her. Things would have been so different if I had only known. I should have been stronger. I should have insisted on having a lawyer look at the documents before I allowed them to steal her away from us, *away from me.* Tears burn my eyes at the memory, and the look in Nat's sad and despondent eyes as they drove away wrecks me every day.

As I wipe the sweat from my forehead with the back of my wrist, the weather unexpectedly changes. Suddenly the sky turns dark; the wind begins to bellow lifting the little tent protecting the mourners in front of my casket. Big fat raindrops fall from the darkened clouds as the torrent wind lifts the little tent causing it to tumble from tombstone to tombstone. Funeral goers scatter, running for safety and protection from the howling storm.

Scanning the grounds, my attention is captured by a leggy dark-haired woman as she approaches the casket. I'm so captivated by the mystery woman, I startle at the sound of the three-volley salute. The reverberation of the seven solders firing their rifles has my eyes briefly turning back to watch as two service men fold the flag which covered my coffin and another soldier recites the *Thirteen Flag Folds poem.*

Turning back to the mysterious woman, I notice that she's dressed in all black, including a black fedora slightly tilted on the side of her head. Black lace veils her face, but I can see her red lips as the wind blows at her.

Her hair is up in a tight coiffure and you can tell her outfit is designer down to the black stilettos on her feet.

A clap of thunder rattles the ground as a forked streak of lightning, brilliant and white-hot, flashes across the now blackening sky, ripping it in half.

The memory of Nash, Nat, and me staring out our front window rises. We'd count the seconds between the lightning flashes and the loud crash of thunder to see how far the storm was away from us. The lightning today has me unconsciously counting now. I don't even get to one before the thunder cracks in the sky. This storm is on top of us. Maybe God is mad I faked my own death. Maybe, he's so mad he'll strike me dead here on this spot in front of... glancing down at the headstone I'm standing in front of. *Ernie Christianson loving father and husband's* grave.

The beautiful blue sky of ten minutes ago is covered with dark cumulonimbus clouds that boil and turn. The wind isn't howling, it's screaming angerly as the skies open. The rain doesn't just fall, it's driving, hard, merciless and torrential.

My eyes flash back to the mesmerizing woman. She nonchalantly opens her umbrella as if this isn't some weird scene out of a horror movie. She's totally unfazed.

Screams and movement catch my attention as more jagged flashes light up the monochromatic sky. Everyone begins scampering, racing from the gravesite, like a bunch of cats being chased by a big, mean dog.

Nash stands stoically; he's staring at the woman too. I don't think he even realizes the little popup tent has just been picked up by the lashing winds, tossed away like an autumn leaf.

Pulling my cap down, concealing my eyes and lowering my head, I pretend to be visiting Ernie Christianson in his final resting place, while keeping my gaze glued covertly to the woman. She's also totally unaffected by the weather, and for a woman in designer clothes that's unheard of. Hell, the people who were just here ran away, seemingly afraid that they would melt under the deluge of rain.

I wonder who she is. Glancing around, I question if she has the wrong grave, but there are no other graveside ceremonies today.

She walks up to the casket, and just stares at it. Long minutes pass, but she doesn't move. She runs her fingers across the smooth surface of the casket as if inspecting it. Then as if it isn't raining cats and dogs, she pulls her umbrella closed and with poise and elegance, sets it on the ground.

Captivated, I can only watch. Water streams off the brim of her fedora. Her head bowed as if praying. The rain continues to pour down, but she still stands there unaffected.

Reaching out, she lifts a rose from the bucket that sits beside the casket. I watch as the rose shakes in her hand. I can tell it's not from the weather. Who is this woman? I never had a committed relationship for this very reason. I never wanted to put anyone in this situation. She lifts the rose to her face, drinking in its fragrance. Leaning over, she sets it on the casket, and I can see her back bowing quickly as if she's breathing hard.

"You Goddamn son of a bitch! I told you not to go," she screams. A sob breaks loose from her throat. The birds in the trees take flight, fleeing from the loud cries that frighten them. "I told you not to try to cheat death, but you didn't listen." She drops to her knees, sinking into the freshly dug soil. Then she starts hurling mud at my dark walnut casket. Handful after handful is slung. Glops of brown goop slides down the polished wood, plopping back down on the soggy ground.

My God, it's Natasha. I didn't even recognize my own sister. I'd only seen her in a dress one other time, at our parent's funeral.

My breath catches in my chest; a lump of emotion lodges in the throat, stealing all my oxygen. I want to run to her, but my I can't. Tears breach their confines and spill down my cheeks. My heart is breaking for the pain this is causing her. I wish there were another way, but there isn't one.

I watch, helpless. Her chest heaves, as she struggles to rake in ragged breaths from her exertion. She's on her hands and knees. "Why didn't you listen?" she's sobbing now, her head is bowed and her whole-body shudders from her cries. "You left me. You left me and now I'm all alone again. We just found each other again, and now... and now I'm all alone..." she shudders. "All alone. You left me all alone. You promised you would never leave me again."

I need to go tell her. I can't allow her to hurt like this. I know she and Connor can keep the secret; I can't keep this from them.

Taking a step toward her, I see movement off to the side. Someone is watching her, and it isn't just Nash. I remember my mission and keep my feet firmly planted in the soggy lawn, watching the stranger as he watches my sister. Christ, never in a million years would I have thought she would have grown up to be so beautiful, poised, and elegant. Not that she wasn't pretty when we were kids, I guess I just keep thinking of her as that little tomboy who had to do everything better than all the boys in the neighborhood.

From the way Nash is looking at her, I'm sure, he hasn't figured out that the woman in front of him is Nat. Nash, gentleman that he was raised to be, sets the folded flag that had been draped over my casket on a chair arranged behind him. Then he steps over to her, placing his hand gently on her shoulder, in a caring and kind touch, but it startles her.

Nash is a soft-hearted man. He was always ready to console and soothe anyone who was hurting, but now... they only have each other.

Unbuttoning his jacket and kneeling next to Nat he places it over her shoulders. His jacket must be soaked too, but at least the layers will keep her shaking body warm.

Straining, I can just make out his words. "I'm sorry, I didn't mean to startle you, I didn't want you to get colder than you are," he says in a soft calming voice. She turns to look at him. I don't think she's recognized Nash either. We were so young the last time we saw each other. We've changed so much. He lifts her veil, his handkerchief in hand. His movement stops as he searches her face.

Suddenly, Nash stumbles backwards, catching himself on a chair. He stares at her, motionless, his mouth slack and his eyes wide with disbelief.

My heart thrashes against my ribs knowing they just found each other again. I have no idea what's going to happen. Nash never said anything to me about it, but I could tell he was in love with her back then and never got over it. He was probably afraid to tell me. God knows, I had threatened enough boys in school.

"Natasha?" Nash gasps out.

Nat tilts her head as if trying to recognize who's in front of her, "Connor?" Suddenly, she lunges at him, knocking him to the ground. Her arms wrap around his neck as her body shudders with sobs.

Nash wraps her into his hold, burying his face into her neck, his body shuddering as he begins to weep. My heart shatters, but it's also strengthened, knowing that they will now have each other.

Hearing a growl, my eyes flash to the man standing at the edge of the trees. He's been watching Nat. His face is red as his eyes squint to slivers. I wonder if he's having a heart attack due to his obesity or if he doesn't like what he's seeing. I glance at Nat and Nash, but movement of the man captures my attention again, and I look back in time to catch his disappearance into the trees.

WHEREVER OUR JOURNEY LEADS US

Nash stands, lifting Nat, carrying her like a small child back toward his truck. Turning, I look for the voyeur, but he's gone. I wonder who he is.

CHAPTER 17

It's not always necessary to translate into words ~ the feelings in our heart ~ Sometimes we need stillness and silence to feel those sensations ~"Breathe" into it ~ bringing awareness to whatever those emotions may be ~ and allow them to surface ~Vishwas ॐ

ALIAH

The sound of the garage door opening brings a smile to my face. I love when Alec comes home from work. But today, he is home early. Neelam isn't even home from school yet.

Hurriedly I grab the remote and turn the television off. During the days I have the simple children's shows on. They are silly, but I do learn a lot from them.

My stomach flips as the hairs on the back of my neck stand on end when Alec's shattered voice pierces the silence.

"Alec?" The butterflies crash to the pit of my stomach, now filled with dread and fear. Alec has never sounded so distraught. My heart falters a beat before running toward the door, toward my husband.

Grabbing me, he pulls me into his hard body. His grip on me is tight I can hardly breathe. He is soaking wet. Why is he wet? Pulling away slightly to look into his face, his eyes are red as if he has been crying. I pull him back into me as he burrows his face into the crook of my neck and weeps.

I do not know what happened today, but it must have been bad for him to come home in this condition. He has not spoken since he has come home, but I know he will when he is ready.

I lead him to the sofa, pushing him to sit. Crawling up into his lap, straddling him, I hold him in my arms to try to soothe him. His face is cradled in the crook of my neck as his body shudders with sadness.

Pulling out of my embrace, Alec finally speaks, and although I still cannot understand him, he has been able to interpret what he is saying from his phone. It is not always correct, but I can usually understand.

I do not understand what he does for work, other than someone has been trying to kill him and his friend named Nash.

I know when he was in Afghanistan, he was supposed to fake his death, and I knew he would have to lie to his sister, Nat and his best friend, Nash. He didn't like that he was going to have to do this, but he felt he had no other choice in order to catch the people who are trying to harm them and him.

He begins typing into his phone as the interpreter begins to speak.

"As you know, today was my funeral, well, my fake funeral, but no one knew that part. Nash was there. God, I haven't seen him look that bad since they took Nat from us."

I sat there and listened, understanding his emotions and grief more than his words.

"She was there, Ali." Alec's eyes meet mine. Tears brim his eyes; his look is one of anguish. I feel so helpless. All I can do is listen to him and hold him. "She was so mad, so hurt and broken and all I wanted to do was to go to her. God, to both of them. I wanted to let them know I was alive, just so they didn't hurt so bad." He spoke the same word he typed into his phone. A frightened look crosses his face. "I saw a man watching them. God, I'm so afraid for them. Whoever is doing this, isn't going to stop until he gets what he wants." Picking me up, he sets me aside as he stands. "Christ! His reach is long, he knew where I would be in Afghanistan. All those people died or were injured because of me." He paces the room. His hands grab and pull at his hair. My heart aches for him.

I walk to where he is standing, staring out the window, I step in front of him. "We protect."

His head jerks to the side as his eyes flick to mine. His brows drawn together. "Hell no!" I flinch, closing my eyes at his stern words. I know Alec would never hurt me, but the memory of the angry soldiers is still lingering in my mind. "I'm sorry Ali." He pulls me into him, but I stiffen at his touch. "I didn't mean to scare you." Pulling away from me, his finger lifts my chin. Tears fill my stinging eyes. "But no, the last thing I want is to put you or Neelam in danger."

"You teach."

"No!" His grip on my shoulders tighten as if fingers dig into my tinder flesh.

"You cannot watch both. I help; you teach," I huff.

"No!"

I take a step back out of his hold and for the first time in my life, I stand up for myself. I hope he understands I just want to help. I do not know a lot about America, and I do not want to be sent back, but I need him to understand, I need to do this for him, for my new family, and for me.

I hate not knowing the language. I want to yell at him for being stupid and stubborn. "I am in America, yes?"

"Yes."

"America is land of free, and free speak, yes?"

He does not answer for some time, but then he looks at me. Fear flashes in his red-rimmed eyes, but I know fear. I have lived fear for the last five years.

He continues to speak as he types and although I pick up a word here or there, I wait for the interpreter to finish.

"I never thought I would find someone who I wanted to spend the rest of my life with, let alone have a family. Then you and Neelam came into my life and I don't want to lose what I've just found." As he cradles my face in his hands and captivates me in his gaze, his beautiful blue eyes glisten. "I love you, Ali, and the person behind this is a madman. He will stop at nothing to get what he wants. He's already killed my parents and has tried to have Nash and me killed. I don't want that fate for you or Neelam."

He pulls me into his embrace, against his hard body. His strong arms wrap tightly around me as he buries his head into my hair and inhales deeply.

I pull away, taking his phone, I switch the keyboard on the translator and begin speaking as type.

"I understand. But I am not looking to fight. I want you to teach me how to protect myself. I will learn more English, and I will get a job beside your sister. Not today or next week, but in the future. You cannot be seen by your sister or friend. I can."

Turning away, I pad to our bathroom and turn on the shower. He is cold and shaking. Hot water will help him, calm him. Then I will help comfort him the way I love too.

CHAPTER 18

Listen to Her body and She will tell you everything you need to know. How to touch Her and where. Where the pleasure is flowing and where it's not. She longs for this communion. She yearns to open and shower you with Her fragrance. She trusts your presence, your wakefulness. Pay attention. Bow. Receive the blessing of Her full surrender. ~Vishwas🕉

ALEC

Never having lived in a home with electricity or running water, Aliah didn't know what to think. Even at the barracks the showers were in a tent. So, the thought of flushing toilets and being able to get a glass of cold water out of the faucet is a new concept for her.

To help her learn English, I placed sticky notes up all over the house. Door, window, refrigerator, stove, and more. Every day, I would point to an object and she would repeat the name. Sesame Street constantly played on the TV with the closed caption running beneath. I figured it was a fantastic way for her and Neelam to learn words and sounds.

Not wanting Aliah to feel uncomfortable. I moved her into the master bedroom. Yes, we are married, but that didn't mean she was ready for the activities of marriage. She's been abused for so long, the last thing I want is for her to think all I married her for is the sex, but God, I want her. The memory of our kiss is what I'll live off until she's ready—if she's ever ready. God, I'm walking around with perpetual case of blue balls.

With school starting in a couple of months, I wanted Neelam to be as prepared as possible, so I hired a bilingual tutor to teach her, so she'll be ready when school begins. She's so smart. She's picked up her new language extremely fast, and I'm so proud of her. She comes home so excited. Chattering away in both Dari and her new words in English, eager to teach her mother.

Neelam's classes are three times a week. I take her to school then come home and work on the case I had consequently died for.

We've been in the states for a couple of months. After dropping Neelam at school I returned to a silent house. Calling out for Aliah, I'm met with more silence. Why is the house quiet? The television is off and there is no sound of the water from the shower running. My heart begins to race as fear courses up my spine. Had I been so complacent that I missed something? Did the person who's trying to kill my entire family find my wife? Searching the house, I run from one room to another, calling out her name, fear and panic etched in my voice. Entering her room, I stumble at the sight in front of me, stopping in my tracks, swallowing the lump of emotion in my throat, as tears sting the backs of my eyes.

Tilting my head, I whisper, "Aliah."

She's lying on the bed; her dark hair is splayed out over the white duvet. I fight to keep my eyes on her face, but I'm a man. A man starving to touch the woman I love. My eyes fall to the little lacy one-piece she is wearing, and I drink her in like a man dying of thirst. The outfit accentuates every lush curve of her gorgeous body. The white lace contrasting with her hair and skin. I can't speak; my mouth is unable to make a sound. The V in front is cut down to her navel, barely containing her breasts, her nipples prominent and dark under the lace. The legs are cut high to above her hips making her legs look even longer. The dark hair of her pussy is shadowed under the thin fabric. All I can do is stare at the beautiful creature in front of me. The woman I've fantasized about for months.

"God, you scared me." My voice is low and raspy with a mixture of fear and lust. I don't know if she understands, but I was so scared something happened to her, I hadn't even paid attention to why she is on the bed in lace.

She points to a sticky note that's stuck to her chest and whispers. "WIFE."

My brows furrow as she repeats herself. "WIFE."

She slowly slides from the bed, padding over to me. Again, she repeats the word. "WIFE." And points to herself.

My heart thunders in my chest, and this time it isn't because I'm afraid. This time is because I've waited so long to have this woman. I've dreamed of her kiss, her taste, the feel of her lush full breasts pressed against me. My dick throbs as she runs her hands up my chest, making quick work of my buttons. She slips the shirt off my shoulders, then her hands slowly reach up and cup my face.

Her eyes are hungry with lust as they search my face. She pulls me closer to her. Our lips finally graze each other's. My breath is sucked from my lungs as my stomach twists with need.

I've wanted her for so long, but she needed to come to me when she was ready, not because I was a horny ass.

Our lips meet. Shyly at first. Her hands still hold my face. My arms wrap around her as I thread my fingers through the long, dark silky locks. The soft lacy fabric of her nightie can barely contain her full, firm tits. Her pert hard nipples press against my chest as my dick painfully pushes against the zipper that restrains it.

I need this woman; the woman who stole my heart that first day on that dusty street and every day since.

Her lips are soft and warm as they caress mine. My tongue sweeps out, tracing the seam of her mouth until it opens, inviting me in. Standing there, I'm afraid to move. I don't want this to be a dream, I don't want to scare her. She's only known dominance and supremacy. I want to show her love, respect, and tenderness. I want her to know that making love is more than sex, more than satisfying a man's longings. I want her to feel the passion. I want her to freely give herself to me because she wants to, not because she thinks it's expected, but God, I'm not certain I can hold back.

Our tongues slide and twist, dancing, making love, tasting. Our breaths are one.

Breaking our kiss, I gaze into her eyes, full of want and need. "Are you sure?" I voice quietly.

She points to the sticky note that has fluttered to the floor. "Wife, yes, please. You, me, bed." Her eyes twinkle as she smiles up at me.

She squeals as I pick her up and carry her to the bed. As much as I want her, this is for her. I want her to know how good making love can feel.

Slipping the straps of her nightie down her shoulders, Aliah lies back down on the bed, leaving her garment gathered at her hips. As I stare down at her—at her lush tits and her sensual curves—my heart swells with the love I feel for her.

She tugs at my jeans, but all I want to do is drink in the sight of her.

Slipping my fingers under the lace, I slowly slip it down her legs revealing her dark curls. She gasps, and my eyes lift to hers. Her tongue slides across her bottom lip as she nods her head. "We don't..."

"Yes, please Alec."

My mouth waters with the need to taste her.

"Please, Alec, clothes."

Standing, I bend and untie my boots, toeing them off before unfastening my jeans and slowly slipping them down my legs, taking my briefs with them. My erection stands thick and hard. Another gasp escapes her lips.

I watch her as I take my length into my hand, stroking myself. Her eyes are dark with lust.

"Alec, please."

Crawling back onto the bed, I position myself above her, but not laying on her. I need to taste her, kiss her, I need to feel her writhe under me.

Resting my forehead to hers, I can't kiss her right now. If I do, this will be over too fast, and I want her to feel good. My hand caresses her thigh, her hip, her ass. Desperate need to feel her is consuming me. There's an urgency to wanting this woman; my wife. Is it just the title of wife? I don't know; all I do know is I feel crazed for her. There's a fire in my soul that's raging out of control with need. My hands slide up her waist, her ribcage... to her breast. Her perfect breasts that fit my hands as if they were made for them. They're firm and taut as I massage them, rolling my thumb over the pebbled tip of her nipple.

Taste, I need to taste them.

Her hips grind into my throbbing dick, and it swells even harder than it's ever been. Little mewls escape her lips as I kiss up her body to her nipple. Aliah's hands find my hair, her tight grip, making my dick throb with desire.

The primal need I have for her has my stomach doing somersaults. My balls ache as they tighten.

When I lick her hardened peak, she moans. Her hips still gyrating on me. Precum lubricates our abdomens. Sucking her nipple into my mouth, I flick her with my tongue and twirl it across her nipple while my other hand massages her other breast.

Taking my time, I kiss down between her breasts, and along her abdomen. Her hands tighten in my hair, and her body tenses. Glancing up at her, I see the fear in her eyes. "Let me make you feel good, Ali." She relaxes her grip as I slip between her legs, spreading them, to kiss her dark curls. Her scent is spicy but sweet. My tongue finds her little bundle of nerves. Her hips buck into me as I swirl my tongue over the little bud. Sliding my tongue between her wet folds. I lap at her juices, craving this new flavor. I'm so hard now it's torture. My dick throbs with the need to be inside her. Her moans are louder; her hips thrust into my face, it won't take much to push her over the edge. Slowly pushing a finger inside her, finding her hidden treasure spot, I exert the slightest pressure. She screams something, but it's in Dari. Her channel tightens as her orgasm rips through her. As she comes down from her climax, I kiss my way back up to her, finding her mouth, kissing her fiercely. Her hands grip my face, her tongue devouring me as if I'm her last meal. She sucks my tongue as if it were my dick and I think I'm going to explode.

Centering myself over her, I push against her and my hard length finds her wet folds without me having to place it there. We fit perfectly together. Slowly I begin to push into her as a rush of pleasure roars through me. I'm not even in her, but I know I never want this to end. "Oh, God, Ali. You feel so fucking good."

She's writhing under me, trying to take me deeper. I push in farther as a lets out a sexy whimper. Her hand reaches down grabbing my ass silently begging to go faster, deeper, harder. Wrapping her legs around me pulling me in, burying me balls deep inside her. She's panting, mumbling words like a prayer. I don't understand them but strive to learn. Her tight little pussy clenches around me and like me, she's on the edge again. "Alec, please."

My lips crash to hers, kissing her savagely as she groans into my mouth.

I reach up and palm her breasts, and massage as she arches into my touch. Rolling my hips, my thrusts are deeper, harder, frantic now with need. Our bodies moving in unison. She arches her back, and her body begins to spasm. With her channel clenching and tightening around me, a scream escapes her lips. My hands are in her hair as I take her mouth not able to get enough of her, needing to taste her again. It's primal. I explode. My orgasm is so hard it brings tears to my eyes.

I growl as it continues to rip through me. "Come for me Ali."

Her body arches as her pussy tightens and spasms, another orgasm rips through her. White flashes of light dance in my eyes as I try to drag in air, my climax ebbing. My mouth finds hers, this time my kiss soft and gentle, hoping to show her how much I love her, and what she makes me feel in a simple kiss.

Her hand caresses my face as a tear slips from the corner of her eye. I'm hoping it was from experiencing nirvana, something I have never experienced before. "Thank you," she whispers.

I roll off her, and she rolls with me, settling into the crook of my arm, and as we drift off, I realize just what she means to me. She's my oxygen, my life, my world. And now that I've had her... I'll cease to exist without her.

CHAPTER 19

THE SHADOW

The nice thing about being me, is that I can do anything I want. I'm untouchable. I'm omnipotent. I can make things happen with a single call, especially when I want something bad enough. That's how I came to possess Natasha Turner, or should I say Natasha Welch.

She thinks she can run from me, from my ulterior goals. Making me look like a fool. *No one* makes Louis Kingston III, look like a fool, not even the granddaughter of the two most powerful *famiglias*.

Little did I know that it would take so long to get rid of the next in line, but finally I have succeeded at that too. Now for the kid who seems to have nine lives. There's nothing I hate more than incompetence; he will find his end, and soon.

Irritated about forgetting the engagement ring this morning, that turned out to be just the luck I needed. Seeing the taxi sitting out in front of the house had me suspicious. This is a gated neighborhood; a taxi doesn't just stop in front of a house unless it has the correct address. It only took a phone call to find out where the taxi was hired to go, and another call to have my jet on standby.

One thing I do have, is the patience of a saint—or better yet, the devil.

Sitting just outside her arrival gate, I sip my Laphroaig; the smokey sweet dram slips across my tongue, leaving a warm burn in its wake. It engulfs my taste buds as it saturates the delicate tissues of my mouth, heating my body as the fiery warmth sinks down my throat fueling my anger even more.

Eyeing my possession, I clench a fist as she quickly strides past the lounge. Pulling a Franklin out of my money clip, I toss the bill on the table, hiding myself behind fellow travelers, keeping my distance, staying out of sight.

My driver is waiting for me when I exit the terminal. Pointing out the taxi Natasha is slipping into, I order, "Hold back and follow that taxi."

"Yes, sir."

Where the hell is she going? Her taxi darts in and out of traffic until it finally pulls into a seedy motel; prostitutes loiter outside their rooms waiting for their next john.

This might be easier than I thought.

Natasha jumps out of the taxi and runs into the office. A few minutes later she exits and grabs her suitcase from the cab. Then she walks to a room and opens the door. Moments after that, she's pulling the door closed and jumping back into the taxi as it speeds off. I make a mental note of the room number. I think I'm going to like torturing her.

No need to follow her; I know where she's going. I instruct my driver to take me to the cemetery. I direct him to stop several feet away from the burial site, and then I get out and make my way to the edge of a stand of trees I can use as cover while I get a good view of all the mourners at this funeral.

If I believed in a God, I would say he or she is angry today. The weather has deteriorated. Dark storm clouds cloak the sun, sheets of rain pour from the skies as if Poseidon himself thrust his trident into the ground causing the earth to shake from the thunder striking the earth.

Standing back in the shadows, I observe the gathering and gage the reactions of all the funeral goers.

The heavens open and the ground shakes as bright swords of light streak the sky with its thundering clash. I knew she would show up, and she's finally arrived. I knew she would do whatever it took to pay her respects to her brother. She strides to his casket with purpose. Elegant, poised, exquisite; my betrothed. She *will* be punished; dealt with for what she's done. Her betrayal *will not* be tolerated, and it *will* be severe.

I watch as the woman who will soon be my wife stands before her brother's coffin. The perfect specimen of a lady. All the schooling I've paid for has made her into what I expect and mandate my wife to be.

The weather doesn't faze her posture as once again Poseidon's triton clashes again into the ground with a loud roar.

Natasha lifts a rose from its vessel, bringing it to her nose. Glancing away, I catch sight of someone standing before a grave in the distance. He's staring at the rained out funeral... at my betrothed. But he quickly looks back at the gravestone before him and his lips move, perhaps talking to ghosts. My eyes dart back to the woman who is now on the ground, her elegant hands buried in mud and muck, all composure and sophistication gone as she slings the liquidy brown glop onto her brother's casket. I haven't seen an outburst from her like this since she was a teenager. This is not how she was taught to behave. This is unacceptable, pathetic, I don't care that it's her brother.

She pays no attention to the soldier standing behind her or the other mourners who scurry away like mice when God rained down on them.

Not having time to waste on any more of this foolishness, it's time to leave to make plans for bringing what is mine back and showing her what will happen if she ever defies me again. I don't care who her grandfathers are; she will obey and submit to me.

I've seen enough. I returned to my car and climb in. "Back to the motel," I say.

"Yes, sir."

Again, the nice thing about being me, is I don't have to get my hands dirty to get a job done.

Upon taking a couple of hundreds from my clip, it isn't difficult to find the pimp of the complex. "I have a proposition for you."

He looks me up and down. His beady little eyes scrutinizing me. "'Chew want?"

Holding up the two bills, I reply to the man who's maybe five foot seven. "I need the girl in room seven roughed up."

"Dis is my stable. Whuch-chew up to?"

"She's my woman, and she likes fantasy play. That's it. I'm not asking for anything else." I flash the bills. "I just want her scared, no permanent damage though."

You could almost see the drool slip down his chin as he licked his lip. He nods, his eyes never leaving the bills.

"She'll be here within the hour. You scare her enough, and there's another hundred in it for you when I pick her up later. I'll be back at midnight, I expect excellence."

Holding his hand out, I drop the bills into his slimy germ-infested hand, not wanting to touch him.

I slide back into my car, and the soft leather seats wrap around me. a wry smile spreads across my face as I consider this will make her think about what she did to me.

"Hotel."

"Yes sir."

CHAPTER 20

THE SHADOW

Excitement bubbles deep inside my dark soul. I'll be her savior; I'll be the one to finally hold her, telling her that I'll be her protector. Yes, I know I'm a sadistic son of a bitch, but she deserves to be punished. She left me... and for what, a brother she hasn't seen in years.

Her life is mine.

She was promised to me.

I stare down at my watch to check the time as we approach the motel. My eyes blink at the flashing lights emanating from the parking lot of the sleazy dive Natasha had checked herself in to. What was she thinking checking into a place like this?

"Park," I bark to the driver.

Lowering my window, I observe the mêlée. Why are the police here? My gaze is drawn to door of Natasha's room. It's barely hanging on its hinges, a hole in the shattered wood has me rethinking at my decision, my method of punishment. I told him not to do anything permanent. Did he kill her? What was I thinking, hiring someone I've never used before?

For the first time ever, the icy cold shivers of fear prickle my skin at the thought of having to tell the *famiglia*. No. She came out her on her own. They'll never know I had anything to do with...

Movement pulls my attention to...

What the fuck.

The kid—Natasha's old neighbor—Connor Nash, emerges through the shattered door, yanking a battered and bloodied man behind him. Fucking hell, the pimp. Turning, Nash strides back disappearing into the room, only to reappear with a suitcase and bag in his hands. My treasure, dressed only in a satin gown, follows behind. The breeze causes her gown to flutter open, exposing her luscious legs, hugging every curve of her body, the body that belongs to me.

She follows behind him, like a lost puppy. It makes me sick.

She's mine, she belongs to me.

I bought her, and no one else will ever have her.

Anger boils up inside me as the kid pulls her into his arms. He's touching what doesn't belong to him. Kissing what is mine.

"Follow them," I bark out to the driver.

Rage builds inside me. I will kill him for touching what is mine.

Murderous thoughts flood my brain.

Strategies, plots, and ideas start to formulate in my head. I will end him. If it's the last thing I do, I WILL END HIM.

CHAPTER 21

THE SHADOW

Pounding on his front door, I struggle to rein in my fury. I've been up all night planning, devising and strategizing a way to end Mr. Nash. I want to make an example of what will happen if anyone crosses me.

The door opens. He stands there in only a pair of jeans. No shirt, no shoes. It's after nine in the morning; everyone should be dressed by now. And to answer the door half naked? This is what she wants, when I can give her the upper crust of society?

"Can I help you?"

Reaching into my pocket, I hand him my card.

Staring down at the card I had just handed him, he points to the sign under the doorbell, reading it, as if I can't read it myself.

"NO SOLICITING."

I squint my eyes as heat from my anger climbs up; searing my face. "I'm not here to sell you anything," I growl out.

"I found Jesus a long time ago. I haven't misplaced him, so I don't need to find him again." His arrogance is infuriating me further.

Huffing out an exasperated and annoyed breath, I seethe. "I'm not here for that, either."

"Again..." He glances back down at my business card. "Louie, how can I help you?" He tips his head, staring up at me with a smug look on his face. No one dares call me that, and I want to put a bullet between his eyes. I make a vow to myself that one day, I will kill him, but this time, I'll do it myself. Enough of relying on others who can't get the job done.

"I'm looking for my fiancée," I growl, my vision flashing red with my anger.

He has the gall to laugh at me, and I fantasize of ripping his fucking head off. "I don't get it. Did she get loose and you're going through the neighborhood looking for her as if she's a lost puppy?"

"Her name is Natasha Welch," I snarl. "She used to live here."

He shakes his fucking head and shrugs his shoulders, lying straight to my face. "I've only owned the place for a couple months. I don't think that was the name of the guy I bought the house from though." He furrows his brows, being a smartass "Did your fiancée have a sex change? Because the guy that I bought the house from... well, he wouldn't have made a very attractive female."

"No," I roar. I'm ready to explode. Sweat trickles down my back as his words enrage me. "She grew up here. I was told you knew her."

"What was her name again?"

"Natasha Welch." He's goading me now.

"Sorry Louie, I don't know anyone by that name. Maybe you have the wrong house number." He swings the door closed, but I shove my foot in the way, blocking it from closing. I'm not finished. I know she's here, and I will get her back.

His eyes dart to my foot in his door as he squares his shoulders giving me a menacing look.

"She stole from me," I snarl. "She stole the diamond from her engagement ring."

"Again, man, I wish I could help you, but I don't know anyone by that name." His brows furrow. "But, I'm curious."

Again, my eyes narrow at what he's about to say.

"If you were engaged, and you gave her the ring, how would that be stealing? Wouldn't it already be hers since you gave it to her? Just sayin," he shrugs his shoulders as if I'm the one in the wrong. "But seriously, I don't know anyone with the name Natasha Welch, and to be honest, I don't know anyone with the last name Welch. Like I said, maybe you have the wrong house. Why don't you just call her or find her on her cell phone?"

Recognizing that I'm not going to get anywhere, I try a different tactic. "I apologize for interrupting your weekend." I'll have his tongue cut out for lying to me. For taking what isn't his.

CHAPTER 22

THE SHADOW

Jenkins is now a permanent fixture in the agency alongside Connor Nash. Being on the inside, Jenkins can readily give me reports on Nash. I want to see how predictable he is. When he goes to the gym, lunch, arrives and leaves. So far, he's unpredictable except that he's found a companion in another agent: Agent Walker.

"I told you I wanted *you* to achieve that role. How are you supposed to get close to him if you're looking in from the outside?

"He's getting married."

Choking on the Laphroaig I had just sipped, the scorching amber liquid, scalds my flaming throat as I hiss, gasping for air. "What the fuck did you say?" I growl out.

"I don't have to be in a goddamn bromance with the sap to know what's going on in his life. I said, he's getting married this afternoon at city hall."

"And you're just now telling me? She's *my* fiancée." Spit sprays as I yell into my phone.

"Like I said, I just heard about it. I'm walking into the courthouse now. I gotta go so I can get scanned."

Hearing the three beeps signifying that my call has ended, I hurl my phone against the wall. "NO!" I roar. Shards of plastic and glass rain down on to the marble floor.

"This is not the end," I seethe. "You'll pay dearly for taking what is mine," I yell.

CHAPTER 23

A woman's intuition is a unique gift developed over thousands of generations to know what's safe, what's important and when it's worth sharing her thoughts. ~Vishwas ॐ

ALEC

Aliah was right, I couldn't watch out for both Nash and Nat. I needed help, her help. She's smart and yeah, I didn't give her the credit due that she deserved. She survived for five years without any help from family or help from any of the villagers so why am I doubting her now? That's a stupid question. I don't want her in the middle of this shitstorm. I don't want her getting hurt, or worse, killed. Being married is something I hadn't ever planned on, but after meeting Aliah, I couldn't imagine not having her by my side.

Leaning against the granite countertop, my mind ruminates any other options that would work, but I can't come up with anything.

A mug of coffee is pressed into my hands. It's warm and its fragrance has me blinking my thoughts away. "Good morning."

Her voice purrs and her fingers skate down my arm and I want to drag her back to bed and fuck some sense into her, but that still won't change anything, I need her help.

"Alright," I sigh. "You're right. I can't protect them both." Her big caramel eyes flash to mine in disbelief. Her teeth sink into her bottom lip, drawing my attention to it and not what I was about to say. She straightens her posture as she listens. "But, if I don't think you can protect yourself, then I'll figure something else out. I won't let you put yourself in a situation you can't handle." She nods but doesn't argue. "Training will be hard. It has to be. You need to be prepared for anything."

"Okay," she says.

"You're going to be sore and bruised, but I won't push you more than you can handle, but I also won't let you work with her if I don't think you're ready." God, I can't believe I'm actually agreeing to this. "Go get some clothes on that you can work out in, something comfortable."

Her smile is so big on her face, you would have thought I just gave her a puppy. She sets her coffee cup down and steps in front of me, batting her long dark lashes. "Thank you, Alec." Kissing my cheek, she bounds off to the bedroom

CHAPTER 24

Find someone who wants to invest in you, learn from you, see you win, support your visions, and fall in love with you daily.
~Vishwas ॐ

ALEC
2007

The hardest part of being a ghost in a town I grew up in, is changing my appearance. I grew out my facial hair and now have a medium stubble beard and I've grown my hair out. I've had a military cut for so long, I hardly recognize myself.

The one thing I didn't want, is for my girls to feel imprisoned in their own home just because of who I am and my situation. We've made a couple of traditions in our home: dates with Dad and girls' night out. Tonight, is my date with my ten-year-old. Harry Potter and dinner is what I have planned for the evening.

Sitting at a quiet booth at a nice Italian restaurant, Neelam asks. "Daddy, tell me about how you knew you were in love with Mommy." I've told her the story several times, but she's a romantic and loves to hear that I fell in love with Aliah almost at first sight, but I oblige her, telling it to her again. Even though she was there, she doesn't remember a lot of her time in Afghanistan. I don't know if that's a good or bad thing.

Pulling my hat down over my eyes and slumping down into the booth, I watch as Nash and Nat walk into the restaurant. Fuck me. After living in the same town for the last five years, this is the first time I've come this close to them.

Neelam's head turns from side to side, searching for what or who I'm hiding from. "Oh my gosh! She's beautiful, who is she?" She continues to stare at Nat.

"Shhh." Neelam turns back to look at me, her eyes wide with wonder. "That's my best friend and my sister."

"Wow," she whispers. "She's so pretty." Her eyes begin to shimmer with unshed tears.

"What's wrong, baby? Why the tears?" Reaching over, I take her hands in mind.

The first tear slips down her cheek. Brushing the tear away with my thumb, she mutters. "If I had a sister or brother, I'd be so sad that I couldn't talk to them or even see them."

Cupping her cheek and wiping another tear away, I press my lips to her forehead. "Baby, the only reason I'm keeping away from her is to keep her safe. I'd rather stay away from her then to have her get hurt." Lifting her chin to look me in the eye, I ask, "Do you understand?"

She nods her head, sniffling and wiping her sleeve across her face.

CHAPTER 25

Fall in love with someone who only has eyes for you, who chooses not to be distracted by anyone else. Someone who is emotionally whole. Someone who has learned that the way of love is to give unconditionally without holding anything back. ~Vishwas ॐ

ALIAH

The last five years has blown away like the grains of sand in my homeland. My Neelam is such a beautiful young lady and so smart and talented, learning English easily.

Strong arms wrap around my waist as I cut celery into small pieces for stir fry.

Warm lips caress just under my earlobe. Desire prickles my skin as the heat of his breath causes my nipples to tighten, chaffing against the lace of my bra.

Dropping the knife to the counter, I close my eyes and allow my head to loll to the side, Alec's warm lips nibble at my tender flesh. Soft mews slip from my lips.

"How much time do we have?" he murmurs.

Forcing my eyes to open, I glance at the clock on the microwave. "Only about thirty minutes. She is at volleyball practice, and Katie's mom is going to bring her home."

The corner of Alec's lips curl into a wickedly seductive smile sending shivers up my spine. Wiping my hands on a tea towel, I tease, dashing out of his grip, knowing he will have me back in his hold in a matter of seconds.

I squeal as he grabs me, hoisting me over his shoulder slapping my bottom with at pop. "Ouch!" I cry out, not from pain, but out of surprise. He strides to our room, tossing me in the middle of the bed. By the time I've stopped bouncing and righted myself, Alec is naked and looming over me. Desire burns in his eyes. Even after several years, I still find myself shy in front of him, but God, he excites me.

"I think you're a little over dressed, Mrs. Turner."

My tongue darts out swiping over my bottom lip as I try to swallow the emotion of my desire. "Well, Mr. Turner, what are you going to do about it?"

Within seconds my dress is on the floor, my bra landing on top of the pooled fabric, and my panties ripped and dangling from his fingers.

Predatory lust fills his eyes, and I am his prey.

He lifts the lacy fabric of what used to be my panties to his nose, and closes his eyes as he inhales an audibly deep breath before running his tongue up my inner thigh to his prize, my panties clutched tight in his fist.

Never in my dreams did I ever think I would be in a life like this, with a man like Alec as my husband, and marrying for love. Before Alec, I thought I would live a very submissive and sad life, serving a man who purchased me like a slave. My only job would be to serve him and bear his children. And after Neelam's birth, even that seemed unlikely. Then Alec fell into my life and saved me.

I writhe under his touch as his tongue swirls and dips deep inside me. His magical fingers massage and tease my breasts and nipples.

A blinding pressure grows inside me as my body convulses and quivers and he pushes me over edge in a toe-curling orgasm. But he doesn't slow; he crawls up my body circling my nipple with his hot tongue, as he thrusts his rigid length deep inside of me. My hips instinctively push into his groin as the heat of his kiss ignites my orgasm, and I cry out as my climax reignites, pulsing and spasming around his hard erection. "Yes, God, yes. Alec now! Come now!"

My teeth sink into the hard muscle of his shoulder as he growls his release. "Oh God, Ali, fuck, fuck, yes. You feel so good. Yes." He collapses down on me as we both pant; our hearts beat with the same rhythm as our bodies once again speak the same language. "Have I ever told you just how much I love you?" He places a kiss on the tip of my nose. "You make me so happy. Thank you for loving me."

"Oh Alec, you are so easy to love."

Alec's lips find mine as we lay in each other's arms, just loving the feel of his body against mine in the afterglow of our lovemaking.

"Mom, Dad, are you home? Mom? Where are you?"

My eyes go wide, afraid of being found in this situation. Alec smiles down at me, nibbling my earlobe before rolling off me. Jumping from the bed, I grab my dress and bra and the ripped lace of what was once my panties and dash into the bathroom. Once I'm dressed again, I step out of the bathroom, flustered, surprised that Neelam is chattering to Alec about being made captain of the volleyball team, while Alec stands fully dressed looking like the god he is as if he hadn't just been inside me not more than five minutes ago.

I finally finish my stir fry, and we sit at the beautiful table Alec bought the day we moved into our home. It is our tradition that we sit and eat at least one meal together. No phones, television, or outside distractions. It's our time to unwind and talk about the happenings of the day. It is how I learn to have a good conversation with others. Although I took English classes, I also decided to follow my dreams and took classes in hospitality and event management. I loved seeing how Alec and my wedding was put together, and I wanted to bring that excitement and joy to others.

My eyes meet my husband's, and I find them filled with excitement. "Husband, my dear, you seem to be hiding a secret."

He can hardly contain his smile. "Well, a little birdie told me a secret and I thought you might be very interested in it..." He taunts.

"Oh? Please do tell."

"Well, I heard there is a new business that just opened that you might like." His eyes slowly look from his fork to my eyes. "I think it might be just what you've been looking for."

"Alec, stop teasing me and tell me." My heart is racing with excitement. I love being here for Neelam, but I also long to be more. I never had the freedoms that I have here. I couldn't go to school or even think of the idea of having a career. Not a job, but something I was proud of.

"Connor just purchased an old rundown warehouse for Natasha, giving it to her for their fifth anniversary."

Scrunching my nose, my brows furrow. "I don't understand."

"It's for her event company. She'll need help putting it together. I thought that if you started with her from the ground level, you could learn everything from the beginning. Gain her trust and friendship."

"Fake my friendship?"

"God, no. Nat never had a lot of friends, just Connor and me. From what information I've gathered, she never made any real friends when they took her either. She was never allowed to socialize with anyone outside of our fake aunt and uncle and of course the guy who she was supposed to marry. It might be difficult at first, but I know you two will become best friends."

"How do you know this?"

A twinkle entered his eyes. "Because I have a deep understanding of both of you. Yes, it's been years since I've been around Nat, but I remember what she was like as a teenager. She longed for that bond. The girls in school didn't understand her and our musketeer relationship. She wasn't the typical girly girl. She was a tomboy."

"Tomboy? What is this?"

"A tomboy is a girl who would rather play active games outside than stay in the house playing dress-up with dolls."

"Oh."

"Anyway, I thought you would like to go and meet her. See if she's needing help."

My body begins to dance around with excited energy. "So, now what? Where do I go! I want to go now. I do not want to miss this chance."

Alec's warm hands grip my shoulders keeping me grounded. "I'll take you by there in the morning."

"You know you cannot do that. You will risk being seen."

His shoulders slump as though he had not considered this.

"When will this mission be over? Because as I see it, it will never be over. You are wasting precious time that you could be having with your sister instead of missing her." Neelam looks from Alec to me, her eyes questioning.

"I don't know, honey." Alec takes her hand in his. "I love her so much, but I'm trying to protect her, and the only way I can do that is if she doesn't know I'm here."

"That's really sad. If I had a brother or sister, I would never want them to think that they were alone. Even if we were fighting." Neelam stares at Alec, her eyes fill with tears.

"You would have made a wonderful big sister."

Alec and I had tried to get pregnant, but I was not ever able to give him a child. I know how much he loves Neelam and I would have loved to give him a son, but God had other plans, although he did adopt Neelam once we came to the United States. It filled me with pride and joy that he would want another man's child as his, but that is just My Alec.

Alec helps me with my resume after Neelam is in bed. I'm so excited. This is a new adventure for me.

CHAPTER 26

ALIAH

With my hair in a long braid hanging down my back, I walk into the dark cold warehouse. There is no signage or information as to what kind of business will be filling the large empty space, but I have my story straight and I'm ready for this new part of my life.

Pushing through the front glass doors, my feet stall as I stand in awe. There is so much potential for all the space inside. Even though I have never worked as an event planner, in my classes, I have seen pictures and I can see in my head just how beautiful and elegant this place can be.

"May I help you?" My eyes dart to the voice as I am caught off guard and my heart stutters with a dash of fear.

Even in jeans and a T-shirt she's stunning. We could almost be sisters with our dark hair and similar body shape, but it's the eyes that catch my attention. Icy pools of blue with silver flecks just like my Alec's. Clearing my throat, I put on my best smile. "I am Ali Tu... Jan, and I would like to work for you." Most Afghans don't have a surname, and I almost gave her my married last name which would have given my identity away. That was too close. I will have to be more careful as I speak. After Alec and I got married, we decided that for safety reasons my last name would be Jan even though I did take his name when I signed the marriage certificate.

"Excuse me?" Her hand perches on her hips and her eyes squint in suspicion.

"I would like to work for you." Extending my portfolio toward her, I hand her my resume.

"How do you even know what type of business I'm opening?" My Alec's Natasha is very untrusting, but from what he told me about her childhood, I can understand why.

"You are going to plan events, yes?" I'm afraid of revealing too much about how I know about her, so I try to avoid answering directly. "When I came to the America, I took English classes to better learn the language of my new homeland, and I wondered what I wanted to do for a career. I thought back to when I got married and the friends who helped me put my wedding together and knew I wanted to do the same for others."

"My I ask where you are from?"

"I am from Afghanistan."

"I hear weddings in Afghanistan last for days."

"Yes, but I married an American man, so I had an American wedding."

Her face relaxed, and she smiled as we began to speak more. "I'm sorry, I didn't mean to ask such a personal question."

"It is not a problem. Afterall, it was because my husband's friends created such a special wedding that compelled me consider this for a career. So, I went to school and received a degree in hospitality and event management. I am a hard worker and want to help you."

Natasha's chest expands as she draws a deep breath, closing her eyes for a moment.

"Are you alright? Can I get you something?" I ask. Not sure what I might have said to upset her.

Her eyes glisten with welled tears. She turns away from me, her hands brush at her face. "It's nothing." She sniffs as she turns back toward me. A forced smile on her face. "You say you're married?"

"Yes, for five years now." I respond. "This makes you sad?"

She gives a small chuckle. "No, it's just. My brother used to wear that same cologne that I smell on you. I'm sorry. I don't usually get emotional, but I miss him, and the scent just brought up memories of him."

"I am sorry. Does he not live around here?" Of course, I know that she thinks Alec is dead, but cannot let on that I am aware she thinks her brother is dead. Still, I need to let her know that I empathize with her. I need to gain her trust.

Pausing, she swallows hard, as if trying to control her emotions. "No," she whispers, shaking her head. He was in the marines and was killed in a bombing five years ago."

"Oh. I am so sorry for your loss, should I tell my husband to change his cologne when I begin to work for you, so you will not be sad?"

Natasha bursts into a laugh. "You're very sure of yourself." She stares down at my resume. "I'm not even sure when I'll be ready to open. There's so much that has to be done first."

"Please, I... what is the word. I work free to help and you teach me."

"Apprentice?"

A smile stretches my lips. "Yes, that is the word. I apprentice for you."

"But that's not fair to you."

"You need me. I help clean and decorate. Your building needs much work. I do the work, and you concentrate on getting event jobs. I have some incredibly good ideas for decorating your place."

She doesn't answer for a bit of time, but then smiles at me before saying, "Okay, fine. But when the time comes that I'm making money, I'll pay you back." She holds her hand out for me. Her fingers are long and tapered, and her fingernails are immaculately manicured. I take her hand, and we shake to our agreement.

"Do you have a copy of the floor plan?" I ask as I pull out a sketch pad. "I'd like to sketch a couple of ideas that hit me when I walked through the door and see if I have the same kind of ideas you have."

"I don't. Hell, girl, I just got the place last week and went to the city yesterday to get my business license."

"Yes, I know. That is how I found you." That much is kind of true at least. Pulling out my phone, I begin taking pictures of the space. The new app on my phone allows me to measure the space so I have a record of the dimensions we will be working with.

Natasha still has not opened up to me since I began working for her a month ago, so I invited her out to dinner hoping she will be a little more at ease with me. It has been weeks of long hours and hard work, and I love it. Alec was right, I do like Natasha, a lot.

After a glass of wine, I ask her about her family. Of course, she has already told me about her brother, but nothing about her parents or her life with her aunt and uncle. Thinking that it would help her, I begin to tell her about my family. "My parents just left me."

"What do you mean, they just left you?"

"I was lucky, they could have killed me for disgracing the family."

"They really do that. They would kill their own child? I thought that was all propaganda."

"Yes, at the time I left, women were never allowed to be outside the home without a male relative."

"How long were you alone?"

"A little more than five years."

"What about the birth of your daughter? I mean, I don't know that much about Afghanistan other than that's was were my brother was killed. Did you go to a hospital?"

Shaking my head, my eyes meet hers. "No, I was from a small village and even if there were a clinic, I didn't have a male family member to escort me, but there was an elderly woman in the village who helped me."

"You don't have any other siblings or family?"

Shaking my head, I take another sip of my wine. "No, most of the men in our village were killed when gunmen from a militia group attacked. I had two brothers, but they were killed. My mother and I were lucky that our father survived."

"Oh my gosh, that's horrible." Natasha's fingers cover her mouth as if trying to quiet her gasp. "What did you do?"

"After the attack, the Western soldiers came to our village. That is where I met Joe, my daughter's father. My parents left shortly after I found I was with child. I dishonored my family. They spared me by just leaving me there alone. The elderly woman next door helped me when she could, and I helped her when I had the means. I would sneak out at night and go to the well and bring her back a jug. Her husband had died the day my brothers had. That was ten years ago."

"How did you survive without anyone to help you?"

Embarrassed at what I had to do to stay alive, I drop my eyes drop to stare my hands, my fingers fidgeting in my lap. "I had to do whatever I could to survive. At night, I would rummage through my neighbors' spoiled food and sneak to the well in the dark to gather water. Then I met my husband. He saved me and my daughter. I've been here in America for five years now."

"What is your husband's name?"

My heart begins to race. Shoot, I hadn't planned for that question. I know if I don't use his real name, I might slip later. I have no other choice but to use it. "Aleczander."

Gasping, she sits up higher in her chair and I have her full attention. Tears fill her eyes. "What? His name is Aleczander? What are the chances that we both know an Alec?"

"It is meant to be." I smile up at her.

Natasha sits in silence as if pondering life's cruel joke.

Her voice is almost inaudible as she begins to speak. "My parents were killed in a car accident. That was thirteen years ago. An aunt and uncle that I didn't know I even had, showed up and took me away from my brother and Connor. Connor was my brother's best friend and is now my husband. They told me for years that Alec and Connor didn't want anything to do with me, and after time, when my brother didn't even call me, I began to believe them." A tear slips from her eye. "My aunt and uncle had me betrothed."

"I didn't think American's believed in arranged marriage." My brow furrows at the thought.

"They don't," she says shaking her head. "But I didn't have a choice."

"I don't understand."

She takes a deep cleansing breath, closing her eyes as if centering herself. "From the time I arrived at their home, I was groomed to be his perfect wife. Educated at private schools, received my degree in hospitality, then began working as an event coordinator to learn how to throw the best social parties for Louis."

"Louis?"

"Louis Kingston the third, my betrothed."

"How did you and your brother reconnect after you were taken and how did you get away?"

Glancing up at me, her eyes glimmer. Her fingers fret with her napkin. "Alec saw my engagement announcement, which mentioned that I was an event planner, but since it didn't say where I worked or even the city I worked in, he called all of the event planners he could find until he located me. Unfortunately, he was preparing to leave on his last mission." Her chin quivers and she bits her bottom lip to stop it. "He died before I got to see him again, before I could hug him and tell him I loved him to his face after thinking he and Connor forgot about me."

"I'm sure he knew."

"I said some horrible things to him that first day he called. I never said I was sorry." I tear slips down her cheek and she quickly brushed it away, as if I wouldn't notice.

"You were his sister. Isn't it an unconditional thing to forgive your family?"

She nods silently.

"But you married his best friend?"

"Yes, after Alec found me, I set up a Google alert for him. I was sitting in my office when I received an alert notifying me a marine by the name of Alec Turner, died in Afghanistan from a roadside bomb. I was in denial at first, but when I it was confirmed that it was my Alec, I knew what I needed to do. I booked a flight and flew out here to say my final goodbye to him. He was the only family I had left." She brushes another tear from her cheek with her slender fingertips.

"I didn't even recognize Connor at first. He was in his uniform, the nice one. I don't know what it's called, but when I walked up to Alec's casket, all I was paying attention to was the box sitting in front of me. I might not look like it now, but back then, I was always dressed in designer clothes, and Alec's funeral was no different. I didn't own anything but designer clothes. I had a reputation to live up to. I was Louis Kingston the third's fiancé. I was his showpiece, and I was to always look elegant and sophisticated.

"Anyway, I was so distraught, I fell to my knees and began slinging mud at the coffin, screaming vulgarities." She glances up at me. "I was never allowed to curse, Louis never allowed it.

It was pouring rain, and I was soaked. The next thing I knew, someone was placing a jacket over my back. It was then that I looked up into the most beautiful eyes. Eyes that I'd never forget. Connor's eyes.

"I wasn't very nice to him at first and made him drop me off at a little sleazy hotel. He saved my life that night." Her face lights up as she speaks of her husband.

"And he was your brother's best friend? And now your husband?"

"Yes. I knew I loved him when we were kids, but I couldn't let him or Alec know. And I didn't think Connor really cared that much. I was just his friend's kid sister." She smiles up at me. "Connor told me later that he felt the same way, but then I was taken. When I realized it was Connor at the funeral, we've been together ever since."

"What a lovely story." I place my hand on hers. "Did Louis come out with you?" I ask.

The color drains from Natasha's face; she's ghostly white at mention of Louis's name. Slowly shaking her head, she closes her eyes. Her voice sounds like a child. "No, I knew for a while that I couldn't marry Louis, so I began saving money and stashing it away. We were living back East, so I snuck out of the house and flew here to my brother's funeral. I just never... well, here I am."

"Did Louis ever find out you flew out here?"

Pursing her lips, she nods. "He showed up at Connor's house the day after Alec's funeral. Louis tried barging through the door, but Connor blocked his entrance, telling him that he had the wrong house."

"And he hasn't shown up again?"

"No. I haven't heard from him in the last five years." She shakes her head as if it isn't a big deal.

I pull in a breath but hold back what I was going to say.

"What? What are you thinking?"

Tilting my head, I bite my bottom lip as I ponder my question. "Do you not find that odd?"

"Odd? Why? I went off the grid. Connor denied knowing me, so when Louis couldn't trace me, I figure he went back home and moved on." Her brows wrinkle with concern.

Bringing my wine glass up to my lips, I take a hefty swallow. "From what you told me, Louis does not seem to be the kind of man to just walk away. If he came all the way out here the day after you disappeared to bring you back home, I do not think he just walked away. I mean, I do not have a lot of experience with men, but the ones I did have were not nice and they never forgot someone who made them look bad. They are like elephants and have long memories. You need to be careful."

CHAPTER 27

ALIAH

Gripping Alec's hand, the nurse escorts us back to the doctor's personal office and not a sterile exam room. I have not been to a lot of doctor's offices, but I know this cannot be good. I am so nervous, my heart thrashes hard in my chest as I attempt to understand what the doctor is saying. "I'm sorry, Aliah and Alec. I've run all the tests I can. This is just one of those complicated diagnoses that we can't treat."

I choke as I try to force air into my lungs. Tears fill my eyes, and I'm stunned with what the doctor has just told us. Alec grips my hand tighter. "There is nothing you can do?" I murmur. The first tear slips down my face.

He looks at me sadly, then his eyes glance downward at the computer sitting in front of him. "I'm really sorry, but there's really nothing we can do."

I nod, and an unwanted sob slips from my mouth. Anguish and disgrace blanket me. Maybe this is my punishment for dishonoring my parents. This is my worst nightmare coming true. My worst possible nightmare. Giving me an uneasily smile, he reaches into his top desk drawer and offers a brochure. I glance down at the smiling happy faces on the paperwork.

I stare without seeing what it says. The paper feels cold, stiff, and revolting.

"Both of you should go over all the options. You'll need to have open communication to help you cope. You need each other to go through this journey. There are support groups that can help you come to terms with it, too."

This is the first time in my life that I am ashamed of being a woman who cannot even give her husband a child.

I can't believe this is happening to me. Five years with someone, five years of trying and that is it; it is done. I will never be able to give my husband what I so desperately wanted to give him. I knew something had to be wrong. We decided to not use any protection, hoping we would get pregnant organically when God allowed it. About two months ago, I asked Alec about going to the doctor to see what was wrong.

The doctor was warm and friendly and ordered several tests. I did not know what to think. I was poked and probed for several hours and felt optimistic when I left the clinic. They talked to us about treatment I had never even heard of, but I felt like whatever was wrong with me was something that could be fixed with a simple medication, or a specific plan of action. That's usually how doctor's offices seem to work. All that mattered was that I was taking an important step in figuring out what the issue was, so I could fix it.

WHEREVER OUR JOURNEY LEADS US

After two months of testing and blood draws, I knew before I even came into the clinic today, the issue was much worse than I ever expected.

CHAPTER 28

ALIAH

Finally, after a couple of months of hard work, we were ready for the grand opening. With all the work and preparation, the thought of a baby has been buried deep in my brain.

The grand opening itself was a huge success. We were able to schedule a few events as the community came into the beautiful space we had renovated.

The showroom is bright and open. Sparkling white tulle flows from the vaulted ceiling. The only touch of color is the rainbow of colored linens and fabrics that hang pristinely in alcoves built into the walls and the linens on the staged tabletops.

Assorted styles of place settings are displayed in large open hutches that line the walls, showcasing china, crystal, and flatware from the elegant to the whimsical to meet anyone's expectations and needs.

Examples of linens are displayed on tables that are placed around the large show room, letting everyone's imagination go wild with possibilities.

Wanting to stand out from other event planners, Natasha decided to set the room up differently. "I was thinking of food stations instead of the usual buffet tables that are over crowed."

"What did you have in mind?"

"Amuse-bouche." Her eye flash to mine, as if looking for reaffirmation.

"That's a wonderful idea. I sketched out an event like that in school. It's easy as far as the food goes because you do not usually have to make as much, but there is a lot to keep the displays full. Buffett tables are so old-fashioned"

"I agree. It should wow our guests with the elegant and creative presentation."

"What did you use in your project at school?" Natasha pulls out a notepad and begins to write down some of my ideas.

"I setup individual portions on small plates, bowls and shooters. Arranging them into tiers using sheets of glass on risers or cake stands. Groups, rows, and levels. Low items in the front and taller items in the back. It's a clean, defined, and well-ordered look. The food is presented in individual containers or utensils and arranged in rows. Not only does this give it a modern, professional look, it also helps with portion control. Most people are more likely to just take one of each item."

"That's an amazing idea. I love it!" Natasha claps her hand in excitement. "So, instead of using the waitstaff to carry trays of food, we can use them to keep all the foods filled, and the cleanup will be a breeze!"

Natasha had interviewed several chefs and finally picked her favorite along with several people to work as catering staff. Their responsibility will be to set up the food and displays, while others will take care of the utensils and small dishes. The different hors d'oeuvres and amuse-bouche were set up perfectly. A long buffet table sits to the side. Clear rectangular vases filled with white twinkle lights act as pillars as large slabs of glass build layers filled with fruits, vegetables, and cheeses. Sliced blood oranges rim the border, as different colored grapes cascade over the edge. It is the ideal focal point.

It is a beautiful evening, and the first time I have the chance to meet Natasha's husband Connor Nash, my Alec's best friend.

"Ali, this is my husband, Connor. Connor, this is Ali, the woman who helped me get this place up and running. She's never afraid to get her hands dirty." I can hardly swallow the lump of fear inching up my throat. Alec and I thought it would be best to keep all my paperwork simple, using my nickname instead of my birth name just for this very reason.

Connor reaches his hand out to me. He stares at me skeptically. "So, Ali, I've heard a lot about you. How you just happen to show up before even knowing what kind of business this was going to be." His eyes squint, he is a very untrusting too. "And how your husband has the same name as Nat's late brother. Is there a reason you're here, weaseling your way into my wife's business and life?"

He takes a menacing step toward me. The hairs on the back of my neck stand on end as flashbacks of my life in my home country shadow my thoughts. I need to remember that he's only looking out for her. Squaring my shoulders, I remember what Alec taught me about showing fear. Not dropping my eyes from his, I tell him the truth.

"As I told Natasha when I first approached Natasha, I had just graduated from college with a degree in hospitality management. There had been rumors that a new shop was supposed to be opening, so I had been checking for different event companies through the Secretary of State and found the application for this place. As for my husband, yes, it is ironic they have the same name. It must have been a common name that year." I tilt my head to one side, my brows furrowed, and gaze locked on Connor's, I snark out. "Is it not common in the United States to study the most common names for the year?" Yes, I am being a bitch, but he is not being nice either. "I am not trying to hide who I am. I loved how my husband's friends made our wedding so special and that is why I decided to take this career path. It is not as if I'm jumping into the career path to stalk Natasha. I have been going to school for over four years to earn this degree."

My anger is getting the best of me, and for the first time, when I am threatened, I stand up for myself, and it feels good. Natasha's hand grips Connor's arm, as if holding him back and silently asking him to stop his interrogation of me. Remembering this is a public event, I lower my voice. "Natasha, I am sorry, but if this is what I will have to be dealing with, then I will need to resign my position. When I left Afghanistan, I made a vow to myself and my daughter that I will never be put in a situation of being bullied again." Untying my apron, I thrust it into Connor's hands, then turn for the door.

The drive back to my home is interrupted with several texts and calls from both Natasha and a number that I do not recognize, and I wonder if it is Connor; but I do not answer any of them. I will look at the messages when I get home. Tears sting my eyes as I wonder if I did the right thing. After all, I was supposed to be there to protect her, but Connor needs to understand that I won't be intimidated.

Days have passed since the grand opening, and I have still not answered any calls or texts from either of them, yet flowers and cards still arrive every day asking for my forgiveness.

Alec pulls me into his arms reassuring me that I did the right thing. "Both Connor and Natasha can be very protective and stubborn. Connor would do anything to keep Natasha safe. He still blames himself for her being taken from us. His heart is in the right place, and we are keeping a huge secret from them."

"Yes, I know it is. I guess it just hurt my feelings that after all I did to help Natasha get her business going, he would think the worse of me. I will not let it go on for much longer."

CHAPTER 29

ALEC
2011

For the last five years I've been investigating Louis Kingston the third and what he has to do with my family, and how my supposed aunt and uncle are involved. But so far, I haven't found any money transfers that would make me believe that they are mixed up in any dirty business. Aunt Susan and Uncle David have a modest jewelry business, but it's always struggled from all the records I've reviewed. It hasn't changed in years, yet they were able to send Natasha to prestigious prep schools and universities. I just don't get it.

I'm missing something. There has to be something more in my mother's journals, and it's not just my aunt and uncle. I've been keeping a close eye on Nash too. He's been working the same case for the last five years. That's not normal. Not to bring down some punk gang. Call it a gut instinct, but I have a feeling it's all related. I have a gut feeling it has something to do with my family, but I'm missing so many pieces to the puzzle. I can't get a clear picture of what's going on.

So, I keep digging.

The good news is, Ali loves her new job and she and Nat have gotten close, even though Nat hasn't volunteered any information about what Nash is working on. She *has* confessed that he's been gone a lot more than usual and she's worried about him.

This isn't the way I wanted our marriage to be, but I don't have a lot of choice in the matter. I have to be a ghost. It kills me that I can't be seen at any of Neelam's school events or concerts like most fathers. I'm always hiding in the back of the room, never being introduced to any of her friends or their parents. Never did I think this mission would take so long. A year maybe, but not years. Both Aliah and I wanted to have another child, but God had other ideas for us. We knew there was an issue when she wasn't getting pregnant, and the doctor confirmed it. After thinking about it though, it would be selfish of me. She's already had to be a single parent to a teenager, I couldn't do that to her with a baby. I can only hide myself so much. A baby is an unknown. Maybe when this case is over and I find out the truth, but for now, I just keep searching.

The house is quiet. With Ali at work and Neelam at school, I pull out the stack of journals and paper that discovered before my last mission to Afghanistan; the documents that had been hidden in my storage unit before I found out my parents had been murdered.

Papers are splayed out over the dining room table, the chandelier radiating its bright rays down on all the pages as I try to make any semblance of sense out of them.

Hunched over in concentration, I re-read my moms' written words, which are beginning to blur. Her formal cursive penmanship has me wondering if cursive is even taught in school anymore. I don't ever think I've seen Neelam bring it home as homework.

Running my fingers through my hair in frustration, I have to believe there must be some hint of what my parents were doing and who they were running from in her writing. Is there a message somewhere in her words? God, I'm going insane trying to figure this out. Who would she think would be reading this? I was a kid when they were murdered and wasn't even born when she wrote in them according to the dates.

Twisting my neck and rolling my shoulders, trying to loosen my stiff muscles, I realize it's time for a break. I need to step away and take some time to clear my head. I walk into the kitchen to grab another cup of coffee, probably the fifth of the day, I decide to make a sandwich to absorb some to the acid turning in my stomach. My eyes burn from the drying light and the constant staring at the delicate cursive of my mom's handwriting. Rubbing my eyes, hoping it will help with the strain of all the tedious searching, I blink a couple of times before picking up my coffee and sandwich and head back to the table.

My toe catches in the fringe of the area rug nestled under the dining room table wrenching me forward. I'm barely able to catch my balance, but not before my black coffee sloshes out, drenching all the papers and journals sprawled out on the table.

"Shit." When I slam my mug down onto the table, the handle breaks off as the remainder of the hot liquid splashes out. I stare dumbfounded at the handle in my hand. "God damnit!" I drop the plate with my sandwich onto the table and dart back into the kitchen, grabbing a handful of paper towels to mop up my mess. How much information have I just lost? Dabbing at the soaked pages, I dry them off the best as I can.

Grabbing the hair dryer out of the bathroom I begin the monotonous task of drying the coffee-stained pages. Picking one of the journals up out of the puddle of coffee it's still sitting in, I fan out the pages, standing them up hoping they won't stick together before I have the chance to dry them. Thank God, I hadn't put creamer in my coffee this time. As I pick the journal up, I notice its inner lining is starting to curl. Inspecting it more, I find a piece of plastic tucked inside. Taking the journal over to the breakfast bar where I it's dry, I splay the book open. The hot coffee must have melted the glue sealing the lining to the cover of the journal revealing an object hidden under the paper. It's clearly a false back. Taking the knife from my pocket, I meticulously slice through the loosened back of the book, carefully revealing hidden documents.

The papers are neatly folded inside the plastic. Pulling the papers out, I gently open them. My brows furrow as I stare down at the yellowed document trying to comprehend what I'm seeing on the papers in front of me. Birth certificates: two of them, but the names are unfamiliar to me. One is for Stella Abella and the other for Marco Robino. More puzzle pieces to fit together.

Spreading the certificates out, my hands hold a shaking phone as I try and try again to take a focused picture of them to send to Grover. I'm not typically an anxious person, but deep down I know who these people are, I just don't know why.

It takes all of thirty seconds for my phone to ring, causing me to jump and almost dropping it.

"Hey, Grove. What took you so long?"

Grover snorts. "Fuck you, Turner." Grover and I have become good friends since my untimely death. "Who are they?"

"Not one hundred percent sure, but if I had to guess, I would say they are my parents—their true identities." Picking up one of the birth certificates, I try to think back over the years and if I ever heard either of the names mentioned, but nothing is familiar. "Can you check it out for me?"

"Of course. Anything new on Nash?"

"Strange you would ask. I have the weirdest feeling that the case he's working on and this case are somehow connected."

"Why would you think that?"

I tell him about the night I followed Nash to the club. I could tell Grover was nervous. "Hello? Grove, you still there?"

I keep staring down at my phone, wondering if I'd lost the call, when Grover finally clears his throat.

"What the hell is it, Grove? What aren't you telling me?"

"We need to sit down and have a beer."

"Fucking hell, Grove. A little difficult to do when you're on the other side of the country. Now stop stalling and tell me what the hell is going on."

"What do you know about the case he's working?"

"Not a lot, just that he's been working it for the last five years. He's been leaving early and getting home late, if at all. If I didn't know he loved my sister the way he does, I would almost think he was cheating on her. But I've seen him, something's wrong. I've never seen him look this bad. He's lost weight, and he appears as though he hasn't slept in the last year. Now tell me what you know."

"As you're aware, we've been keeping an eye on both Nash and your sister. With what you had found in your mother's journals and the attempts on both yours and Nash's lives, we're thinking the same thing.

"Not long after Nash joined up with the agency, he met a couple of agents. One of them, Walker, is actually my brother. Then he met another agent, an agent who was a plant, a rogue agent. We're trying to find out what he's up to and who he's working for.

My brows pinch together as I play back what Grover just said to me. Did I hear him correctly? "Excuse me?"

"Walker is my brother. My kid brother actually. The kid is a genius and a master in martial arts. Anyway, you're correct in thinking there's a connection to your case. As I said, there were two agents he met. The second is the one we think tried to kill Nash and you."

"What the fuck? How did he get in? Why didn't any of his military records get flagged? Do you understand just how fucked up this is?"

"I do, and that's the reason they planted Walker."

"We need to end this. Nash needs to know."

"Turner, this isn't any different from what you did with Aliah. You trained her to protect your sister, to watch after her. Walker is doing the same with Nash."

"Damnit, it is different!" I roar.

"Turner, the case Nash is working on involves a guy who strangled and raped his brother's fiancée in front of him. Walker's expertise is psychology, criminal justice, and linguistics. He can protect them both. He can watch Jenkins..."

"Is that the fucker's name who's been trying to kill us?"

Pacing, my anxiety level through the roof, I want to throw something. Palming my mug, I draw my arm back to throw it when my eyes land on the words printed on the side of the cup, and the delicate handprint. 'WORLDS BEST DADDY' My eyes burn as my shaking hand carefully sets down the mug that Neelam made me for Christmas their first year in the States. Closing my eyes, I take a deep breath to calm myself. My chest aches, it's so tight. I need to trust that things will be alright. It isn't as if we don't have people constantly watching Nash and Nat.

Grover has fallen silent, but he finally responds. "Yes, plus he's trying to get at Nash's witness. Let Walker do his job. If I didn't think he could do it, I'd have him pulled out. But we need this. We need him in there. He's our eyes and ears. God, Turner, he's my kid brother. If thing go fubar, his life is on the line too."

"At least give me a little more about Nash's case."

"I don't know much other than Mark, the assets brother, had been locked up in some mental hospital, but they let him go, said he was cured. But within forty-eight hours of his release, his family home burned down killing his father and the father's mistress. I'd say he was cured. Only a few people know about him. He's the one that got Maison, his brother involved and is now Nash's asset. I agree with you, I think there is some correlation between Nash's case and your parent, I just don't know what it is yet.

As I exhale the breath I was holding, his words hit me. His brother's life is on the line too. "Fine. We'll do it your way for now, but I need to be kept in the loop on what's going on. This is my family too."

I open the junk drawer in the kitchen and pull out the superglue. Spreading it on the broken handle of my mug, I then press it together and try to calm my breathing

CHAPTER 30

ALEC

My focus the next several months will be solely on Nash and his asset. Grover filled me in on what he had found out about the kid Nash has been protecting. I can't imagine what this kid, Maison has had to go through because of his brother.

Maison evidently has an identical twin brother who came down with a mental illness. Grover's brother, Walker, filled him in on the type of illness he has, which includes feeling more superior than all others, like a god and he has his eyes set on his twin brother.

There has to be more then what I'm seeing. This isn't the Nash I know. Something's happening. Nash isn't coming home at night, and I'm wondering what going on. Concerned not only for Natasha but for Nash as well, so I decided to follow him.

It's early evening when he arrives at Saber Elite, the club his asset, Maison Keller owns. For needing to be out of sight, Keller has done just the opposite. Having just built a club that everyone is dying to get into, he and his partner are in the headlines a lot these days. Ever since the clubs opening, there have been lines of hopeful patrons anxious and eager to get in, not caring about the long lines to get it. It's like nothing I've seen before. Well, except for the grand opening of an In and Out Burger.

Parking three cars back from where Nash has parked at the curb, I watch as he walks to the head of the line, flashing something at the beast of a man behind the velvet rope. Flipping his dark sunglasses up to get a better look at what Nash is showing him, the man nods, dropping his glasses back down on his nose and unfastening the purple rope that keeps the excited onlookers at bay.

I've never been here before and as I wait for Nash to exit, I take in all that is Saber Elite. I have to say, it looks spectacular. Black and white lights illuminate the marquee on in front of the building, as purple neon washes over the big double front doors decorated with a unique wrought iron modern-day mission design that matches the stacked flagstone façade on the outside the building.

Maybe one day, I can bring Aliah here... One day.

I check my watch again and wonder how long Nash will be in the club. It's been a while and he hasn't come out yet, so I decide to risk checking out his truck. I keep my eyes on the front door of the club as I stroll up to his truck, flipping my keys up and down in a controlled action, then drop them when I'm close and bend over to snatch them off the ground, attaching a tracker under the bumper as I stand. The tracker will be the best way for me to follow him in the middle of the night if I need to find him.

I'm just getting back to my car as Nash pushes through the door of the club accompanied by an extremely angry looking man, who's yelling at Nash as he follows him to his truck. I take in a long harsh breath, that was way to closed. From the photos that I've seen in my investigation, the enraged man is Maison Keller, Nash's asset.

After Nash leaves with Maison, I activate the tracker and watch as they drive around in a random, seemingly aimless pattern, and I know Nash is making sure he's not being followed. Finally, he parks and I pull in down the road from the craftsman style home in a quiet neighborhood. Keller exits the truck as Nash waits for him to enter the house. I glance at my watch an hour later as Maison slowly walks back out to Nash's vehicle. I watch as they pull away from the curb.

I flick the switch on the tracker as it begins to blink and beep once again, letting Nash have the head start.

Several minutes have passed when I finally put my truck into gear, following the red dots on the map into another neighborhood, I pass a house, but don't see Nash's truck and wonder if he parked in the garage. Both Nash and Maison are standing at the front door, while another man holds the door open, so I must be at the right place.

I pull into a driveway. The house has a for sale sign in the lawn and looks vacant. I get out of the truck and look in the windows and see the house is empty of furniture. Good, no chance of someone yelling at me for parking in their drive. Creeping through the front yard of the neighbor's house, I'm glad for the shrubs that line their fence. Listening, I strain to pick up the conversation.

"I was told you had a witness to hide, so I came to watch him for you," says the man at the front door.

"You can go, Jenkins. I'll stay here with him." The hairs on my body prickle as I hear the name of the man who has been trying to kill both Nash and me, knowing Nash has no clue who this man really is.

"No, man, I've got you covered," Jenkins replies.

"How did you even know I was coming here?"

I'd like to know the answer to that question as well. Jenkins hesitates as if trying to come up with an answer.

"I heard about the fire and his brother, so I figured you would house him here."

I replay my conversation with Grover. He said his brother just found out Mark was released from the mental hospital. He allegedly burned his childhood home down. There was no information on how the fire was set. Grover also said no one knew Maison had a twin brother, so how does Jenkins know?

After a lot of arguing, Jenkins walks out to his car and leaves. Not more than ten minutes later, I watch Nash pull out of the garage of the safe house. I can see his eyes searching for anyone who might be watching before heading in the opposite direction Jenkins left from.

Back in my car, I watch the little red dot bounce on the map, allowing Nash a head start, I recognize the direction and know exactly where he was going. His parents had a cabin in the woods. We used to go there when we were kids. We would have parties up there because we could always see anyone coming up the long gravel road. It's a long drive to the cabin, so I stop and grab coffee before leaving the city limits. The sun is just coming up, as I pull onto the side road leading to the cabin. I can't drive to far in without being noticed by Nash, but from where I'm at, I can watch for anyone coming and going.

It's mid-morning when I receive a call from Grover. "What's up, Grove? We just talked yesterday. Are you missing me?" I chuckle.

Grover's voice is raspy and thick. Concern seeps through him. He clears his throat before he speaks. "There was an explosion this morning."

My heart sinks as my stomach roils at the thought of losing Natasha. "My sister? Is she okay?"

"God, sorry Turner, yes, she's fine. According to my contact, it was a safe house that Nash took his asset to. They're looking for their bodies now. I'm sorry, Turner."

My heart is pounding out of my chest, emotion clogging my throat as I try to speak. "They aren't there." It's a rough whisper that escapes my lips. Unshed tears burn my eyes as fear courses through my veins. "I followed them. They did stop by the house, but Jenkins was there. He made up some bullshit story about how he knew Nash would be going there and tried to convince Nash to leave the asset with him. Nash refused and Jenkins finally left. Nash left shortly after Jenkins. It's obvious that Nash doesn't trust Jenkins either."

CHAPTER 31

ALEC

The case Nash is working on has to do with witness protection. Maison, his asset, has had several different identities. Not that Maison did anything to Mark, but the brother's disease has made him envious of his own sibling.

Walker said that Maison and Mark were extremely close as children and into their early teens, then Mark snapped, and he began lashing out at everyone, but more so at Maison.

The report on Maison that Grover shared with me included information on his family and how dysfunctional it was, which seemed to aggravate Mark's symptoms. A philandering father, and a mother who wouldn't stand up for herself, didn't help either of the boys learn how a real relationship works.

When they finally took Mark to the doctor, they were told most adolescents grow out of this kind of disorder as long as there was some sort of therapy. Unfortunately for everyone in Mark's way he didn't go to his therapy sessions.

According to the report, Mark was out to destroy Maison, using his name in some big drug deal. It wasn't difficult for the agency to find Maison, but when they brought him in to interrogate him, they soon could see he had nothing to do with what he was accused of. And of course, he had no idea why he was brought in. During the investigation, they found that Maison had an identical twin brother. After Maison told them about his brother's illness, they knew there was only one way to clear his name unless he went in and helped catch the leader. So, Nash made him an asset.

No one outside the interrogation room knew Maison had a twin brother, and since Mark had used Maison's name it was easy to hide that knowledge. Mark had been experimenting with drugs, add that to his mental issues, the agency knew they couldn't use him in court, which left them, Maison.

Maison agreed to help as long as his brother received the care he needed in a good facility, with no possibility of being discharged. Unfortunately, the facility Mark was locked up in found he was cured and saw no reason for holding me. Somehow all his court paperwork was lost or missing, allowing him to just walk out after they saw an improvement in his behavior. He was never supposed to get out.

Walker just found out they let Mark out and didn't notify anyone. Not his family and not the authorities.

He's now murdered his father and his father's girlfriend and burned his parents' house down. Luckily, a neighbor rescued the mother.

The agency inserted Maison just long enough to gather the needed information, then they had to keep him alive to testify.

Luckily, there were a few informants, but every time they got close to a trial, a witness either recanted, or worse yet, went missing. That was five years ago, and I don't think they've even come close to closing the case.

CHAPTER 32

ALEC

I'm tired, and I miss my family. I've been following Nash for the last couple of weeks. There are so many moving parts to what's going on. I just need down time, and to be honest, I don't know how Nash has done it for so long.

Aliah is already in bed by the time I get home. I strip out of my clothes and crawl in behind her; pulling her warm naked body close to me. Nuzzling my nose into her long silky hair, and breathing her in, I whisper into her ear, "I love you, please never forget that."

Slowly shifting, she turns in my arms to face me. Her warm hands cradle my face pressing her forehead to mine. "I understand you are worried about Nash and Natasha. They need to be your priority right now, but I miss you, miss your touch on me, the way you make me feel. Maybe it's my insecurities, but sometimes I wonder if you are getting tired of me."

A sliver of moonlight shines through the curtains and I see her eyes pool with tears. My chest aches at her words. "God, no, Aliah,

I love you so much it hurts. I'm so sorry for neglecting you and Neelam. I've been so preoccupied about everything going on with Nash and wanting this all to be over that I've ignored you." Pulling her into my arms, I press my lips to hers.

"Show me that you still love me, Alec. Show me that I can still make you happy."

"Let me show you just how much I love you. Slipping down under the sheets, I worship her body with my tongue, tasting and licking until my need for her can't be stopped. She's so wet and hot as I sink into her, feeling her need for me. No words are said as we make love, our two bodies joining to make one, bringing our souls back to each other.

The next morning, I receive a distraught call from Aliah. "Alec, Nash is missing," she heaves out in a panicked whisper.

Fuck. "When was the last time anyone has heard from him?" I need to stay composed, to hear everything Aliah says.

"No one has heard from him in the last couple of days. Natasha is concerned it has to do with the mission that he has been on. She does not know what to do."

"How does she know? There have been several times that he hasn't come home recently."

"He usually calls her during the day, but he hasn't called. I see the fear in Natasha's face.

"I'll find him. Try to keep her calm."

"Okay. Please be careful Alec."

But I can't promise her anything, because I don't know what the circumstances are. "I love you," I say then end the call.

Thumbing through my phone, I open the app for the tracker and see Nash's car has been sitting in the same place for a while: Maison's house. Calling Grover, I notify him of where Nash's car is and hope he can get someone there quickly. I feel helpless, not being able to do anything. My chest constricts with fear for my best friend. God, this has to end.

Pacing, I wait for any news. Then I receive the news I never wanted to hear. Nash has been shot. He's lost a lot of blood and they don't know if he'll make it, and I want to curl up and die with him.

Fucking hell, is this what it was like when he was told I was dead? How could I have agreed to this? This was wrong on so many levels.

Turns out Nash was shot in the abdomen. They rushed him into surgery to repair the damaged organs and blood vessels. Luckily, nothing major was damaged by the bullet. I think he's part cat with the amount of lives he's had.

Natasha hasn't left his side. I feel helpless. I want to see him, apologize to him for lying to him, but if I do, I know that this mission will be over and we'll wind up in the same situation, not knowing who is behind this whole mess. I have to rely on Aliah and what information she can bring me.

Over the following weeks, Nat remained by Nash's bedside while he was in the hospital. Aliah brought her food and visited with her, but Nat never really talked or ate any of the food that was brought.

I'd learned that Jenkins showed up at Maison's house and more or less kidnapped him and no one knew where either of them was.

For several weeks Aliah continued delivering food to Nat after Nash had been released from the hospital. She knew it was the only way to check up on both of them. She said he's been in a real foul mood, threatening to go back to work early if Nat didn't stop hovering and go back to her event planning business.

A few days after the doctor released Nash to return to work, Aliah received a desperate call from Nat. Nash left her, said he didn't love her anymore.

Bullshit. I know better. In fact, the idea had crossed my mind as well. I'd do anything to keep Aliah safe, but I knew she wouldn't understand, and it would devastate her.

CHAPTER 33

ALIAH

I've been taking care of the shop for the last couple of months. After Connor was shot, Natasha stayed with him. First at the hospital, then at home until the doctor released him back to work. Then he did the unthinkable; he left her. I may be new at relationships, but one thing I do know for certain is that Connor Nash loves Natasha. He must be afraid of something. Something that could get her hurt. That is the only reason he would walk away.

"He called me," Natasha sobs out on the other end of the phone. "He called me and told me he missed me."

My heart sinks. It was a bastard thing he did, but how do I tell her to walk away when I positive he loves her. "I am sorry, Natasha. Did he mention why he is doing this? Is it because of the case he is working on?"

Her voice hitches and I hear her sniffle on the other end of the line. "No, he hasn't said anything other than he doesn't love me anymore."

"And do you believe him?"

"I don't know what to believe now," she cries out. "I would say no, I don't believe it, but he's been acting so strange lately." She hiccups a ragged breath again.

"It's time for us to do something for ourselves! We are going out! We have worked our asses off to get the business going and we did an amazing job. It is time for us to celebrate," I say, knowing she will try to stop me.

She sighs. "I don't think so Ali. I really don't feel like going out."

If I don't take the upper hand, she will not go. "Tough, you do not have a choice. I will drag you out myself if I have to. It is time to cut loose. I do not think I have ever seen you relax, so, like it or not we are doing it. There is a new club that opened up downtown, and I have been dying to go."

Silence comes from the other end of the phone. Then Natasha's voice, quiet and unsure. "I've never gone to a club before. My aunt and uncle were extremely strict. I was never allowed."

"Well, to be honest, I never have either. I was not allowed to go outside or even to the market without a male relative. I lived for years in the dark. I did not have the choice. So, this is a first for me too, and we are going to have a blast."

Natasha never spoke freely about her childhood until the day after Connor left. It only took a plate of chili cheese fries and several raspberry lemon-drop martinis for her to tell me everything. She told me about her childhood, her parents, Connor, Alec and his death, Louis, her aunt and uncle, then finding Connor again at Alec's funeral.

It was then that I realized Natasha wasn't a job anymore. She was a friend. My best friend. Something that I have not had since I was a child. Yes, Alec is my best friend too, but having a girl friend is different. It is like how the girls back on the base were with me. It was something that I never knew I needed but desperately wanted.

It has been a long week, and I am excited that tonight Natasha and I are going to Saber Elite. I do not know a lot about it other than it recently opened, and it is *the* place to go.

The plan is to leave after work, hoping to beat the late-night clubbers. "So, let me see what you brought to wear tonight," I ask. I feel like a schoolgirl clapping with excitement. Glancing around, I look for a garment bag or something she might have a change of clothes in.

"What are you looking for?" she asks, tilting my head as if not understanding my question.

"Where is your garment bag with the clothes for tonight?" My brows furrow thinking I missed something.

"Was I supposed to wear something different?" Natasha stops straightening the linens hanging in their alcove, a confused look on her face.

My mouth falls open.

"I... I just figured I would remove my jacket and wear what I have on now." She glances down at her business suit. The skirt falls below her knees and my God, she has on sensible shoes. There is nothing wrong with her outfit for work, but to go clubbing in? No way will her matron clothes be appropriate.

I just stare at her wondering if she's just joking.

"You cannot be serious?" I huff out as I study her, my eyes roaming up and down her body.

"Ali, I've never gone to a club before. I don't have a clue what to wear."

"Honey, we are not going to a meeting, we are going out to dance and maybe pick up a man for you." I struggle to keep the panic out of my voice. Fear flashes across her face.

"I... I'm married."

"Natasha, hun, so am I, but we are going out to have fun, we are not going to church or meeting a potential client. Besides, he is the one who left you, yes?" Insecurity lights her eyes. "What? You think no man is going to notice you? You are beautiful! I guarantee you that we won't be there five minutes before you have men buying you drinks and asking you to dance" Her eyes drag up and down my body "Oh, and by the way, we are going shopping at lunch for a new outfit. This is not a Halloween party where you dress up as a school matron. Besides, I have to use some of the information that I've read about in my romance novels," I wink at her before turning and walking out of her office.

Her mouth drops open as if I insulted her and my opinion on her attire. She begins to say something, but I am out the door before she finishes, saying over my shoulder, "Love ya, hun!" and wink at her.

At lunch, I pull Natasha out of the shop. Finding a little boutique, we walk in and I get a room for her. She has killer legs, that will drive all the guy crazy if she wore a little skirt, but we settle on a pair of black skinny jeans with a white midriff tank and a cute form-fitting leather jacket and a pair of little black leather ankle boots with a spike heel. The white tank contrasts perfectly with her dark hair, which she pulls back off her face in a high ponytail. She finds a pair of gold and black beaded chandelier earrings, and I apply a red lip stain to her lips, so she won't have to reapply it all night.

She looks amazing.

"Do you like it?" I ask.

"Other than the top is short, I feel comfortable and I'm almost excited about going out tonight." She has a sparkle in her eye. "I have to say that, although I haven't gotten Connor out of my head and probably never will, you have a way of preoccupying my thoughts."

"Good, isn't that what friends are for?"

Pulling up to the valet, Natasha hands him her keys. It seems like hundreds of people are standing in line to get in. I hope my idea works, otherwise we might not ever get in tonight. Everyone is dancing to the loud music streaming over the outside speaker while they wait in line.

Grabbing Natasha's hand, I drag her, dancing my way up to the big hulk of a man, standing in front of a purple velvet rope at the front of the line. I cannot read his expression as his eyes are hidden behind wraparound black glasses. He is a hulk of a man and I wonder if his suits are custom made because I don't think any big and tall shop would carry his size. His biceps stretch the fabric of his suit jacket, and if I were anywhere else, I would think about crossing the road so I would not have to approach him, but what's the worse he could do... say no?

Natasha tugs at my hand and whisper yells. "Ali..." She glances at everyone waiting patiently in line, who are now shouting at us, "...we can't just cut."

I'm tall, but the man standing in front of me is enormous. Reaching up on my tippy toes, I motion that I want to say something, and he leans down so I can speak into his ear.

Glancing at the building, as he ponders my question, I am struck by the grandeur of the building. None of the buildings around it come close to its opulence.

"Have fun, ladies," the man with the deep baritone voice says as he unlatches the purple velvet rope allowing us to walk in. His smile is warm as he lets us pass.

"Thank you, Jonathan." I run my hand down his massive arm giving him a wink. Excited, I grip Natasha's hand as we walk the red carpet to the front door, flipping my hair over my shoulder and adding a little extra swing to my walk.

Natasha turns toward me, surprise filling her eyes. "How..." Her brows pinch together. "Do you know him?"

"No, but where I come from, if you do not try, you will never know. What is the worst thing that could have happened? He could have said no, and we would have had to walk to the end of the line. I am not a conformist." Another large man pulls the big front door, and I feel as if I am entering another world. The hallway is dark but lit by little-LED lights leading us to the large main room. Loud music reverberates around us.

Wrought iron wall décor echoes the wrought iron design from the front door and is lit from behind with the same purple, red and white lights.

The room has multi-level seating areas. The dining area overlooks the dance floor. Red leather horseshoe booths around black acrylic tables line the purple walls. A long sweeping acrylic bar, lit with purple and red lights, line the opposite wall. The same mission design illuminates the club's name from behind the bar. Long strings of twinkly white lights dangle from the ceiling, balls covered in tiny little mirrors hang around the room casting prisms of rainbow colors that bounce off every surface. Clear acrylic rectangular pedestal tables outlined with LED lights dot the outside of the dance floor as red, purple, and white lights flash to the music. This gives me so many ideas for events.

I cannot stop looking around. Everywhere I look, there is something different that I did not notice before. I just want to walk and explore. This place is amazing.

Natasha points to an empty booth, and we each take a seat there. Within seconds, a server is in front of our table asking for our order.

As the lights flash to the beat of the music, I see the wrought iron spiral staircase and wonder if it leads to a special VIP area. Three bird cages for dancers hang next to the DJ's stage. Scantily clad dancers move erotically inside, and I wonder what it would be like to be in one of them. Each cage is made of intricate wrought iron and spotlights shine on them showcasing the dancers.

"Wow, this place is just... Wow," Natasha says over the music. Our server returns with our drinks. Natasha pulls out her credit card to have a tab started, but the server shakes her head. "Oh, do you not carry tabs here?" A look of surprise is Natasha's face.

Our server leans into us. "Your tab for the night has already been paid."

My eyes scan the area for anyone acknowledging us but see no one.

"Who?" Natasha asks.

"He didn't tell me his name, just told me to tell you to have a good time."

There's nothing else to do but to bounce with excitement. "See, I told you," I say, bumping my shoulder to Natasha's and taking a sip of my drink.

After finishing our first drink, we head to the dance floor. As we dance, a man comes up to Natasha asking her to dance. Her eyes flash to me as she sinks her teeth into her bottom lip, but then nods her head accepting his offer.

I feel I am responsible for Natasha, so I keep my eye on her. I watch as different men approach her, and as Connor flashes his badge at the men, flicking his thumb in a move out gesture. He gives me a look to not say a word, and it just reaffirms my thought that he didn't leave because he didn't love her. He left to protect her. Natasha is none the wiser as to what has happened to every man who has asked her to dance, and I suppress a smile.

Natasha and I dance to a few songs before returning to our table and as before, our server is there with new drinks. Even though I have never been to a place like this, I have read enough to know that you never leave a drink unattended.

WHEREVER OUR JOURNEY LEADS US

By the third drink, it is obvious the alcohol is affecting Natasha's coordination not to mention her inhibitions. I stopped drinking at two so I could keep a clear head, but she keeps asking for more.

After her fifth drink, she is having a hard time standing. "Come on, Ali." Her words were more than slurred. "I wanna dance s'more." From what she told me about her past, she has never been a drinker. Maybe a glass of wine with dinner, but never more than two. Louis, the man who her aunt and uncle had betrothed her to, always told her, *'Proper ladies never embarrass themselves by overindulging in alcohol.'* She begins to giggle as we walk back to the dance floor.

"What are you laughing at?"

Her eyes are glazed over as she continues to giggle. "Louie the prick." As if remembering his rules.

She stumbles, grabbing for anything to keep her standing, but there's nothing around to hold on to. I try to catch her, but she is too heavy for me.

Out of the corner of my eye, I see a flash of somebody. Before hitting the ground, Connor catches her, lifting her into his strong arms. He gives me a stern look before carrying her out of the building. This is a secret I will not tell her.

CHAPTER 34

ALEC

Aliah is taking Natasha to Saber Elite. I give Grover a heads up so he can get the word to his brother Walker and he can trickle it down to Nash.

Hiding in a booth, I search the crowd for anyone suspicious. I lower my head and study my drink as Nash strolls through the door of the club and walks over to a man sitting at the bar. From what Grover has told me, Walker was going to be here keeping an eye on Nat until Nash arrived. He doesn't look good. In fact, he looks like shit. Dark circles accent his eyes, and his clothes hang off him as if he's lost weight.

Staring at Aliah and all the men clambering around her, I think just how lucky I am, and how much I love her. I want to stride over to her and show everyone she belongs to me and only me.

I can only imagine how Nash feels watching all those men grab at his wife and not be able to do anything about it, because I want to cut the hands off of all the men touching my wife.. I realize he's doing it to protect her, but seriously, he's an ass.

He surreptitiously uses his badge to repel all the men with their tongues dragging the floor for her. My sister grew up to be a gorgeous woman, and God I miss her.

Natasha begins to stumble and fall, but as if he could sense it, Nash is there to catch her, lifting her into his arms as Walker grabs her things from their booth and follows Nash out the door.

That's my green light to walk onto the dance floor and take my wife from the man who has his hands on her; he begins to argue until she wraps her arms around my neck and drags me to her lips. She nuzzles into my neck, whispering into my ear. "Meet me home, my love and make wild passionate love to me."

Aliah pulls the valet ticket from her wallet. We walk out separately just in case someone is watching.

Although Neelam is fourteen now and we haven't had to worry about a babysitter for a while now, she decided that she would stay at a friend's house tonight.

Jumping over my back fence, I creep through the scrubs and watch as Nash carries Nat into the house. Suddenly, I notice Walker striding my direction, his gun drawn as he advances toward the back of the house. His gun is focused in front of him. I only have seconds before he will see me. Walker is just turning the corner of the house as I disappear back into my yard and slipping through the sliding door, I close it just as I see the shadow of Walker coming to the fence.

Because I wanted to keep an eye on Nat and Nash, we bought the house directly behind theirs. I'm glad we did. This way, I always had my eyes on her, and could protect her at a moment's notice.

CHAPTER 35

NOW

ALEC
FOUR MONTHS AGO, ~ 2018

Months have turned into years, and Grover informs me the case with Nash finally have a court date. *Hallelujah!! There is a God.*

The court date is in a week. Maison—who now is going by the name of Liam has been hiding out and is on his way back. Hopefully, nothing will happen to him before that, because I can't take this any longer.

According to Walker, they have a surprise witness who's been hidden away for years. I wonder who it is. Walker wouldn't tell Grover. And honestly, I don't think the guy they have locked up is the real guy. I'd bet my life he's just a pawn, because from what I've been told, he has nothing to do with my family.

CHAPTER 36

ALEC
THREE MONTHS AGO

Something's happening. There's only a couple of days till the trial, and from what Grover relayed to me, Callie, Maison's—I mean Liam's ex-fiancé, her husband Kai, and one of her sons were kidnapped from their home in some kind of home invasion. They knew the house was being guarded because they kill one of Nash's men. *Fuck me!* They're holding them for ransom. Liam.

My stomach drops well aware this case hinges on Liam's testimony, no Liam, no case. All these years, years I could have been with my family, my sister, and best friend. Years wasted.

Grover has kept me up to date with everything that's been going on. I feel helpless. There's nothing I can do but wait.

It's the night before the exchange, and as I lie in bed holding Aliah tight to me, I would give myself to protect the woman in my arms.

As dawn wakes, Grover calls with news. I'm surprised. I thought the rule was to not give into ransom demands. Nash is doing something I never thought he would do. After years of sacrificing not only his marriage, but also sacrificing himself for his job, for the man he's protected and almost died for, he's going to give Liam to the kidnappers to save Callie and her family. It's hard for me to believe he's doing it. Does he have another plan? Does it have to do with the surprise witness?

Standing in the kitchen, staring out the back window at Nat's house. I try to piece together all the possibilities of the day. I've seen Nash with Liam. He's more than an asset to him. Liam is Nash's friend, and maybe that's why it's so hard for me to understand how he could just sacrifice him.

Aliah comes up behind me, her arms wrap around me. It's her touch that allows me to take a breath and relax.

I turn, and our eyes meet. "I don't want you going into work today."

Tilting her head, she furrows her brows. "You know I have to go in. I need to be there just in case something happens. This is what you trained me for."

"I can't risk something happening to you." Cradling her face in my hands, my forehead drops to hers. "I don't want anything to happen to you," I say as I press my lips to hers.

Pulling away, her look is one of resignation. "This is my job to watch after your sister because you cannot. I understand you have other people looking after her from the outside, but I am the only one on the inside. I could never live with myself if I fail this one mission. This is my honor to your family. Please, I must."

"And I would never forgive myself if I lose the only woman I love." I beg with my eyes, but I realize her mind is made up. There's no stopping her.

Aliah goes to work as usual, as if nothing is different. I have extra protection on Nat. If they're willing to take a mother and her family, just because she once was engaged to him, they won't hesitate using other tactics them from trying to stop Nash any way they think possible.

The trial begins today, and I don't think they will leave fait to just Callie and her family.

CHAPTER 37

ALEC
THREE MONTHS AGO

The trial is over but not without maelstrom of gunfire and death. I've been told Jenkins was killed, but it still doesn't make sense to me. He didn't have the financial backing to do all the things he did.

Still not one hundred percent sure that Nat is safe, I patrol her house. It's been a long day and so much was revealed. I just need to be sure she's okay.

It's almost midnight when I jump the fence, into Nat's back yard. I'm just coming around the side of the house as a Tahoe pulls away from the curb but then screeches to a jerky stop. I can hear the sound of the car being slammed into park. Shit, it's Nash. He doesn't even wait for the vehicle to come to a complete stop before leaping from it and running toward me. I quickly bound over my fence and into my house. I peer through the curtain as he continues searching for the unknown. As he reaches for his shoulder, my back-porch light shows him wincing in pain I was told he was injured today in the melee. Grover told me they were ambushed in the parking structure of the courthouse.

The secret weapon was none other than Mark, Liam's brother. According to Grover, Mark had been put on a trial drug several years ago. He'd been monitored while he'd been locked away in a mental hospital. Long story short, it worked, and he was able to testify along with Liam.

I also found out that Jenkins, the FBI agent that was suspected of being the mole in the agency, was the kingpin, but it doesn't feel right. It was too easy. God, what am I saying? It hasn't been easy, but it just doesn't fit. Someone had to fund him. I know the trial is over and Jenkins is now dead, thanks to Liam's girlfriend, Finn, but I still have to go with my gut instincts. This isn't over yet.

CHAPTER 38

There's power in love.

ALIAH
PRESENT TIME – THE WEDDING

Today is Finn and Liam's wedding. I had met them on a day Natasha was out of the shop. Liam is the man who Connor had been protecting. I believe he is called an asset.

Over the years, Liam and Connor have become close friend and, in the process, Connor had told Liam about Natasha and that he was still in love with her. They were hoping I could help them get the two back together. Liam feels guilty for the destruction of their marriage. In fact, they came to Natasha after finding out she was an event planner to help them with their wedding. What they needed from me was to keep Connor and Natasha separated until Finn was to walk down the aisle. I've worked enough weddings to know how I could make this work, and I was all too happy to help, because I too think they need to be back together.

Liam and Finn's wedding is not large; in fact, it's rather small. Normally I do the smaller events, but since they had asked for Natasha personally, she was going to handle it.

It was when I met them that I found he was the co-owner of Portland's most posh nightclub, Saber Elite, the club I took Natasha to. I was surprised that their wedding was so small, but neither of them have a lot of family, and both he and Finn, wanted something more intimate. What surprised me more, was that his ex-fiancée Callie, the one who had been kidnapped, is sitting in the audience and one of her sons is the ring bearer.

Both Liam and Finn are so sweet. She is beautiful, very much the "girl next door." And no one would ever guess that he is owner of such a prestigious establishment.

All I told Natasha was that Liam and Finn have asked to help them with a special surprise for one of their attendees. Little does she know she is the surprise.

Due to not only what happened a few months ago during the trial and home invasion, but because they are celebrities in their own right, they have hired extra security.

"Ahem." Turning, I see one of the beefy security men trying to get Natasha's attention as I help another one with his boutonniere. His low baritone voice catching her attention.

"Excuse me, Ms. Turner." He looks as though he's never been to a wedding before. "Could you help me with this flower thing, please?"

She smiles up at him. "Yes, of course, and it's called a boutonniere." She made sure security looked as if they were part of the wedding party. Each man had a boutonniere pinned to his lapel with hidden mics in them. Earpieces were hidden in their ears.

I thought Natasha was going to freak when Finn and Liam told her they wanted to get married within the month. We have thrown events together fast, but this was not just some random person, Liam owns a well-known club. If it goes bad, it could damage her reputation. The thing is, I know even if there were problems, they would never give a bad review because they came to Natasha for one reason only. Our biggest issue was the venue, and if we could even find something suitable for them.

We got lucky, because Finn is a fashion designer and wanted to design and make her own gown, and oh my gosh, it is stunning. The dress Finn created fit her personality perfectly. It is a bohemian style and quite simple. Her train is not long, but the look is light and airy with the chiffon skirt. She glides as she walks and the effect on the fabric is stunning. Simple white flowers decorate her hair which is in a loose knot. Wisps of hair curl and flow, framing around her face. The bodice is a French lace with a sweetheart neckline that continues over her shoulders in a unique racerback design. The lace she ordered for the dress was held up in customs and delayed the wedding a few extra weeks, but the effect was worth the wait.

She thought about changing the type of lace for the dress, but she had dreamed of this day and would not compromise, even for lace. Unfortunately, we lost the original venue due to the delay, but they did not care where they got married, they just wanted to be married.

Finn and Natasha became good friends over the weeks they have been working together on the wedding.

Natasha walks to Finn's dressing room as I make sure the men are standing at the altar. Before anyone had arrived, we had installed long opaque white fabric panels to conceal the chapel from the atrium to hide Finn until it was time for her to walk down the aisle. Once all the guests arrived, the panels were released allowing the fabric to conceal us from the guests but more important, from Liam and Connor.

Handing Marley, Finn's best friend and the Maid of Honor, her bouquet, Natasha positions Luka; Callie's youngest son and the ring bearer, at the front. He will be the first to walk down the aisle. Pulling the satin ropes, the curtain lifts and separates revealing the cute little man.

Luka begins to walk to the front of the chapel. The hum from the people in the chapel heightens as this cute little boy, with his dark curly mop and his rolled-up Khakis with suspenders, strides down the aisle to Liam. As I watch Luka, my heart aches at the regret that I couldn't give Alec a little boy like him.

Needing to brush that thought of babies from my mind, I force myself to remember that I have a job to do. The panels are lowered once again, and I motion for Marley to stand and wait for the panels to open again. Once again, they are lifted, and she begins her walk.

Once the fabric panels are lowered to conceal Finn, we wait for the music to begin.

Natasha readjusts Finn's train, then motions for the curtain. Finn, her face bright with a smile, begins to walk down the aisle.

The curtain remains drawn as Natasha and I admire Finn gliding down the aisle to the very enchanted Liam. My eyes flash to Connor, who turns ghostly white, and he almost stumbles. Is he going to pass out? His eyes are trained on Natasha.

Liam turns to Connor, a wide smile spreads across his face as he asks. "Something catch your attention, friend?" Everyone in the audience turns to see what Connor is staring at.

"Fucking hell. Nat!" Conner mutters, the pastor's mic picks up their conversation as Finn and Liam just smile at each other knowing their plan has worked.

Out of the corner of my eye, I can see when Natasha recognizes Connor, because like he did, she loses her balance, and I grab her, keeping her from falling.

Her face is void of color as the blood drains from it. "Oh God, Connor," she whispers as she grabs the wall trying to steady herself but misses. Still with a grip on her, I lead her to a pew in the atrium to have her sit.

"Natasha, are you all right? Geez, it seems like everyone is a little unsteady today."

She hasn't seen Connor in years. I am surprised they never ran into each other since they live in the same town. I know she is in shock, but I think this is what she needs, which is the reason I agreed to help Liam and Finn with this little surprise for the both of them.

Tears fill her eyes as she takes in a long shaky breath and whispers, "Ali, I have to leave. I'm not feeling well. Please make my apologies the Finn and Liam."

"Are you sure you will be alright to drive?"

"Yes, I'll be fine." Holding her arm, I help her to stand. It takes her a few seconds to gain her balance before I release my hold on her.

Grabbing her emergency kit, she rushes to her car.

Glancing back down to the front of the chapel, I watch as Connor slaps Liam's shoulder before running down the aisle. As if remembering he had the ring, he turns, tossing the box to Liam who just laughs.

My attention remains on Connor and Natasha as Connor rushes up behind her. She is throwing her bag into her car, but startles, clutching her chest with a shaky hand. "Jesus Christ son of Mary!" she exclaims. "Connor, you scared the shit out of me."

He chuckles, which brings a smile to my face, because I don't think in all the years I have known Natasha, I have ever heard her curse. "Still have that trucker's mouth I see."

"I have to go." Natasha tries to move around Connor, but he blocks her from leaving.

"But the wedding isn't over yet."

"I... I'm not feeling well." Her eyes fall to the ground. I notice she cannot look him in the eye.

Not wanting to be caught watching this very personal moment, I hide behind the chapel doors, peeking out from the edge.

Connor lifts her chin with a finger, her eyes still not looking at him. "Hmmm, you look rather good to me. In fact, you look amazing."

Her eyes flash to his as she squares her shoulders and the quiet pristine woman transforms into a cold, hard, ice queen. I've never seen this side of her.

I jump with surprise from the sound of her hand slapping Connor's face.

"You fucking coward, you lost that right when you walked out on me and broke your vows," she roars.

Connor grabs her, threading the fingers of one hand through her well-coiffured hair, the other hand cradling her face. His lips crush down on hers. She pushes at his chest, fighting his hold, before biting his lip making him growl, but I do not think it was an angry growl, more one of longing. Pulling away, he wipes at his mouth. A trace of crimson smeared on his fingers.

Once again, he drops his lips to hers as a deep guttural growl resonates from his chest, loud enough that I could hear. His tongue slides over her lips as his hand slides down to the small of her back, pulling her body to his. Her body softens, molding to his. Her hands grip his hair, pulling and tugging him closer, as if he was everlasting life and she was dying. Both of them lost in the moment and I wonder what she is thinking.

Tears begin to fall down Natasha's face, as they pull away from each other. Connor leans in to kiss them away, whispering, "I'm so sorry Nat..."

Natasha's fingers cover Connor's lips. Taking a step back, she slips under his arm and slides into her car. "So am I."

Starting her car, she pulls away, not ever turning back, and even though I'm the interloper here, my heart aches for what I know each of them are feeling.

Connor stoically walks back into the chapel as I pretend to be doing something other than watching their intimate moment.

CHAPTER 39

ALEC

Aliah calls me filling me in on the wedding and how the surprise Liam and Finn had planned for Nat. I wasn't all that excited about it, frankly, because I'm still fucking pissed that Nash hurt my sister. Yes, I realize that in his stupid head, he thought he was saving her, but let's be real here. No one could have protected her better than he could. But instead, he had someone else watching her.

Glancing out the back window of my house, I notice the flashing lights from a police car and wonder what's going on. I can't just hop the fence, someone could see me, especially if something is going on. Jumping into my car, I drive around the block and pull up to the curb, rolling down my window to hopefully hear the conversation. Nat is in her car; an officer leans down to speak to her through the window. I notice her garage door is open. I'd driven by earlier today and it was closed. I wonder if that's the reason she's still sitting in her car.

After writing in a little notebook, the officer enters the house through the garage, disappearing inside.

Nat rolls her window up, waiting for the officer to return. He's in the house for quite a while before exiting the house and walking over to Nat.

The officer speaks to her for a few minutes, I can only pick up a couple of words he's saying, that he didn't see anything out of place. the officer nods at Nat before getting back into his car and driving away. I don't like this. Call it a gut feeling, but I know something's wrong.

Nat pulls her car into the garage, closing the door before getting out of the car. Good girl, you remembered.

CHAPTER 40

ALIAH

Connor slowly wanders back inside the chapel. So many expressions cross his face as he comes face to face with Finn and Liam's mischievous smiles. They glance behind him; their faces fall in disappointment.

As Connor congratulates them, his phone rings, and he pulls it from his jacket. The color once again vanishes from his face; his smile is no longer evident. Who is on the other end of the line?

Holding a finger up in the universal sign of "just a minute," he swipes at his screen. Then he turns and strides to the chapel exit. "Hold on Walker, I need to get to an area that's quiet."

Leaning against his truck, he begins to speak. "Walker, are you still there?"

I pretend I'm packing my things to see if I can overhear anything. His head falls as I hear him drawing in a deep breath. I wish I could hear both sides of the conversation.

"Could she have left it open by mistake?" he asks.

I need to call Alec.

"She didn't go inside did she?"

Oh, my goodness, someone must have broken into her house.

"Good. Good girl." His stature seems to relax, exhaling a sigh of relief.

"What do you mean?"

Again, he tenses. Then he's jumping into my truck, gravel flying as he barrels out of the drive.

Pulling my phone out, I call Alec. He answers quickly. "Aliah, what's going on. Nat just returned home."

"I'm not sure. Connor just sped out of here. He received a call from someone about Natasha. It sounds like someone broke into the house. There's something wrong. The person on the phone said something that freaked him out, and he panicked and left."

I can hear Alec's phone fade as if he's receiving another call. "Ali, Grover is calling, I have to get this."

"Yes, of course."

I end the call and put on a fake smile feigning everything is alright when I know otherwise. This could be the end of this whole horrible and sad story, but with most horror stories, comes death. And for the first time in years, I'm scared of losing not only my husband, but any part of his family before he has the chance to reunite with them.

CHAPTER 41

ALEC

Flicking my phone to Grover, my hand shakes at what he's about to say. "Grover, tell me what's going on, Ali just called me."

"It's Louis. He's back." Grover's voice was strong and emotionless. He broke into Nat's house, leaving the garage door open. When she got home, she called the police, but that's not who she got. He rigged it. He had a fake cruiser come out. He was even able to get ahold of a real uniform."

"Yeah, I saw him go into the house," I say.

"Well, he was just a hired man." Grover pauses, and I'm afraid of what he's going to say.

"What? Tell me. What are you afraid to say?"

"I think he's in the house."

Just as Grover tells me my worst possible fear, Nash's truck screeches to a halt in front of the house. As he jumps from the truck, Nash has his gun drawn as he reaches the front door.

My heart slams against my ribcage and I have to remember to breathe as my skin prickles with nervous anticipation. Unholstering my gun I feel beads of perspiration slip down my back. My eyes shift around, searching for any movement as I make my way to the front door. The last thing I want is to be ambushed.

Standing at the front door, I finally hear the voice of the man who I believe is responsible for the destruction of not only my family, but the deaths of my parents. "Well, well, well. I do believe it's been a long time, Mr. Nash."

I can't see him from where I am, but I'd bet my life, the voice I hear is none other than Louis Kingston III. Fucking hell.

"You've been an extremely hard man to kill and look at you now. All dressed up in a tux and nowhere to go. If the mortuary is good enough, they might not even have to remove it off your dead body for your funeral," he quips, and I can hear a gasp from Nat. He must have her in his grip. Maybe even holding a gun to her, knowing what I do about the man. "I wondered how long it would take you to get here. You made surprisingly good time."

"Louie, it has been a long time. Still holding a grudge, I see?" Even though it's been a long time since I've worked with Nash, I understand exactly what he's trying to do. He wants to piss Louis off, but I hear the hint of fear in his voice.

"You have no idea just how long I can wait. I can be a very patient man. You see, she was promised to me when she was a young child."

I risk peeking around the corner just as Louis runs the muzzle of the gun down the side of Nat's tear stained face as if caressing it.

"This plan started years ago, and I've waited patiently until she was ready." His gaze drops down at Nat, then flashes angrily up at Nash. "You took what was mine," he snarls. "You soiled her. She was pure, and you took that from me."

The puzzle pieces are coming together. The letters and journals from my mother.

"What do you mean since I was a child? I only met you after..." Nat's voice goes quiet. "You were at my parents' funeral," she says, recognition in her voice.

"Hmmm, I knew you were smart," he huffs out. "It's a story that started over twenty-three years ago."

"But you didn't know her twenty-three years ago," Nash states, obviously confused.

"You and that meddlesome brother of hers." He points the gun at Nash as he speaks. "You were getting too close, and we had to move our plans up sooner," Louis admits.

"What did you do?" Nash's voice is a low growl.

Nat's brows furrow as if trying to understand what's happening.

"Was it gambling? Were you holding their marker?" Nash has no clue about my family and where they came from or who we really are.

A sadistic laugh erupts from Kingston.

"Tell me, Louie, why Nat?"

"Aw! Now you're letting your mind work in the right direction."

Nash begins to walk, his gun aimed at Louis.

Louis turns his body, holding Nat to him as a shield. His gun pointing at her head, he keeps Nash in front of him as he walks farther into the living room.

"I figure the aunt and uncle owed you something and the only way of getting your payback was them getting ahold of Nat. I would have said human trafficking, but you had years to sell her and you didn't."

"Very good, Mr. Nash. You're smarter than I gave you credit for. The funny thing is, Mr. FBI agent, Jenkins was *my* plant, he worked for *me*." His voice is smug and condescending. "I knew everything. It's funny what you can get when you have money and power." His sardonic laugh chills my blood.

"Her parents, well, they were the easy ones to get rid of, but her brother on the other hand, now that took some serious planning. And you, you were supposed to die with her goddamn nosy brother. Hell, you must be part cat with as many times as I've tried to have you killed."

My lips turn up as I've thought the same thing about Nash. But my stomach sinks at his confession. Yes, I suspected he had something to do with my parents' deaths, but now I know he did. *Keep your focus, Alec, you can enforce your revenge later.*

Peeking out from around the corner, still not wanting anyone to see me, I watch Nat as realization hits. Her beautiful blue eyes go wide as her lips part in a gasp. Her back straightens and her chin lifts. Her eyes flash to Nash's, locking with them. Spinning, she jolts out of Kingston's grip. "You killed them? You killed my parents and brother?" she shrieks. "You son of a bitch!" Nat turns on Louis, her fist crashing into his face. Blood gushes from his nose. Louis squeals like a pick. His hands automatically fly to the broken appendage, and he drops his hold on her.

"You fucking bitch!" he shouts as he struggles to wipe the tears from his watering eyes. Blood sluices with the salty secretions.

"You stupid, stupid girl. You could have had an easy life, you just needed to obey me."

"I'm not a submissive, nor will I ever be. I would rather die than be your fucking slave." Cold fury tinges Nat's voice.

"Your choice." Lifting his gun, he points it at Nat, and without hesitation, Nash dives for her, shielding her from the blast of the gun. She falls to the ground, Nash landing on top of her. I don't know who was hit.

I don't even think as I pull the trigger. Both Nash and Nat are still on the ground. Nash is moving, but Nat lays motionless. Fuck! Nat!

"Nat." Nash is struggling to move, wincing, and groaning from pain. Is he too late? The stench of death fills the room. Smoke curls from the end of my gun as I stand, stunned at the words of the man I just killed.

So many thoughts jumble through my head. The mother fucker admitted to killing my parents. He stole my sister from me, and he tried to have me killed. Hell, almost everyone thinks I am dead, which is how I got the advantage.

A moan brings my thoughts back. Nash is on his knees searching Natasha for injuries. "Nat, baby, wake up. Please God, please." His focus is solely on Natasha. He cups her face, stroking it lightly with his thumbs, placing kisses over her face. Stupid fuck, he hasn't even realized that the man who shot at him is lying dead on the floor in a heap.

Natasha gasps as her eyes startle open, fear etched across her face. "It's okay baby, I have you."

It's then that Nash finally glances over to the fat man on the floor. Jumping up, he holds up his gun, pointing and searching for someone he never thought he would ever see again.

Me.

CHAPTER 42

ALEC

Nash turns, finally noticing the man lying in a heap on the floor, a hole between his eyes oozing blood, and the stench of death lingering around us.

"Nash?"

I should have been more vigilant regarding my surroundings when a voice from over my shoulder pulls my attention away from the scene in front of me. A voice full of concern. Turning, I see a man who has to be Grover's brother, Walker. When I glance back at Nash, his brow is furrowed, his eyes are full of shock and disbelief.

Nash's hand reaches up, gripping something under his shirt the way he would grip his dog tags when he was nervous or stressed. Shaking his hand, he drops them as if they just burned him, and sticks his fingers into his mouth.

He loses his balance, falling to the ground, a myriad of questions, confusion, anger, and pain, etched in his face.

The room is eerily quiet as Nash searches my eyes. They flash from Nat to me. I know I look different from the last time we saw each other. I have a dark beard now, and of course, I look a lot older.

Nat is in shock. Her face has no color in it as she shakes her head in disbelief. Tears are streaming down her cheeks as her hand covers her mouth in distrust.

"Alec?" Nash tilts his head, as he studies me. He guardedly stands, slowly and apprehensively moves toward me, still not believing who's standing in front of him.

Now that I know Nat isn't in any imminent danger, the anger that has built up inside of me at what Nash did to my sister comes to the forefront. As he approaches me, I pull back, letting my fist fly into Nash's face; yelling; letting years of frustrations take over. "You mother fucker. That's what you get for taking advantage of my sister."

Nash flies backwards knocking into a shelf as trinkets and small framed pictures tumble to the ground with a clatter. The sound of shattering glass has me glancing down.

Reaching up to his jaw, he stares up at me, apparently still not believing it's me standing in front of him.

After sluggishly getting to his feet, he stands in front of me, watching me as if I'm a mirage.

"You deserved that." I pull my arm back again and throw another punch, but this time, he blocks the hit, while still staring at me.

Nodding, he says. "You're right, I deserved that. But I love her. I've always loved her. That has never changed."

"You goddamn left her. She was unprotected. For eight fucking years, while you ran off and did your own thing. You forgot about her. And for what?" I spit out.

"To protect her." His voice is quiet. "I always had someone on her, someone in the shadows. She came home early today, and I screwed up. I missed it. I thought the threat was gone months ago."

We both glance over to Nat; she's still sitting on the floor, her eyes wide and full of tears.

Walking to her, Nash kneels beside her to help her up. "Are you alright? Did I hurt you when I landed on top of you?"

She crooks her head to the side. Her eyes stare disbelievingly at me. I know I look different. My hair is long, just past my shoulders, as is my beard. Taking her by the hands, Nash helps her stand.

She walks over to me, stands in front of me, and slaps me hard across the cheek. "You bastard!" she screams. Fuck, she hits me so hard, my head whips to the side with the force. "You promised me. You promised that you would never leave me! You broke that promise." Turning to look at Nash, she murmurs. "And you broke our vows. You promised in front of God and our friends, for better or for worse. You both lied, and I want you both out."

"But—" Both Nash and I say at the same time.

"No!" she yells. "Neither of you trusted me enough to let me make the decision for myself. I'm not the prepubescent little girl who was ripped away from everyone she knew. I'm a woman who has made it on her own when everyone walked out on me. So, get the hell out and get this fat fucker out of here too."

Walker is still standing silently behind me. "I've called it in. They're sending people over to take statements."

"Thanks, Walker," Nash replies. He turns, looking back over at Nat.

"I said get the fuck out of my house," she screams.

Nash's jaw clenches at her harsh, angry words, and he takes a step toward her, but she holds up her hand.

Her eyes glimmer with unshed tears, and I can see she's fighting to keep them from falling. "You walked out on me and never looked back. How does it feel? Does it feel good to know the only person you ever loved doesn't give a damn about your feelings? What you did to me broke me. I never want to see you again. I won't tell you again. GET. THE. FUCK. OUT!" she spits.

I can see Nash's demeaner shrink away. He sucks in a ragged breath as his eyes glisten, and I understand just how bad he feels, because I hurt her worse than what Nash did. I purposely kept myself from both of them. Nash squares his shoulder — he won't leave until he says his piece.

"I did what I did to keep you safe. Maybe I should have done things differently, but at the time, I thought it was the right thing to do. I wanted you to find someone who was safe. Someone who didn't have a job that could target the only person I loved." His voice is quiet, and it quivers as he speaks, but I agree, she needs to hear it. "I love you, Nat, I have loved you all my life. I wouldn't be able to live with myself if they got to you."

She steps over to Nash, beating his chest hard. He winces in pain, tears pool in his eyes as he presses the palm of his hand to his chest. Something isn't right. He looks pale. "And how's that working for you?" She turns, thrusting her hand to point at Louis. Nat glances down at her hand and gasps; it's crimson, covered in blood. Nat screams out as Nash's eyes roll back into his head and he falls to the ground. "Nash!"

CHAPTER 43

ALEC

"Connor? Oh, my God. Connor!" Nat cries out as she falls to her knees, cradling Connor's face in her hands. Tears stream down her face.

I slip my phone out of my jacket and try to dial, but I keep fat fingering the numbers on the pad; I can't stop shaking.

My eyes lock on Nat. She's lost. In shock. Staring at nothing.

Walker jumps into action, dropping to the floor beside Connor's lifeless body. Blood pools under him.

I don't understand, he hadn't been bleeding, but now all I can see is blood.

Walker tries to get Nat's attention. His voice is quiet but stern, but she just stares at him. Gripping her arm, he snaps his fingers in her face. "Natasha, I need your help." Her eyes flash to Walker's.

Her head barely moves as she nods, drawing her arm across her face to wipe the tears away, streaks of black smudge her face.

"Sorry, I'm here. What do you need?" she says, hiccupping through her sobs.

Walker makes sure he has her attention before he speaks. "First, I need scissors. I need to get his jacket and shirt off." Standing there, I feel hopeless as Walker applies pressure to Connor's chest.

Nat jumps up and races from room to room gathering the list of items Walker has asked for. In short order, she runs back in and carefully lays a blanket over Connor's legs, dropping the rags on the floor beside Walker. Then she's off again, heading into another room for more supplies. When she returns this time, she's carrying a large bowl of water. Steam curls and twists with her movement as she sets the bowl on the floor beside Nash's head.

Walker has cut Connor's suit off, and I take a step toward him when I realize he has a flak jacket on. What the fuck? Why would he be wearing a flak jacket to a wedding? Walker flips it up over Connor's head giving him access to his chest.

Nat gasps when she sees the hole in Connor's chest. Walker is holding one of the washcloths over his wound to stop the bleeding.

Nat kneels beside Connor, dipping a rag into the water, wiping it across his face, talking to him as she takes his hand in hers. "Connor open your eyes," her voice is just a whisper, as she repeats her words over and over. Leaning down, she cuddles into the crook of Connor's neck. "Baby, please come back to me. I'm not ready for 'forever' to come. Please, baby, open your eyes."

Finally hearing the sirens, I step to the door to escort the paramedics in.

The EMTs roll their gurney next to Connor. He's ghostly white and still hasn't regained consciousness. Nat begins to move out of the way, but Nash's grip on her hand gets tighter. His eyes flicker open. His voice is a hoarse rasp. "Don't leave me. Please, Nat. Please don't leave me."

"I'm right here Connor. I'm right here."

The paramedics load him on the gurney after putting some sort of gel patch over his wound and covering it up with gauze.

Grabbing Nat's arm before she steps into the ambulance, I say as I pull her into a hug that I've needed to do for so long. "I'll follow you." God, this feels so good, I don't want to let her go. "He'll be alright, he's strong and has gone through a lot worse." Brushing her tears away, she just nods, turning to step up into the ambulance.

CHAPTER 44

ALEC

I close my eyes and take a deep shuddering breath before walking back into the house. I'll be questioned, but I'd rather get it over with sooner rather than later.

The man who arrived just after me is standing at the front door giving me a questioning look. Stepping toward him, I reach out my hand. "Alec Turner."

Taking my hand, a smile curves his lips. "You look pretty good for being dead for, what, sixteen years?" He chuckles. "Walker. I used to work with Nash at the agency and have tried to keep an eye on your sister for him when he couldn't."

Quirking a smile, I respond, "I believe the circumstances and details of my death are highly exaggerated."

"Well, I would say that is very obvious and I'm sure there's a very long story behind it."

"Longer than I wanted or expected. But yes."

Two black Suburbans and a coroner's van pull into the driveway and as if timed, all the doors open at once. Six people step out striding toward us.

The medical examiner stops in front of us. "Body?" is all he asks.

Pointing over his shoulder, Walker says, "In the house, can't miss him."

He nods at Walker, steps toward the entrance but not before donning protective clothing as not to contaminate the scene.

While the medical examiner is still in the house, another man approaches us. "Walker, it's been a long time. How are you involved and who is this?"

Walker begins to introduce me when a marine officer approaches us. "Master Sergeant Turner, I hear your assignment might have finally come to an end?"

I watch out the corner of my eye as Walker's eyes widen and his brow lifts in surprise. I'm sure the reaction from Nash will be tenfold.

"Yes, sir. It will be in my final report, but, yes, the subject was aiming to shoot Agent Nash's wife. I felt I didn't have any other option but to take the shot. He had already fire at her when agent Nash jumped in front of her."

The officer reaches his hand out to Walker. "You must be Walker. Grover has told me a lot about you. I heard we lost a good man the day you retired from the agency."

"I'm sorry, you have me at a disadvantage?" Walker queries.

"Yes, of course, Major Bryant," he says by way of introduction. Walker takes his hand.

"Major Bryant, this is Special Agent in Charge West, he was my supervisor when I was with the agency," Walker advises.

The two men shake hands then turn to each of us as if we have the answers to life.

Moments later, the coroner and medical examiner wheel the gurney out of the house. A large black body bag lays on top.

The major unzips the bag, as both he and West glance inside. Bryant's mouth twists as he peers down, examining the body inside. His brow creases as his big dark eyes find mine. "Hmm. Perfectly between the eyes," he mutters to himself. "I don't want this falling apart, so if you two need to get your stories straight..."

"No sir, that won't be necessary, there was really only one shot I could take, and I took it. I won't change my report or pretty it up. It is what happened."

"And the knowledge that Agent Nash's wife is also your sister?" West questions.

"That's irrelevant. This was a hostage situation. Nash tried to reason with him, but he refused to drop the gun."

"And Nash's injuries?"

"Unknown sir. He dove for his wife to protect her when the gun discharged hitting Nash in the chest. If you don't mind, sir, I would really like to pick this up later, so I can get to the hospital to be with my sister."

"Yes of course."

I call Aliah on the way to the hospital, filling her in on what happened and letting her know that the threat was over, and we were finally going to be out in the open.

"I'm on my way to the hospital. Nash was shot."

I hear and audible gap coming from Aliah. "Oh my gosh, is he going to be alright?" Her voice crescendos as she asks about Nat "What about Natasha?" Concern invades her voice as it begins to quiver.

"She's good, a little shook up and confused, but she went with Nash in the ambulance."

"What was Natasha's reaction when she saw you? And Nash's?"

A smile curls my lips as my hand gravitates to my cheek where she slapped me. "Let's just say she was not very happy that I lied to her for all these years."

"Do you think she will understand why you did what you did?" She sounds forlorn. "Do you think she will forgive me?"

Aliah sniffles, and I'm aware that she's concerned about losing a good friend as the realization hits her of what will happen to her when Natasha finds out who she really is.

"Give her some time. Let's wait until Nash is better, and then we'll cross that bridge. You were a good friend to her, that hasn't changed. You were never just an employee."

CHAPTER 45

"When we face our fear of death and slow down our busy lives, we come to realize our relationships are precious, a part of life's foundation. Knowing this fact helps us to understand that death's true purpose is to teach us how to live." ~Vishwas ॐ

ALEC

I don't remember the drive to the hospital. Yeah, Nash has been shot before, but he only has so many lives. Stabbing at the elevator button, I wait my turn as well wishers cram their way into the small enclosed moving box. Gripping the handrail, I close my eyes as I count the dings as it carries us upward.

Stopping at each floor to let people out has me agitated and restless. I need to know how Nash is. I haven't received any information. Not noticing the elevator didn't open correctly aligned with the floor, my toe catches on the threshold of the car, thrusting me forward into the reception desk. "Oh, my goodness!" cries the little lady behind the large monitor. "Are you alright?"

I manage to catch myself on an empty wheelchair being pushed by a young girl. After my heart starts beating again, I take a deep breath, I nod, then ask directions to the waiting room. Pointing down the corridor, I stride down the long hallway, the sterile blend colors on the walls numbing my anxiety coursing through me.

Pushing through the glass door of the waiting room, I search each face, each chair, for someone I used to know, but she's not here. Christ, I wasn't that far behind her, was I? Could... No, I'm not going to go there. He has to make it, but fuck, all that blood. God, I'm so fucking sick of death, so done.

Moving to the woman behind the desk, I ask. "Connor Nash?"

Her eyes pin me with a sympathetic smile. "Are you a relative?"

I lie, because he is my brother, always has been, always will be, divorce or not. "He's my brother," I choke out.

She nods as her fingers tap away at the keyboard sitting in front of her. Glancing up at me, her face is expressionless. "Mr. Nash is still in surgery. His wife is in the chapel if you would like to wait with her." She gestures down the hall.

My eyes sting, as I blink the tears away. "Thank you," I murmur, following the direction she points to.

I think about everything I've learned about our parents and realize there's a lot we have to talk about; who our parents were and why they were really murdered. Not to mention our supposed aunt and uncle who started this whole thing, but for right now, my sister is more important. She needs me now more than ever, especially if Nash... nope, fucking hell, I won't go there.

Stained glass windows to my right draw my attention, and the sign above the door confirms I've arrived at the chapel.

The chapel is empty as I walk in, and I wonder where Nat is. It only takes a moment before I see her head pop up and turn toward me. She's on her knees, praying, something I haven't don't for a long time. I think it's about time to get back into the habit.

Not knowing if she even wants to see me, I hold myself back from running to her, instead cautiously walking toward her. She jumps up from where she's been kneeling and runs to me. I hold out my arms, and she falls into me as I wrap her into my embrace, pulling her tight to me. I've missed her touch, her smell, her; my sister, my Nat. I kiss the top of her head as tears stream down her face; hell, they're streaming down mine too. "This is Nash... Connor. He's been through worse, he'll be fine. Although I'm going to hit him again for taking advantage of my little sister."

Nat pulls back so I can see her face, her beautiful face, as she smiles up at me grabbing my beard giving it a light tug. All I can do is smile at her. We might get through this. "Hey, I'm just as mad at you too." She wraps her arms around me again, and I pull her back into my tight grip, not wanting to let go. Never again.

The door squeaks, causing us to pull out of our hug. As I glance over my shoulder, my heart catches in my throat. A man in scrubs approaches us, and I realize it has to be the doctor. I can't read his face, other than her looks tired and I'm not sure if that's a good thing or not.

Nat begins to tremble as I take her hand in mine.

"Mrs. Nash?"

Tears again begin to slip down her already tearstained cheeks. She just nods at the doctor.

"I'm Doctor Hughes, I've been attending to your husband." The doctor motions for a pew, and my gut rolls; this can't be good. "Let's sit down."

"No. No. No," Nat cries out, as she begins to collapse to the floor. Catching her, I guide her onto one of the pews then sit next to her. Burying her head into my chest, I hold her tight as she begins to sob.

"Mr. Nash is very lucky." Lucky? What the fuck? What's going on? The guy has no expression on his face. He tells us to take a seat, and now he's saying Nash was lucky?

The doctor holds out his hand. I reach for whatever he's giving me.

The chain dangles over the side of my hand. I stare disbelievingly at the cold metal, reading the inscription. My dog tags. I thought they had been lost in the blast. Why does the doctor have them?

I lift them by the chain examining them. "These are mine." My brows furrow in confusion.

A quiet whisper comes from beside me. "They were given to Connor at your funeral. He's never taken them off." Looking at the tags, I notice an indentation in them. "What happened to them?"

The doctor smiles down at us, and I'm trying to understand what he's so happy about.

The doctor reaches his hand out again, and I hold out my palm automatically, jumping in surprise as he drops a small metal object into it.

"What is that?" Nat asks.

Picking it up in my fingers, I show it to Nat. "It's a slug."

"A slug? Like the slimy thing on the ground?"

"Seriously?" She really must be out of it to ask such a silly question. Staring down at her, I raise a brow at the obscurity of her question. "It's a slug from a gun." Focusing on the small piece of metal and the dog tags, I drop the small slug into the divot in my dog tags. My eyes flash from Nat to the doctor.

"Mrs. Nash, these tags," the doctor says, pointing at the chain in my hand, "saved your husband's life."

Her eyes fall to my hand, tilting her head in confusion. "I don't understand. You told me to sit down. That always means bad news."

"Heavens no, Mrs. Nash. Your husband is very much alive."

It's all coming together. My heart is suddenly shocked back to life as it skips a few beats.

The doctor gives a soft chuckle. "You just looked so weary, I thought it would be best for you to sit."

"He's alive?" she whispers. "And he's going to be alright?" Her eyes light up, glimmering with tears. This time, happy tears.

The doctor smiles as his whole face lights up. "Yes, barring any complications. Yes. As I said— oomph."

Nat throws herself at the doctor, knocking the air from his lungs and wrapping her arms around his neck. I almost start laughing at the doctor's expression. I don't think he's ever had anyone react this way to his news before.

"Can I see him?" asks Nat.

The doctor is still as stiff as a statue, but then begins to relax.

Stepping back away from us, the doctor smiles and replies, "Of course. He's still in recovery, but they'll be moving him to his room soon. I can have one of the nurses take you both to his room if you would like. It might be a little more comfortable to wait for him there."

CHAPTER 46

ALEC

We follow the nurse like a couple of lemmings. Fear and apprehension has Nat clasping my hand like a vise as we're led through windowless hallways lined with unmarked doors. No signs tell us where we're going or where we came from. Weaving in and out of the maze of corridors, I'm glad I won't be leaving Nash until he's released. There's is no way in hell I would ever find my way out without a map.

Sliding a large glass door open, the nurse stands aside, inviting us into an empty room except for the one wall that's lined with machines. Nat's hand squeezes mine tighter as she stands motionless, her grief-stricken eyes stare up at me. This is a side of her I've never seen. She's always been so strong, even when our parents were murdered.

Her shoulders tremble as her body begins to shudder. I think the shock of the day has finally hit her. She's ghostly white, and I wrap my arms around her, pulling her tight to me and never wanting to let her go again.

Even with her red-rimmed eyes and tear-stained cheeks, I can't stop staring at what a beautiful woman she's grown up to be.

"Nat, God, I've missed you so much. I've been so scared for you."

The noise of the sliding door opening, startles me, and instinctively I push her behind me, shielding her from any danger.

A woman in purple scrubs steers a bed through the glass door. IV bags filled with different colored fluids—one being blood— hang from a shiny metal pole at the head of the bed. Moving quickly out of the way of the bed, Nat and I maneuver to see Nash. He's skin is ashen except for the dark purple shadows that rim his closed eyes. Glancing up at Nat, I note that her eyes glisten with unshed tears, her lashes flutter as if trying to blink them away.

The nurse diligently works to attach Nash to the different machines, pushing and flipping switches making them come to life, filling the room with the ominous noises of all the apparatuses letting us reassuring us he's is still with us.

Nat reaches for him, but then stops, dropping her hand to her side. Her eyes drinking in the man lying motionless in front of her. "Talk to him honey, touch him, let him know that you're here," says the caramel-skinned woman in the purple scrubs with dancing green frogs, standing at the head of his bed. Her words bring a slight smile to my lips. She has a friendly, warm smile and kind eyes.

"Will he hear me?" Nat asks, almost begging for her acknowledgement.

Her head turns to glance at the machines. "Yes, hun, I do believe he will. Touch therapy is the best," she says, laying her hand on Nat's arm. "It's sometimes called 'laying on of hands' and is thought to promote healing, and the voice of a loved one is known to calm and induce more efficient breathing, allowing more oxygen into the body for quicker healing. I saw it as soon as you began to speak. His oxygen levels went up and he started to take deeper breaths. He knows you're here." She pats Nat's arm before leaving the room.

I step to one side of Nash, as Nat steps to the other. Reaching a shaky hand to his face, Nat's trembling fingers caress the curve of his cheek, tracing his brows and down his nose, to the bow of his mouth, her tongue mimics her touch on his lips.

"Connor open your eyes, baby," she says, taking Nash's hand in hers. My eyes flick to the machines that begin to flash, the sound of them speeding with her words. She continues to speak as she runs her finger up the bridge of his nose and over his brow again.

"Would you like some coffee?" I ask. I walk to stand behind her, placing my hands on her shoulders, massaging the knots in her tight muscles. As she rotates her neck, I continue to rub the tight sinew there, feeling her relax under my touch.

Then I leave in search of some hospital brew returning after a trip to the lounge with a couple cups of coffee. Pausing, I stare through the glass door of Nash's room. Nat's eyes are closed; her head is resting on her hand that's still clutching Nash's. I'm sure she's exhausted from all the day's events, not to mention the shock of seeing Louis, and then discovering that I was alive after years of being dead.

Slowly sliding the door open, I hear a rough raspy voice that could almost make me cry. "Nat."

"Mmm," Nat moans. No, she's purring; angling her head at the touch from Nash.

"You always did purr like a kitten when you were petted."

"That's my sister you're talking about, you son of a bitch." I step through the door, setting the cups of coffee down on his nightstand.

"She's my wife," he growls.

Nat begins to stir, but still hasn't realized Nash is awake.

"You left her for your Goddamn job!"

"I left her to protect her. If you care so much, where were the fuck were you? You faked your death, then suddenly you show up sixteen years later and you criticize me? How fucked up is that?"

Nash's monitors begin going off. Lights flash as the alarms grow louder and louder.

"STOP! Stop the yelling and that fucking beeping."

"What is going on in here?" Swinging around, I find the nurse wearing the purple shirt with frogs standing resolutely at the door. "Do I need to call security?"

Nash and I stare daggers at each other when suddenly Nat jolts her head up taking in her surroundings, blinking in confusion.

"Way to go, boys, you woke her up. You both should be ashamed of yourselves," the nurse reprimands us.

Nat's eyes flash to the nurse as she pushes buttons and fiddles with knobs on the machines to quiet them. "If you set the alarms on these machines off again, I'll make you leave." She gives us a stern look.

Jumping up out of her seat, Nat stumbles backward. I'm not sure if it's the shock of the day, but her eyes are locked on mine as if she hadn't remembered I was back. The nurse catches her, keeping her from falling to the floor.

Her eyes fall to her hand, examining it. She stands there catatonic, staring down at her fingernails. She gasps at her blood-stained nails as if just remembering the earlier events of the day. All the blood drains from her face as I rush to her side, trying to help her into her chair, but she pushes me away, stumbling to the door. Hurt and confusion mar her face.

Running to catch up with her, by the time I reach her, she's sliding into a cab. Her sad eyes find mine as I watch her drive away.

I spring to my car and get in. Then I go to the one place Nat would go when she was upset. I've followed her there several times since she made her way back home.

Our plots are quite different from where they used to be, and there are several additions that she's never seen before. I can smell the freshly cut grass as I walk out to the lake. She's standing in front of our family's funeral plots. I watch as she views our parents' headstones then looks at the new grave markers in the same vicinity. Her head tilts as she begins to read them, and a second later her brows pinch together as if trying to understand.

"Aliah Turner. Who the hell is that? *Amazing and caring mother and wife. DOB: February 8, 1982.*" She runs her fingers along the top of the black carved granite.

A loud sob escapes her, as she falls to the ground. Her body shuddering with uncontrollable sobs.

Kneeling beside her, I say. "I figured both you and Nash would put your own sentiments on your headstones." My voice was quiet.

Her eyes find mine as she glances up at me, tears streaming down her face as she speaks. "I don't want to put anything on it. I just want him back. I didn't get the chance to tell him I love him. God, I didn't even get to say goodbye. What kind of person am I?" she sobs.

"You are the most loving and caring woman I have ever known and loved." Nash's low husky voice came from behind Nat. He ran out after me, sliding into my car before I even had the chance to start it. Nat's head swings abruptly to see Nash.

She stammers. "They said you were..." Her head falls, not able to finish her statement.

"Gone?"

She nods her head, still not looking up.

"Nurse Bledsoe called me after I had checked myself out against medical advice and told me you had called and spoke to the desk nurse. She said you might have misunderstood the statement about me being gone. She said you hung up before she was able to pick up the phone and apologizes for the mistaken news of my death."

She slowly stands, moving to Nash.

"She said, unfortunately, you are still married to this stubborn, obstinate and mulish man."

She playfully slaps at his arm. "You divorced me. We're not married anymore." He winces. "Oh fuck, I'm sorry."

Nash chuckles. "I probably deserve that."

"But you left me, you said..."

"I know, and I am so sorry for that. I hope one day you'll be able to forgive me. If I could go back, I would have been honest about what was going on. I just didn't want you to get caught up in the middle of this. But it seems this started long before you and me. I never saw this coming."

She lunges for him as he wraps his arms around her, holding her tight.

CHAPTER 47

A strong person loves, forgives, walks away, let's go, tries again, perseveres... no matter what life throws at them. ~Vishwas ॐ

ALEC

Turning my back on my sister and Nash, I walk down to the edge of the lake, staring out at the shimmering water.

Running to catch up with her, by the time I reach her, she's sliding into a cab. Her sad eyes find mine as I watch her drive away.

I sprint to my car and get in. Then I drive to the one place Nat would go when she was upset. I've followed her there several times since she made her way back home.

I never thought coming back would be so strained. Nat will hardly speak to me, and Nash, well, what can I say? I should have asked him what his feelings were for Nat. It wasn't as if I couldn't trust him with her, I guess I was just afraid of the change in our friendship. but then Mom and Dad were murdered, and she was gone, I guess at that point it didn't really matter what his feelings were, we both just wanted to find her.

My phone vibrates, taking my mind off my past. I smile as I see Aliah's beautiful face, her sparkling caramel eyes smile up at me and my heart fills with love for this woman. It's been sixteen years since we first met and my love for her grows stronger every day.

"Aliah, my love, God, I love you so much. So much has happened. How are you?"

"I have been very concerned for you, Alec. Are you alright?"

"I'm sorry, Aliah, I should have called. Nash had himself released from the hospital and he and Nat are talking."

"Will he be okay? And have you told her yet?"

"Yes, he'll be fine, and I can't wait to tell you what the doctor figured out. You'll love the story of how he survived, and no, I haven't told her yet. I thought I'd pick up some takeout and bring it home for the family. We can all sit down and have a nice long talk. Will that be okay?"

"That will be nice. I am sure she will be very surprised."

"Yes, that's an understatement. I've got to go, love. I'll be home soon. Bye, Aliah, I love you."

"I love you too, Alec."

Dropping my phone into my jacket pocket, I feel two sets of eyes staring at me. I look up at them, I think it's time to have a chat. Besides, now that I'm no longer employed, I need to figure out what I want to do when I grow up.

"I think it's time we sit down and talk. Not just about us, but what I found out about the secrets in our family."

"You mean other than the wife and child you have?" Nat says, giving me a knowing smile.

"That's where my life not only ended but it began that day, too. But there are other more important things we need to discuss."

"Where are you staying?" Nash asks.

Stammering over my answer, I'm concerned this won't go over very well. "We... ahh, we actually live behind your house."

Nash's interest is pricked. "Were you sneaking around Nat's place?"

Closing my eyes, I nod my head, relenting. "We moved in right before you moved out. At the time, I didn't understand why you were leaving her when it was clear just how much you loved her. Anyway, that's how I got away from both you and Walker. I just jumped my fence."

"And your wife? Where did you meet her and how long have you been married? Plus, you have a daughter." Nat's questions hang in the air. I don't want to have this conversation out here in the open.

"I think it would be better to have this discussion somewhere private and quiet. Your place is still a crime scene, so why don't we go to my place?"

"And your wife? I'm sure she wouldn't want you to surprise her with unexpected guests," Nat questions.

Taking Natasha by the shoulders, I reassure her, "Aliah will love you. You are my sister, my family. We'll pick up some Chinese and have a nice dinner and get to know each other again. I'll fill you in on what I found out about David and Susan and we'll see what the plans are for making them pay for what they did." I pull her into my arms. "I love you, Nat. I'm glad we're back together again. And I hope you will forgive me for not coming back sooner. I just had to quietly keep my secret to keep you safe."

Nat nods as tears shimmer in her eyes. "Don't you ever do that to me again."

"Deal."

CHAPTER 48

ALEC

My stomach twists in knots as my chest constricts my air intake. I have no idea what kind of reaction Nat will have when she meets my wife. She didn't take it well when she realized I had lied to her for all these years. How did I seriously think she'd react when she found that my wife, her best friend, had been working for her for several years and never told her who she really was. Fuck me, this isn't going to be good.

Nat and Nash were stopping off at the store to pick up some wine, while I picked up the Chinese. I have a feeling we'll be needing a lot of wine tonight. Hell, we might need something even stronger than that.

Grabbing the several bags of takeout, I bring them into the house, setting them on the kitchen island. Aliah comes up behind me, wrapping her arms around my waist and nuzzling into my back. God, I'll never grow old of this. She's always had a way of calming me, and together we'll get through tonight as well.

Turning in her arms, she has a mischievous look in her eyes. "Let us forget about this sister and brother-in-law stuff, you need to make love to me." She quirks her right eyebrow; her lips curve up in a seductive grin.

I can't help but give her a big smile that spreads across my face, loving how playful she is. "Baby, there's nothing I want to do more." I lift my head to the sound of the doorbell. "But I think it's going to have to wait." My lips crash to hers, taking my breath away. God, I love this woman. "You ready?"

She nods, but I can tell she's apprehensive.

Opening the front door, I welcome Nat and Nash into our home. "Come in, Ali is in the kitchen getting the food ready."

"That's funny, I have an Ali that works for me." They follow me into the kitchen. "It isn't very often that you hear that name for a..." Nat stops at the entrance of the kitchen. Ali is anxiously biting her lip as we enter. "Woman." Her voice is a mere whisper as she sees Ali.

"Wait... You're... You were at... You're married to...." Nash's eyes bounce from Nat to Aliah and back again trying to figure out what he's seeing. "Oh fuck."

Nat's brows pinch together in confusion. "Okay, so is this an episode of the Twilight Zone? Because my mind is about to blow a gasket." Nat asks as Aliah hands her a drink.

"I made you a lemon drop martini, hun. I thought you might need one tonight," Aliah offers.

Nat takes the drink, tipping it to her lips and doesn't stop until it is empty.

"Nash, this is my wife Aliah."

"Please call me Ali. It is very nice to officially meet you. I thought it was very noble and gallant of you to protect Natasha the way you did at Saber Elite. You are an incredibly good man."

"You knew he took me?" Nat's eyes are wide with surprise.

Chuckling, Aliah replies, "What kind of friend do you think I am? Do you really think I would not look after you? You were an innocent. You never were allowed to go out, let alone drink. I knew who Connor was. I was watching him watch you the whole night. He would chase all the men away from you. Then when you passed out, he carried you to your home. I knew just how much he loved you. And yes, he is a very gallant and honorable man."

After we finish eating, I excuse myself to my office grabbing the files I'd accumulated over the years. Laying some of the more important paper on the table I begin to explain what I had found out.

"So, this is what I have. Get ready for your mind to be blown. Mom and Dad were two parts of rivaling families. They were like the Capulets and Montague's. Their families were sworn enemies. When they met in college, neither of them knew each other's true identities. They fell in love. Then they found out who they really were, they were distraught. They knew their families would never allow the union, so they changed their names and moved to the other side of the country. Walking away from everything and everyone they knew and loved.

"Somehow, after being off the grid for years, they were found. Aunt Susan *is* Mom's sister. David thought by marrying Susan, he could start reaping the financial rewards of the family to grow his jewelry business. He wanted to weasel his way deeper in the mob, so he offered you up to Louis for a price.

Louis also wanted to get in. He needed help laundering dirty money. He had several illegal dealings including the one with your asset Liam. Louis knew if he married into the family, he could work both side of the two families since we share both bloodlines.

Susan and David knew I'd never leave with them, so they gave up trying to convince me and took you." I glance over at Nat's emotionless face as she tries to absorb what I'm saying. "Since we have the blood of both families, they thought it would force the families to unite. But before your nuptials, you ran away due to my untimely death, something they hadn't planned for. I'd imagine Louis kept you on a tight leash and never thought you'd have the guts to trade the stone of your engagement ring in for cash and also to have the wherewithal to swap it out for a very close replica of glass.

"Long story short, they were afraid you and Nash were getting too close, so they had to adjust. They killed Mom and Dad to get to you." My voice hitches in my throat, as I'm suddenly overcome with sadness. "They wanted you pure. If he had married you and you bore an heir, it would have changed his future. Not only are you from both bloodlines, but if he married you, his line now mixed with both families, would instantly raise him to next in line for the head of both families.

"I have to say, this Louis guy was a real piece of work. I don't know how much he shelled out to have us killed, but it had to have been a lot."

"I always thought it was Jenkins." Nash cringes at the name. "He's the reason the case took so long to get to. By the time we finally got it scheduled, I'd left Nat in hopes that Jenkins wouldn't harm her. Little did I know at the time that it was Louis behind everything. No wonder they had the financial backing for this whole thing.

"God, all the innocent lives that were lost. And for what? It's not like any of those mercenaries meant anything to the mob, they were just collateral damage. And my friend Liam and his family got caught in the crossfire," Nash states.

"Oh, God!" Nat exclaims. "Maison is Liam."

I nod, urging Nash to explain further. "His real name is Matthew Leary. He's had several names, but it was Maison when I was shot by his brother Mark and then when I turned him into an asset, I had it switched to Liam Tate. He's a remarkably close friend, but I didn't even tell him about you." Nash looks over to Nat. "Until the trial. He told me I was stupid for leaving someone who I loved the way I love you and not giving her a choice. To be honest I had no idea it would take so long to close the case, but then it did, and I sure as hell didn't want you getting hurt. I really did have good intentions." A forlorn expression settles on Nat's face.

"So, what do we do about Susan and David?" Nat's voice is quiet. I watched as she tries to process what I had found out.

"The authorities are going to reopen the investigation into Mom and Dad's deaths and I'm sure, with a little convincing, the driver will sing like a proverbial canary. Now that the case is closed and Jenkins and Kingston are dead, he shouldn't have anything to fear. Between that and Walker's and my testimony, I'm hoping they'll be taken into custody."

"How did you meet Ali?" Nat's eyes light up, begging for information about her friend and coworker.

"Prior to being deployed, I'd been investigating Mom and Dad's deaths. I was also investigating why Susan and David wouldn't let you stay with Nash and me. Nash's parents had already offered to let you stay with them so they wouldn't breakup the family more than it was. I did a DNA search on us when I couldn't find anything about our ancestors. I didn't believe the first lab test, so, I had the lab guys analyze the findings. They even rerun the test. They found the same information I had found. Once they realized it was me, they did the DNA on, and found that I had the two bloodlines, we started to look further into Mom and Dad's deaths.

"It was my last mission, or so I thought at the time. Nash, you'd been sent home with a gunshot wound. Another failed assassination attempt." My eyes land on his. They're tired and shadowed with dark rings; he's overexerted himself today and, by all rights, should still be in the hospital.

Nat slaps at Nash's arm. "Would you please stop getting shot! I'm tired of hospital chapels."

"I aim to please," Nash quips. We all chuckle as he gives her an apologetic half smile.

"Anyway, there were several times that both you and I got incredibly lucky and survived near death mishaps." The room is silent at my words as I stare at him. "So, when we put it all together, Major Bryant changed plans. A new guy came with us to cover for Nash. He told Major Bryant that he'd been approached by someone who needed me to disappear. That's when we decided it was time to follow through on my death. But Grover, my battle buddy, wasn't the only one who had been bribed. By the way, Grover is Walker's brother."

Nash's eyes widen with surprise.

"You mean all this time we were being fed intel from brothers?"

"Yeah, I know," I say. "Anyway, Major Bryant put me on one last mission, I just didn't realize it would take this many years.

"It was supposed to be a peacekeeping mission. We were in Afghanistan visiting different villages, bringing them supplies. The buildings were bombed out, and there were very few rations. We were playing with the children and handing out candy. You know how it is, it wasn't the first time we went into villages. Anyway, I saw a little girl sitting in the doorway. She wasn't playing with the other children. Instead, she stayed close to her mother. I glanced up at her mother, my Aliah, and my heart stopped beating. She took my breath away." I stare at Aliah. Tears fill her eyes. "She was and is the most beautiful woman I'd ever seen." I glance up into my wife's stunning cognac eyes and just how lucky I am. She smiles at me, and I feel like a little kid.

"I had candy in my pocket and kneeled with my hand out offering it to the child."

"Neelam?" Nat offers up the name with a quick glance at Aliah.

A proud smile spreads across my face. "Yes, and I can't wait for you to meet her. She's smart and beautiful like her mother and has the most unique blue eyes you have ever seen.

"Anyway, after taking the candy, there was an explosion. I lunged for the little girl and her mother, knocking them to the ground and covering them with my body. The building we were in protected us from the blasts, but it caused the building to begin to collapse on top of us. I was afraid I'd crush them, so I propped myself up with one hand, only leaving one to protect my head. Needless to say, I was struck in the head and blacked out."

Clearing his throat, Nash asks, "Your dog tags?"

"To be honest, I'm unsure how they fell off or were taken off, but they ended up around someone else's neck. And though it was hard for you," I glance at a teary-eyed Nat. "It allowed me to be invisible. No one knew the mission I was on except Major Bryant. When the explosion happened, it gave us the perfect opportunity for me to die, which was the plan all along."

"Baby, you were going to tell me about your dog tags and Connor." Aliah runs her fingers up my arm.

"I'll never stop believing things happen for a reason. So, evidently, when I was laid to rest, Nash was given my dog tags. When Louis shot him, the bullet hit the tags, causing the slug to ricochet away from all his vital organs and vessels."

"You're always watching my back bro." Nash claps me on the shoulder.

Nat yawns, her eye glassy with sleep. "I think it's time to get Nat some sleep," Nash says, wincing as he stands.

"I think it's time for you to rest as well. Don't play the martyr. You need to heal. Then I want to pick up where we left off sixteen years ago. It's time to make our business a reality."

Nodding, Nash takes Nat's hand and walks to the front door. "Christ, it feels good not having to look over my shoulder."

"Amen, brother," I say, and I take Nash into my arms. Tears well in my eyes. "I've missed you, man. God, I thought I was too late the other night. Too late to say thank you for your sacrifice these last eight years and for taking care of my baby sister."

Nash wipes his arm across his eyes. "I love her, I always have."

"I know."

Leaning down, I place a kiss on Nat's cheek. "I love you, sis. Go home and take care of this man."

"I love you too, Alec. Thank you for always being where I need you."

CHAPTER 49

I want love, passion, honesty, and companionship...
sex that drives me crazy and
conversation that drives me sane. ~Vishwas ॐ

ALEC

For the first time in God knows how many years, I feel like I'm finally free to live again. I can breathe without having to look over my shoulder.

I can finally take Aliah and Neelam out to dinner, to a movie. Hell, I can walk around town and watch Neelam graduate from college.

Emotions catch in my throat with the realization of what I've not only missed in my life, but how much I've missed with Neelam. Yes, I'm aware she didn't know any different, and her life here was far better than the life she was living, but just how fair was it? I make a promise to myself that I'll do everything in my power to make my ladies feel special and loved for the rest of their lives.

It's been a month, and I'm beginning to feel like a real person again. Nash and I have finally submitted all our paperwork to the state to start our security business. It's only taken sixteen years.

Where to start. I've been hiding for so long I need to reacclimate myself to the real world. I'm never going to hide again.

Nash moved back with Nat, and it feels like old times again. He hadn't told her that he never finalized the divorce, and even though they were still married, he asked her again. Aliah is putting all the plans together so this time I can walk Nat down the aisle.

Nat forgave Aliah, and their friendship has gotten tighter which is nice since we're backyard neighbors.

Nash and I found an office close to Nat's warehouse, and we signed the papers on it today. It's real; we've finally made it. Our dream is finally coming true.

On the way home, I make a slight detour.

Running my fingers through my hair, I can't believe the difference a haircut can make. Yes, I've had my hair cut over the years, but it's been fifteen years since my hair was this short. After Afghanistan, I began to grow it longer as a disguise. That and my beard. I decided it was time for a change and what a change it is. I look less like a mountain man and more like my old self. Although I did decide to keep the beard, but now it's more of a scruff and trimmed to perfection. God, I hardly recognize myself in the mirror. I look younger but older all at the same time. Laugh lines are carved into the skin around my eyes. This is the new me.

I can smell dinner as soon as I pushed though the garage door. I'm not sure what it is, but it smells amazing. Music is playing in the background, and I stand there watching her like a voyeur, moving to the beat.

Her back is to me, her hair is loose, cascading down her back to her waist. It's raven black, almost blue, and I love the way the lights glimmer off it. She usually has it braided, but God, I love it down, flowing like a waterfall, and I long to bury my face in it.

I must have made a noise, because she turns toward me. She sweeps her tongue over her bottom lip before sinking her teeth into it.

I'm caught, mesmerized and unable to move. She captivates me. Her eyes are huge pools of melted chocolate as she takes in my appearance. Her hand slips down her throat. Her neck is so delicately curved, and I know God made that neck just for me. I could spend hours just kissing and tasting it.

Our gazes collide and never let go as she walks over to me. She must have just worked out; she is still wearing a sports bra and shorts that have my dick straining behind the zipper.

Gripping my hair, she jerks me down to her mouth, grinding her hips into my hardening length.

My arms reach around her, lifting her. Her legs straddled me as I take decisive strides to the bedroom without breaking our kiss.

I have an insatiable appetite for Aliah. All she had known of sex was dominance and force, but after that first time, neither of us could get enough of each other. Our sex life was and is incredible. We've fucked in every conceivable place and position. The bed, on the floor, against the wall. Hell, we even did it on the spin cycle. All I can think of right this minute is that we're not naked yet.

Grasping at the edge of her bra, I lift it up and over her head as she wrestles with the buttons of my shirt. Placing her feet on the ground, my fingers find the waistband of her shorts, sliding them down her long-tapered legs.

"Lie down, baby," I murmur.

Lying on the bed, she slips to the middle, giving me a shy smile. Still after all these years, she's bashful every time we begin our foreplay.

I don't get insecure very often, but today is one of those days. I need to know she's mine.

I stand at the end of the bed, my hands touch and massage her legs; up her hips to her breasts. They're heavy with need as I press my lips between them. "God Aliah, I love you so much," I gaze up at her. Dropping my head, I press my lips to her stomach. "Why me?"

I once again look up at her. Her eyes are hooded, heated. "You made me yours that day in the street. I knew the minute your eyes met mine. Your soul spoke to mine, and I knew it to be." Her fingers curl in my hair, and she uses this to pull me to her. "I loved you from that moment, and I would do anything to make you mine."

I kissed my way down her body as she spread her knees apart for me. "Oh, God, Alec." I didn't answer, my lips were busy as I kissed from one hip to the other then the seam of her thigh, breathing in her fragrance. It is intoxicating. I know her taste, her sweetness, and I long to savor her on my tongue again.

Sliding my hands down her hips to her hot wet center, I spread her velvety lips open desperate to drink from her. My lips press against her opening, as my tongue sweeps between her slick folds plunging into her hot center, lapping at her, parting her farther. She gasps, gripping my hair, moaning with each push in and out. My thumb finds her hard nub, and I rub it. Her hips begin to grind into me. She's close as she writhes under me, little mewls whispering from her lips.

I slide my middle finger down her seam, thrusting into her as my tongue circles her clit. She whimpers as her pussy clinches down on my finger. She's franticly tugging at my hair. "Stop, please Alec, I want to come with you inside of me, please." I glance up from between her thighs and then crawl up her body, and my mouth crashes down on hers as I push into her.

This is different what I'm feeling. It's as if we've moved into a different stage in our life. The honeymoon stage is long gone, but this is more than the exploratory stage. This is our souls uniting as one, it is magical as our bodies move in unison. I can feel her body begin to quiver and for the first time she screams as her body shatters. "Alec, yes, yes, oh God! I love you so much, Alec." She was always so self-conscience, she never cried out when she came, but hearing her cry out like she's doing now, has me so turned on I can't hold back any longer as I erupt, exploding inside her. I don't ever remember a time I came so hard, not even as a horny kid.

Bracing myself on my forearms, I place a soft kiss on her swollen lips as I gaze into those golden pools. "I love you so much Aliah, I don't know how I got so lucky to find you."

WHEREVER OUR JOURNEY LEADS US

Tears fill her eyes at my confession. I kissed her, tasting her tears, claiming this new stage, reclaiming us.

CHAPTER 50

Find someone who makes you realize three things: one, that home is not a place, but a feeling. Two, that time is not measured by a clock, but by moments. And three, that heartbeats are not heard, but felt and shared. ~Vishwas ॐ

ALIAH
TWO MONTHS LATER

Nat liked the little chapel that Liam and Finn were married in so much, she decided it was there that she wanted to get married too.

Not only was it quaint, but it was there that she and Connor found each other again. Yes, they had some major hurdles, one being her ex-fiancé and let us not forget that Connor was shot... again. But people would have to be blind not to see how much they love each other.

I play a double role today; first as the Matron of Honor, and second as the wedding coordinator.

My stomach flutters with nerves. I don't understand why, other than I'm the one in charge of making sure Nat and Connor's wedding is perfect. Reaching into my emergency bag, I grab a couple of pink chewable tablets that are supposed to calm my stomach. Yes, I should have eaten this morning, but I needed to make sure today is everything that Nat has wished for since she didn't get it the first time around. I need to relax. *You have this, girl. This is your thing, and you are good at it.* I take a deep breath to calm myself then swallow a mouthful of water to rinse the chalky taste from my tongue.

The chapel is all dressed up. White tulle and rose swags down the aisle blocking everyone from walking along the delicate lace floor runner.

Knocking, on the dressing room door where Connor, Alec, and Liam are, I let them know it's time to find their places at the front of the chapel before rushing to Natasha's room. Connor and Liam have become very close friends and of course it only makes sense because without Liam and Finn's little secret at their own wedding, Natasha and Connor would never have gotten back together again.

Slipping into Natasha's room, I'm surprised when I see Neelam standing there. Tears fill her eyes. She's been away at school and wasn't going to be able to come back because of finals. My brows pinch together with confusion. I then see Natasha and Finn standing off to the side watching my reaction as the sound of the photographer snapping her camera blends into the background.

Out of the corner of my eye, I see Natasha's gown hanging on the mirror, but then pause. My mouth is agape. I must be losing my mind. I had been in here earlier helping her get into her dress. No, her dress has three-quarter sleeves and the one hanging is sleeveless with a high neck.

Then I notice the bouquets. One with dusty pink roses with ivory and burgundy rose accents and the other burgundy with dusty pink and ivory rose accents. Did I accidently order an additional bouquet?

My eyes flash to Natasha. "What?" My head tips to the side trying to understand, when I realize Natasha has her dress on. She has a mischievous smile on her face as she bites her lip. Her eyes glance to the other dress that hangs on the standing mirror. "Wha... It is... I don't..." Neelam steps to me, taking my hand in hers as Natasha and Finn scurry over to the mirror.

"Turn around," Neelam whispers as she turns me, unzipping my dress.

"I... I do not understand." My mind is racing as my dress slips down my shoulders, pooling on the floor at my feet.

"A long time ago, you told me about not having any friends or family at your wedding, well, when you walk down the aisle today, you will have a chapel full."

Tears fill my eyes, knowing she is right. Yes, the soldiers who came and helped me with the wedding were wonderful, but I could hardly speak English and there wasn't anyone there for me, but today, I have everyone here for me.

"And the dress?"

Finn smiles up at me. "I hope you like it. I took some mental notes when Nat was looking at all the different styles for herself. I listened and asked a couple of questions and put together a dress that I thought you would love." Finn had moved to Oregon to begin her career in sporting wear but found she has an eye for bridal gowns when she made her own gown.

Both Natasha's and my dress are similar but vastly different. Natasha's dress has baroque lace covered with thousands of beads. It hugs every curve and elongates her silhouette. It has a traditional look that juxtaposes a daring, plunging neckline with long sleeves and open back with twinkling ivory beaded straps. It is so classic, so Natasha. Connor will be lucky if he doesn't pass out when he sees her, and I can't wait.

As I step out of my Matron of Honor dress, the girls have me almost naked before I slip into some of the prettiest panties and bra that I've ever seen. I take my shoes off, and they slip the dress over my head as it easily slips over my curves.

It is a gorgeous A-line gown with a lace bodice and high neckline and the matching lace back. It is sleeveless and accentuates my shoulders. The flowing tulle skirt is adorned with matching lace appliques and buttons. It fits me like a glove. I do not ever think I have worn anything so beautiful.

Turning to look at the girls, I find them just staring at me. Feeling self-conscious, I try to glance in the mirror, but they are blocking it. "Does it look bad?" I ask.

Natasha's fingers cover her mouth as Neelam quickly hands her a tissue to dab her tear-filled eyes.

Finally, Neelam speaks. "When I was a little girl and you married Daddy, I thought you were a princess, but that doesn't even come close to how beautiful you are today." She hands me a tissue too as I fan my hand trying to stave off my tears.

"Okay," Finn says. "We have to hurry. She quickly removes the braid from my hair and pulls part of it up but leaves part of it down in wispy ringlets around my face. Then she reapplies a little blush and lip stain and gloss.

"Did Alec know about this?" I ask.

"No, we wanted to surprise both of you. Neither of us wanted to miss each other's weddings so we figured this was the easiest way to enjoy it."

"I do not even know what to say, other than thank you."

"How about, let's get both of you to your men!" Finn says, giggling.

CHAPTER 51

I'm amazed when I look at you. Not just because of your looks, but because of the fact that everything I've ever wanted is right in front of me. ~Unknown

ALEC

"I'm what?" I thought I was hearing things when Nash handed me a tux that looked just like his. I thought we were going low key, then he told me that I was renewing my vows.

"Nat and I want to witness you and Aliah getting married. We thought there was no better time than with us. I mean, Nat and I are still married and we're renewing our vows.

"Alec, I think it's cool that Nat and Connor wanted you to share this day with them."

"I just feel very unprepared," I mumble.

A knock at the door draws my attention away from the thought of not knowing what to say.

Liam strides to the door, opening it just a crack.

"Yes, I have an appointment with Mr. Nash and Mr. Turner," comes a voice from the other side.

Liam turns, shrugging his shoulders, but he has a mischievous look on his face. He can't keep the corners of his lips from curling up. What the hell is he up to? He pulls the door open, and a man walks in carrying a briefcase cuffed to his wrist.

Now I'm genuinely curious.

Lifting his unchained hand toward the table, he says, "Shall we?"

Raising a brow, I, glance over at Nash. "Oh, for Christ's sake, sit the fuck down." Liam huffs. "This is Mr. Randall. He's here to make sure you show your wives just how much you love them."

Mr. Randall pulls a key out from his pocket. First spinning the dials on the combination lock on the front of the briefcase, then unlocking the padlock.

Curiosity has me leaning over the guy's shoulder as Nash leans over the other. "Please gentlemen, take a seat."

Exchanged baffled glances, we dutifully obey.

"Mr. Tate has asked me to help you with a sensitive matter." Opening the sleek aluminum case, he pulls out a black leather tray, covered with a velvet lined cover. Removing the fabric, he reveals glimmering stones atop gold bands of all shapes and colors, buried deep down between black satin pillows. I almost gasp at the sight. I've never seen this much opulence in my life. I mean I've been to jewelry stores before, but these stones sparkle and shine so much more. I've never bought Aliah any jewelry other than the ring I bought her for our wedding and that was never a real wedding ring.

"Wow!" I say reaching but thinking better of it and yanking my hand back.

"What's the first ring that catches your attention? The one that makes you want to touch it?" asks Mr. Randall. "The one that tells her you will love her forever."

My eyes haven't left the white gold solitaire with the rose gold scrollwork on the front and back sides, with a small diamond centered below the main stone. The wedding band has the same scrollwork, but it has a row of small square diamonds circling half the band. It's stunning. Without giving it a second thought, I lift them from their confines. "This is it. This is the one. It's perfect for her," I say, glancing up at Mr. Randall.

The more I think about it, the more I want to tell her I would do it all over again, but this time, I'm going to be a present husband. All I ever wanted as a husband and father was to show just how much I love the two most important ladies in my life. I realize our situation isn't like any other, but I hope they know just what they mean to me. Without Neelam here today, I'm feeling a little off kilter. Afterall, it was her that drew me to her mother. I truly wish she could be here to witness us getting married again.

A tap at the door has me pulling my tux jacket on and fastening it. Aliah. God, she's here to see me. Wait, it can't be Aliah, she has to be getting ready too.

A shiver of excitement shoots through me at the thought of seeing her walk down the aisle to me again. My skin prickles with goose bumps. "Gentlemen, it's time. Please follow me." The pastor gives me a knowing smile as he turns and begins to walk away.

My heart skips a beat at the thought of what's about to happen.

When we got married before, I had a day to think about what I wanted to say, but today, I'm going to have to be spontaneous. Can I do that? The lump in my chest disappears, because my feelings have never changed. I love her more today than that day fifteen years ago.

Taking a deep cleansing breath, I relax, envisioning her as she walks toward me down the aisle once again, savoring the look I hope to see on her face when I slip her new ring on her finger.

CHAPTER 52

"Live your life from your heart. Share from your heart. And your story will touch and heal people's souls." ~Vishwas ॐ

ALIAH

I cannot contain the nervous smile that flourishes across my face. I think about the ring I had picked from the man with the briefcase. It was like in movies, with the shiny stainless-steel cuff around his wrist. This is a wedding not some busy city street.

I was not able to get My Alec a ring when we first got married, not that is was in my culture to give rings, but today, I want to give him something that shows him just how much I love him.

I knew the perfect ring as soon as the man, Mr. Randall lifted the fabric exposing the shiny treasures. The white gold with stripes of rose gold was striking. Black diamonds are channel set through the center making it exceptional and unique.

"Oh, Ali, that is so Alec. He'll love it." Natasha pulls me into a hug, whispering. "Ali, I'm so happy I'm finally going to truly be your sister, and that dress looks amazing on you, you're absolutely glowing." She pulls me to her again giving me an air kiss and I realize this is what a real friendship feels like.

Pulling Neelam aside, I take her hands in mine, swiftly blinking so I do not wreck my freshly made up face to the tears that are threatening to fall. Staring deeply into her eyes, she squeezes my hand. "What is it, Mom? Is everything okay? I'm sorry..."

I don't let her finish. I understand she is doing this for Alec and me. Although our first wedding was a wedding of necessity because of our situation. I was unfamiliar with the culture and the American rituals to genuinely enjoy everything around me. Now that I'm doing this as a profession, I understand the meaning behind it. "I would like you to walk me down the aisle and give me away." Tears fill my eyes as I fan my face to keep them from falling. "It would mean so much to me."

Unshed tears glimmer in Neelam's eyes, and I realize I have caught her off guard. "You want me..."

Cradling her face in my hands, I nod. "You were always my first love. You have been there for me in every moment of my life when I had no one else. Now I want you to give me away to the only man who I will ever love. Please say that you will do me this honor."

Neelam, nods, pulling me into a tight hug. "Yes, of course I will give you away."

Staring into her sparkling blue eyes, I kiss her cheek. "You are my beautiful blue gem, my Neelam."

CHAPTER 53

Make me that part of You that can never be separated ever again.
~Vishwas ॐ

ALEC

Okay, so I'm nervous. I thought I could overlook the feeling ricocheting off my brain, but I can't.

Glancing over at Nash, I see he's just as nervous as I am. Bumping his shoulder flicking a brow at him, I am rewarded when his face relaxes. Then the music begins.

I watch as both of Callie's boys walk down the aisle. Keller, Liam's son with Callie, and Luka, her youngest. Both boys are going to be trouble with the girls, with their dark moppy curls and their individually distinguishing eyes. Keller with bright blue eyes and Luka with emerald green. They already have the walk down, as they strut down the aisle in their black tuxedo pants and suspenders, white button-up shirts, and bow ties; one burgundy and the other a dusty rose.

As they make their way down the aisle, Keller stands in front of me and Luka in front of Nash. Next to come down the aisle is

Finn, Liam's wife. The music changes and my heart beats a frantic tempo at the thought of seeing Aliah.

I wish Neelam could be here. If I had known, I would have made sure she was here, even though she had her finals this week.

The curtain is drawn and, an audible gasp leaves my lips as Neelam and Aliah appear at the opening. By some miracle, or more likely manipulation by our friends, Neelam is here! And Aliah... My heart is in my throat at her beauty. She looks like a princess, her ivory gown contrasts with her golden skin and I can't wait to touch her. Yes, I know she's mine and has been for fifteen years, but goddamn, what this woman does to me.

She and Neelam stop feet away from me, and I can't take my eyes off her, and I swear on all things holy to make things right with her. I want to take her places we've never been able to go dancing, movies, hell, just to dinner on a date.

My thought is interrupted as the pastor asks, "Who gives this woman to this man?"

"I do," Neelam whispers.

Taking a step toward them, I lean over, kissing Neelam on the cheek before reaching my hand to my beautiful wife and escorting her to her position.

Once back in my spot, the music changes and again, the curtain is drawn revealing Nat in an elegant gown with long lace sleeves and a long train dragging behind her. Nash fights to stay, not only standing, but from running to her and my heart floods with love. Our family is back together. Finally.

The pastor motions for Aliah and me to come forward. She

hands her flowers to Neelam and take a step so we're facing each other. Staring into Aliah glistening eyes, I say the words that are in my heart.

"Aliah, although we've been here once before, I owe you a do over. I want to show you what a real husband is like. Not just in name, but in action too." Glancing over at Neelam, I motion for her to stand next to Aliah. "Neelam, I haven't been the father you needed or deserved, and I'm sorry for that, but I loved you both so much I couldn't leave without you. I just didn't know that I would have to hide for such a long time, and I'm sorry for that. I hope that someday I can make it up to both of you. I want to relive a moment in my life that I will always be proud of. A moment when I knew we all belonged together.

"Neelam, I hope you know that I love both you and your mother with all my heart. It was you who caught my attention, but it was both of you who stole my heart.

"Aliah, in you I have found my best friend, my confidant, my lover, my inspiration, my better half, and my soul mate.

"You have already taught me so much about the kind of person I want to be, the kind of parent I want to be. You love with your whole heart and soul and give all that you have whether it is deserved or not, whether it is appreciated or not, whether it is returned or not.

You are the strongest person I know. No matter what life has thrown at you, you have been able to thrive and prosper. You have an amazingly positive attitude, and your good humor is infectious, even to an old grump like me.

"I am far from perfect, this you know, of course, but you accept me for who I am and love me for my flaws not in spite of them. I know that you will always support me no matter what this life throws at us, even if you don't agree with me.

"I promise to always cherish you, honor you, respect you, be true to you and love you with every fiber of my being.

"I promise to protect and take care of you and Neelam and to hold you both in the palm of my hand for all the days of my life."

I reach my hand out, and Keller drops the rings in my hand.

Taking Aliah's hand, I slip off the ring I gave her fifteen years ago, moving it to her right hand, then sliding the new rings onto her finger on her left hand.

CHAPTER 54

ALIAH

I do not want to drop my eyes as Alec says his beautiful words, but I need to see why he is removing my ring. I mean I got him a ring, but that was because I never had the opportunity to get him one, but he got me a lovely lapis ring.

My eyes fall to my left hand as the warm metal slips up my finger. My breath hitches, catching in my throat when I see the rings My Alec has placed on my finger. Tears sting my eyes and the amazing gift he has given me.

Suddenly, my stomach roils. I am going to be sick. Tears spill down my cheeks as I cry. "I am sorry," before running toward the bathroom.

I feel like Cinderella as I grab my skirts and run as fast as I can, reaching a toilet just in time.

"Mom? Mom, are you alright?"

Neelam pushed through the bathroom door picking up my skirts out of my way as I retch. "Oh, Mom." She rubs my back the way I have with her.

Alec is at the door, panicked. I hear Nat at the outside door speaking to Alec. "Let me check on her, I have her kit with some water and mouthwash. Give me a minute."

More tears fall down my face and I afraid I have black smudges streaking down my cheeks. "Oh God, I just ruined your wedding," I cry

"You didn't ruin anything, and it's your wedding too." Natasha hands me a bottle of water, then pulls out a makeup wipe. "Here, let me get you cleaned up. How are you feeling?"

I take a sip of the water and rinse it around my mouth then spit it out. "Actually, I feel fine. Nothing like what I had been feeling."

Handing me a sample bottle of mouthwash, I swish it in my mouth. "Mommm," She draws out the word. "Just how long have you been feeling like this?"

Furrowing my brow, I stop the gargling, thinking back to when I felt normal. Spitting, I glance up at Neelam, confused. "A couple of weeks I think."

Natasha is on her phone, her fingers flying over the keys.

"Mom, could you be pregnant?"

Shaking my head, tears begin to fill my eyes again. "Damnit, I just cleaned those smudges. Let's get your makeup touched up," Natasha says, pulling out a pallet of colors.

"Mom?"

"Honey, I had several tests done several years ago." Gripping her hand, I close my eyes as Natasha uses a foam puff to even out my makeup. "They said it would be almost impossible to get pregnant. We tried for so many years and it just did not happen."

A tap on the door has me opening my eyes.

Natasha opens the door a crack, coming back with a grocery bag. Reaching into the bag, she pulls out a little rectangular box. Staring down at it, my eyes widen flashing up at her.

"I..."

"You know we're all thinking the same thing."

I'm speechless at what to say. I just grab the box and rip the end open letting the contents fall into my hand.

Could I really be pregnant? After all these years. Shaking the thought out of my head, I push the metal door open. "Um, I think I am going to need some help." I do not know what I was thinking. My gown fills the tiny room.

Working together, we manage to get me out of the dress so I can pee on the stick.

Natasha and Neelam help me slip my dress back on while we wait for the results. I am sure of what the answer will be, God knows I used enough of them.

Natasha finishes my makeup touchups and I can't put it off any longer. "Let's get this over with so we can finish the wedding and forget this little part of..."

Staring down at the little stick, it has me pausing. "What does it say?" Neelam steps toward me. Her hand flies to her mouth, gasping. Now tears are streaming down her face.

"No, it cannot be correct, I was told..."

"Mom, I've seen all kinds of things when I was in nursing school. Where's the second test you did? If it's negative, then we'll get another one."

I turn to grab the second test, my eyes drop to the little stick resting in Natasha's hand. Tears fill her eyes, but a smile lights up her face as she whispers, turning the test toward us. "Positive."

Oh my God! I cannot believe it; I am going to have another baby. Alec's baby. "Please don't say anything, I need to tell Alec. Promise?"

"Yes, of course," they both say, nodding their heads.

"And do not look guilty, this was just a mild case of..." I raise my shoulders in a shrug. "...food poisoning, yeah, that is it, food poisoning."

The bathroom door squeaks as I pull it open. Alec is hovering, a scared and concerned look etched into his features.

"Baby, are you okay?" he cradles my face, looking into my eyes.

Nodding, I give him my best lie. The first and only time I have ever lied to him, but it will be well worth it. I will call it a white lie. "Yes, I think I have a little food poisoning."

"Let's get you home then," he says, wrapping his arm around my waist.

Frantically shaking my head, I pull out of his hold. "No, please, I want to stay, I'll be fine. This is so special for us, and I want to see Natasha and Connor get married."

"Are you sure? If you're not feeling well..."

"I will be fine," I say, grabbing his biceps.

"If you're sure." He skeptically tilts his head, looking deeply in my eyes, and I put my best face on.

"Yes, I want to remember every single second."

Taking my hand, we walk back into the chapel. Everyone stands as we walk down the aisle. Natasha, Connor, and Neelam follow us as we take our places again.

"Well, I guess it is my turn now. Thank you everyone for your patience." I say, turning to face our friends and family. "But I had a good reason for running out."

Taking Alec's hands and staring deep into his sapphire blues, I speak from my heart.

"Fifteen years ago, I could barely speak any English, and I was living in a grim situation. Then you came into my life, showing me how gentle and kind a man could be, something I never knew. It did not take me long to fall in love with you and your kind, loving, and caring heart.

"As I have told you back then, I call you 'My Alec' because you are my everything. You still are

"I say these vows not as promises but as privileges. I get to laugh with you and cry with you; care for you and share with you. I get to run with you and walk with you; build with you and live with you."

"Alec, you are the one I want to spend the rest of my life with, my best friend.

"One smile from you brightens my whole day. But most importantly, you are the love of my life and you make me happier than I could ever imagine and more loved than I ever thought possible.

"I promise to love and care for you, and I will try in every way to be worthy of your love. I will always be honest with you, kind, patient and forgiving. I promise to try to be on time. I promise to never steal the covers unless, you are hogging them. But most of all, I promise to be a true and loyal friend to you.

"I will grow old with you and never stop growing with you. Through hard times and good times, through sickness and health, I will always be at your side.

"There is only been one thing that I failed at giving you. That is until today." Taking Alec's hand, I press it to my stomach. There is a loud audible gasp coming from our friends and family. "It was not food poisoning. It was morning sickness." I watch as Alec's eyes widen with comprehension of what I have just told him.

Tears fill his beautiful blue eyes until they spill down his cheeks. "I will love you for all the days of my life." Taking his left hand, I slip the ring on his finger, but I think he is still in shock over my revelation.

The wedding continues with Natasha and Connor, but Alec cannot seem to stop touching me, kissing me, and pulling my face to his. Kissing me as happy tears continue to roll down his cheeks.

I turn a look around when I hear a throat clear and then laughter coming from our audience. As I stare up at the pastor, he announces. "I would like to introduce Mr. and Mrs. Connor Nash and Mr. and Mrs. Alec Turner."

The crowed applauds and roars with congratulations as we walk down the aisle.

Unable to control his excitement, Alec swings me around in his arms. "I love you so much, thank you."

When Alec sets me down, Connor slaps him on the back. "Congratulations, brother."

"You knew and didn't tell me?" Alec growls.

"If that's the worse secret I was holding, let's call it even."

"Deal." Alec pulls Connor into a big hug as we are surrounded by our family offering their congratulations.

EPILOGUE

If you have faith and believe everything happens for a reason, it will make the really tough moments in your life mentally easier to handle. Do good. Help others. Be positive. And ride out the tough time. Something good is on the horizon if things aren't going right, right now. Life always balances itself out. ~Unknown

ALIAH

The last eight months have flown by. My pregnancy has not been textbook, as Neelam says. She finished school and graduated not long after we renewed our vows. She is now a nurse, and I am so proud of the woman she has become.

Zane Michael was born a couple of months ago, and he is truly a gift from God. He was early. They said it was due to my age and the issues I had trying to conceive, but I knew he would be alright even when they rushed him off to the neonatal intensive care unit. My Neelam was there to watch over him, and Alec was there beside his two children.

It will not be long before My Alec becomes an uncle. After renewing their vows, Natasha found out she was pregnant.

SM STRYKER

I never thought I could be so happy as I am right now. Life is not always easy. In fact, sometimes we have to fight for what we want; believe and trust in a higher power that we are given what we long for.

Never stop believing in what you want.

The End

For a preview of When You Loved Me, continue reading2

SYDNEY
FOUR YEARS EARLIER
"THIS IS YOUR LAST WARNING, HAND OVER THE INFORMATION YOU HAVE OR YOU'LL REGRET IT!"

Terrified, I turn, searching for anyone who looks suspicious. My hands tremble, shaking the piece of paper like a leaf in my gloved hand.

My heart thunders against my ribs, blocking my airway as bile once creeps up the back of my throat; tears sting my eyes.

I don't understand

I don't know what they want, and even if I did, what am I supposed to do with it?

I told Dad about the notes a couple of weeks ago, but he hasn't found any leads. Handing me a box of gallon size zipper bags and some black latex gloves, he said. *"If you receive any more notes, put a glove on and place it into the zipper bag."* He smiled, trying not to scare me, but the smile didn't show in his eyes. I knew it was serious, but I never thought just how bad it would get. *"Try not to touch it. I'll see if I can get prints off it."*

Then I received the knock on the door.

Kyler and I were cuddled up on the couch in the family room watching a movie. Although it was a kid's movie, I loved the bond the main character had with his late brother's friends and a big inflatable robot his brother built.

"I can't believe your dad got me into the police academy. It's what I've always wanted to do. Are you excited about studying photography?"

"I am. I've learned a lot with courses I've taken online and at the local community college, but I can't wait to learn more."

Lifting my chin, Kyler gazes deep into my eyes as he whispers. "I love you Sydney."

Reaching up, I palm his cheek. "I love you too, Kyler. I hope you'll always remember that."

I remember the picture on the screen of the TV when we paused it. The big robot grabbing and cradling the boy as they fell from a window; left forever in a freefall. He held the boy in a tight embrace to keep him from getting hurt.

Glancing at my phone, I was surprised that someone would be at our door this last at night.

Mom and Dad were on their nightly walk on the beach, leaving just Kyler and me. We had just graduated and didn't have to get up early, so we were enjoying one of our first nights as carefree adults.

"Were you expecting anyone?" Kyler asked as he hit pause on the remote.

Shaking my head, my brows pinch together wondering if I missed part of a conversation with my parents about company coming to visit. But I don't know who it would be. My parents were the only family I had. "No. Maybe it's Ms. Beasley needing to borrow something. I can't imagine my parents forgot their keys."

"Oh! Maybe she brought over some of her mac and cheese. That stuff is the bomb!"

"I know, right? It's the best." Both Kyler and I walk to the door. Glancing out the sidelight, the smile on my face falls when I realize it's not Ms. Beasley, but deputy police chief Dixon.

As the chief of police, I think nothing of it. It isn't anything unusual for an officer to come to the house to speak to my father when he's at home. Opening the door, I'm surprised at serious look on chief Dixon's face. Instead of his always friendly smile, his face is somber, his eyes red rimmed, and his face blotchy.

I'd never seen this expression on his face before. Tilting my head as I wait for him to speak, his eyes look anywhere but at me. It's then that I notice the police chaplain standing behind him.

Kyler's hand grips mine, giving me a reassuring squeeze. "Sydney, Kyler, may we come in?" His voice is quiet as he cleared his throat.

Moving from the door, they both step into the house. "My dad isn't here right now. Was he expecting you?" I ask, still not understanding his expression. My eyes flick between Dixon and the chaplain.

"Let's go sit for a moment." Kyler pulls me to the sofa in the living room. My stomach roils knowing but not wanting to acknowledge why the Dixon is standing in my house with a department chaplain and I realize this isn't a causal visit for my father.

This is more.

This is official.

Something happened and they're here for me.

My heart slams against me ribs in a rush of crashing blows in my chest as the blood thrums in my ears. Kyler grips my hand tighter understanding that the news we're about to be told is bad. All the while red noise is all I can hear roaring in my ears.

Silence filled the truck as Kyler drives me home from the cemetery.

The winding road from the cemetery overlooks the Pacific Ocean.

My home.

The place I thought I would always live.

My happy place.

The place that was filled with all my memories.

The place that I thought I would once eventually run as the bed and breakfast.

My parents' dream once my father retired.

I see it as if it were in slow motion. A black SUV with dark windows, swerves into our lane. "Fuck!" Kyler yells, his arm swings across my chest in a protective move, pressing me hard against my seat as he tries to control his truck.

My mouth opens as I try to scream, but nothing escapes my lips. Kyler slams his foot hard on the brakes as smoke from his tire's curls and twists behind us. We hit the gravel on the shoulder, as my eyes immediately fall to the jagged cliff below. The turbulent ocean water below pounding the rocks.

They won.

They said they would kill everyone I loved if I didn't give them what they wanted.

They won.

We're going to die.

Kyler's truck fishtails before coming to a skidding stop. We're both panting. Kyler's eyes are wide with fear and concern. Unbuckling my seatbelt, Kyler pulls me into his lap, cradling and rocking me like a child.

Tears blind me.

"Oh my God, Sydney, are you alright?" Pushing me away, he cups my ghostly white face, brushing the tears away I hadn't realized I'd released. "We could've died. It was if whoever that was tried to run us off the road."

I just stare at him. They did this because of me. First my parents now Kyler and me.

There's only one option.

I'll do anything to keep Kyler safe.

SYDNEY LEAVING ON A PLANE

New beginnings are often disguised as painful endings.

SYDNEY

"Are you sure you don't want me to come with you? I don't think it's a good idea for you to be by yourself." Becca, my best friend turns to face me. Her wavy brown hair pulled up into a messy bun. Her soft brown eyes full of concern, her mouth pinches together as she lays her hand on my arm. The constant flashing of red and yellow lights flicker through the windshield as rushing vehicles wedge between parked cars letting passengers out to rushing for their flights. I had nothing of importance to procrastinate over, so I decided to arrive at the airport early. Maybe I'd sit in the bar and have a drink or three before boarding my flight and think about what I want to do with my life. "I can rush home and grab a few things and come with you. I mean, your flight doesn't leave for three hours." Her brows knit together with concern.

Giving her hand a squeeze. "I'll be fine, Bec. This will be good for me." I give her a reassuring smile. "This assignment will be good. While I'm back there, it will give me the chance to finish the work my parents started on the house.

Who am I kidding? I hated the idea of going home. I'd escaped the small country town swearing never to return. Small town living was something I'd never wanted. All the gossip, everyone up in my business and worse, all the memories.

"But what are you going to do about the texts? What if he doesn't stop?" Becca's brows raise in concern, her head tilts in a questioning movement.

Shrugging my shoulders, my fingers nervously run through my hair, my lips pinch together. "I don't know, I just I have to do something because no one is safe. They found me here and I've been off the grid. I'm just tired of running. I'm older and if they get worse, I'll call the police right away. I'll be fine."

"And Kyler?"

A knock on my window has me jumping out of my skin. "You're not allowed to sit. Move on." An officer with a neon orange and yellow vest crosses his arms, my hand clutches my chest holding my heart in.

Nodding my acknowledgement, my hand hesitantly pulls the cold shimmering handle of the door open, blinking away the burning in my eyes. "I have to go. I'll call you when I get there." Grabbing my suitcase from the backseat, and my backpack filled with all my camera gear, I walk toward the terminal. Glancing over my shoulder, I watch as Becca inches her car away from her valued location at the curb, disappearing into the sea of cars fighting for her spot.

Exhaling a sigh, I shrug my backpack higher on my shoulder, wondering the same thing. What about Kyler? I'm sure he hates me, but I didn't have a choice. I had to get away. It was the only way to keep him safe.

Kyler might be over me, but I don't think I'll ever be over him. He was my biggest regret.

Finding a little bar after checking my luggage, I spot a small table in a dark corner. The last thing I want is to be around chatty people. I just need quiet and time to ruminate on the past. The server is at my tableside quickly. "What can I get you started with?"

"A lemon drop please." Her smile is pretty, but her eyes are tired, and I wondered if she's working her way through college as I had. The long hours, late nights and having to get up early for class in the morning, sucked. I don't miss those times. They were brutal. All I wanted was to get in, get out and be done with college.

Becca had moved shortly after I had to be with me, and as much as she liked to party, that really wasn't my thing. I had plans. It's funny how life changes in the blink of an eye.

My life had been all planned. I knew what I wanted to do. Then fate stepped in and shit on all my plans, turning my who life upside down.

All starting with the notes.

"Is there anything else I can get you?" The server slides my drink in front of me. God, how long had I been daydreaming?

"No, this is great for now, thank you."

"Just motion for me when you're ready for another." Giving me another sweet smile, she turns, walking back to the bar. Did I look I really needed another drink? Or does she think that I needed the liquid courage to fly?

Three drinks in and the need to pee, not to mention it's time to board, I pay my tab and search out the closest bathroom.

The jet is already full as I find my seat hoping I don't nail somebody in the head with my backpack. I stuff my treasured backpack full of my camera gear under my hopefully not needed floatation devise before tightening my seatbelt.

Peering out the window, I watch as the cart piled high with all our luggage is pulled up alongside the jet; our luggage being flung haphazardly onto the conveyer belt carrying our precious belongings into the belly of the aircraft. This is why I carry on my camera gear. I paid just about as much for my camera gear as I did my degree. I won't let some gorilla toss it around or better yet drop it.

My eyes are heavy as I close them, dropping my head back against the headrest. My ears highly attune to the banging and clunking of the doors and hatches being opened and closed as the prattling of the fellow passengers intensifies.

We had just finished our fourth bottle of wine; Runaway Bride is playing on the hotel big screen. Our hotel suite is huge, it was the size of the most envied apartment, but this is what Ryan wanted for Emma, so who was I to argue, after all, she was getting married tomorrow. I don't understand why they brought that particular movie. Why not Father of the Bride or My Best Friend's

Wedding? Emma was never the running type. She and Ryan found each other as freshman in college and four years later, they're getting married.

Sweet Home Alabama was always my movie? I've always loved that one. Although I never married Kyler and I'm not from Alabama, I did run away from my small town needing to get away. It wasn't just the small town. *Hell, I wouldn't have even thought about leaving if it wasn't for the notes or the memories of my parents; the cold morgue where Kyler held me as I identified their bodies. The look in Kyler's eyes—hell, everyone's eyes—as I stumbled out of the cold dark bowels of the hospital and left the coroner's office. Kyler supporting me to stand, to somehow walk out to his car.*

Emma is giggling, pulling me from my memories as Anna and Megan are swooning over Richard Gere. Becca refills my glass again. "I swear you guys better not let me sleep through the alarm," Emma says in a slight slur.

"As if," Becca huffs, as she carefully staggers back to the kitchen. "Oops, another dead soldier," She giggles dropping the empty wine bottle into the trash, eliciting a loud clattering crash as the bottle smashes against the other empty bottles.

This is our last hoorah, well at least for a while.

It's late, and I'm finding it hard to keep my eyes open. But there's no way in hell I'm falling asleep first; the last thing I need is for my bra soaked in water and stuffed in the freezer.

A giggle bubbles up in my throat as the memories of growing up in a small town and one of our infamous sleepovers Becca and I had, before life played a cruel joke on me. *We were high school freshman. A couple rom/com movies, a lot of pizza, popcorn, and candy later. I thought for sure I'd get sick. "If this is what college is like, no wonder the freshman fifteen hits you so hard."*

Everyone had finally fallen asleep except Becca and me. Bras soaked and currently being frozen... check. Next, we sprinkle glitter in their hair and over their exposed body. We tried not to laugh knowing it will take a good week to get it all washed out of their hair if not longer. It's a good thing we're such good friends. We were just finishing with the glitter when something hit the window. Shrieking, I slap my hand over my mouth. The lid was still off the ultra-fine glitter that was clutched in my hand as it sails out everywhere. My face, hair, clothes. Did I say everywhere. Geez, it's even in my mouth, coating my tongue and the roof of my mouth. I'll be a freakin' unicorn shitting glitter for a week.

Becca grabs my hand dragging me outside, tears roll down her face. She's laughing so hard I thought she was going to pee herself.

Keeping my eyes closed so I didn't get the glitter in them, she pulls me out onto the front lawn. "What the hell hit your window? It scared the shit out of me." Bending over slapping at my face and flicking my hands in my hair to hopefully shake the glitter from my body, I freeze when I hear the low timbre of the gorgeous boy who's turning into a beautiful man.

"We thought we'd come over and crash your sleepover." The rich baritone of Kyler Wiley's voice had goose bumps peppering my skin.

Oh. My. God!

Slowly lifting my face toward the voice of the boy who I've had a crush on all year, and he sees me like this? I think I'm going to die!

Little prisms of light dance in my eyes as the streetlights hit the remaining glitter still caked on my face. Kyler's hands are stuffed into the front pockets of his distressed jeans. My tongue brushes across my lips when my eyes fall to the rip at his knee. His T-shirt hugs the hills and valleys of his chiseled chest and I fight the temptation to slide my fingers down them. His flannel button-up hangs open as if it were a jacket.

I begin to gag as the glitter coats my tongue. Spitting, my hands automatically lift to my mouth as I try to wipe the sparkling mess out of my mouth.

"Um, Syd, you do realize you probably have more of that shit on your hands and you're just putting more of it in your mouth."

My eyes lift to Kyler's, a cute smirk twists his lips. His tongue sweeps across his lip as mine mimics his, and again, more glitter... Ack!

I stare as Kyler walks over to the faucet. My eyes trained on his backside. God, those jeans look good on him. I swear drool slips from the corner of my mouth.

I don't know if it's because of the glitter or the way he looks as he bends over turning the water on. GAH!

Quickly I wipe at my face, but again... UGH... glitter.

Dragging the hose over to me, he holds it up to me.

"Try to rinse it off your hands first, then wash your face." Running my hands under the ice-cold water, scrubbing my them together, I wash the majority of the glitter from my hands before cupping them together and filling them with water and splashing my

face. Lastly, after filling my mouth with water, I swish it around and spit it out.

The ground begins to glimmer from the prank that seriously backfired on me.

Opening my eyes, they fall to my feet, before sliding up my legs to the ratty sleep short and threadbare tank. I had taken my bra off and hid it just in case I had fallen asleep before anyone else. Fat chance that will happen now. I don't think I'll sleep for a week after tonight.

My eyes land on my chest. My dark pink nipples, hard and prominent as they protrude through the tight thin material of my top. My eyes flash to Kyler's face. His eyes are focused on my chest. No, on my nipples that blatantly scream, 'look at me'. His eyes suddenly flash to mine as a hint of a blush covers his face.

Abruptly, he turns his back to me as if embarrassed, swinging the hose which, he's still holding on too as he turns. A squeal escapes my mouth as the stream of water hits my chest soaking my already see-through tank, and cold water sluices down the front of me. Frightened at what made me scream, Kyler swings back around as the water from the hose, still in his hands, once again douses me.

Meanwhile, Becca is standing back out of the way with Mackenzie—Mac as his friends call him—laughing so hard tears are streaming down her face. She's bent over laughing as Mac replicates Becca's reaction.

"A towel would be great, Becca." I couldn't help the sarcasm that dripped from my shivering voice.

Still laughing, she says, "Oh, yeah, sorry." She clears her throat as she and Mac disappear into the house.

Looking down at my chest, you could see everything. Heck, you couldn't even tell I had a shirt on. Quickly I wrapped my arms around myself trying to hide. "Shit! I'm so sorry Sydney." He drops the hose, removes his flannel shirt, and wraps it over my shoulders.

"Thank you," I say through chattering teeth.

Our eyes lock.

And yes, I do read trashy romance novels, but it's like they say. There was a connection. We didn't have to say anything, it's as if our eyes were talking, as though we were communicating with our souls. His hand cups my face. His thumb brushed across my cheek as his scent from his shirt floats around me. I'm dizzy with stimuli overload. My heart races in my chest and I can't breathe with the lump in my throat.

My first kiss.

Oh my God. My first kiss! And it's with Kyler Wiley.

Leaning in, his lips are an inch from mine. His warm breath whispers across my face. Our eyes are searching. Closing my eyes, leaning forward, our lips...

The sound of a text on my phone pulls me from memory lane. Why am I thinking about Kyler? That was four years ago and I'm sure he's moved on, not to mention, he hates me.

I know why I was thinking of him. I miss Kyler.

Wine has definitely been flowing free tonight and I wasn't feeling a lot of pain as I sashayed over to my phone giggling. My newly filled glass of wine sloshing over the sides.

"Is that one of the guys you've been seeing lately, hoping to hook up before you skip town?" Becca asks in a seductive tone.

Giggling, shaking my head. "Nope, he has a *special* ringtone." We all bust out laughing again.

"Don't even understand why you even have your phone on," Emma's eyes are hooded as the alcohol consumes her. "Your phone is disrupting my concentration on keeping my buzz on.

Glancing down at my phone, not recognizing the number, I'd been getting messages about the photo shoot that I'd been hired to do back home.

Glancing at the clock, I'm surprised anyone would contact me this late though.

Staring at the text, it wasn't like the others. This text took me by surprise and changed everything in a heartbeat.

Pulling up my messages my eyes scan over the words boldly staring at me. The carefree drunken smile dies on my face, instantly sobering me. My body heats as the pounding of my heart echoes in my ears. Tears sting my eyes as I try to blink them away.

"God, Syd, what is it?"

Not able to answer, I just shake my head and continue to read as the first tears roll down my cheek.

The message was a series of photos. The accompanying message simply said.

Unknown texter: "You think moving to the East Coast was going to stop me from finding you?"

The photos were of Kyler, the inside of my parents' home and of the girls and I at the rehearsal dinner tonight. Fuck, they're here.

My brain couldn't comprehend the message; it simply couldn't compute. "What the hell is going on?" There was no questioning the legitimacy of these messages and pictures. They had found me. After four years of silence, they were back.

My heart slams into my ribs taking my breath away as all the blood drains from my face.

Unknown texter: *"You thought you could run and hide. Think again."*

Unknown texter: *"I guess what happened to your parents wasn't enough of a threat. Guess who's next."* A photo of Kyler followed the text.

My stomach roils as nausea ravishes me. Running to the toilet, I throw the lid up just in time to deposit the contents of my stomach.

Becca follows quickly behind me holding my hair back as Anna hands me a bottle of water.

Another photo of Kyler pops up on the screen.

Me: *"No, please. Tell me what it is that you want. I don't even know what you're looking for."*

Each message, each photo was like a knife being thrust into my heart. Tears spill down my cheeks. Anna's wedding is only hours away.

"Oh Fuck, Sydney. What are you going to do?" Becca whispers. "You can't go back there. It's one thing to go for a quick photo shoot, but this..."

"I don't have a choice. He has pictures of all of us. I can't risk it. I won't."

Me: *I'll fly out tomorrow, but I need to know what I'm looking for. At least give me a clue.*

The girls, my best friends, are now all huddled around me. "I can't just not go. I'll do anything to stop this." A sob escapes my lips. "How did they find me?

I wait for a reply, but nothing comes.

So here I am, flying back home.

SYDNEY ARRIVING HOME

SYDNEY

The flight to Oregon was long but as I drove to the house, I grew up in my insides began fluttering with excitement. When did that happen? I'd never thought I would come back here. Maybe it's the returning to what I know. The idea of getting away from the noise and the stress of the city sounds appealing. I just need and try to relax, forget about the last couple of days; hell, the last four years.

I called the property management letting them know I wouldn't be needing their assistance any longer and that I would be moving back into the house. Luckily, since most of the tenants were vacationers and only using the house for weekends and since the home is fairly expensive to rent due to the size of the house, there were only a couple of dates I would have to work around and hopefully I will have the bed and breakfast up and running by that time and I will honor their reservations.

The hazy golden sun is slowly rising in the sky as I drive into town. I'm exhausted and just want to sleep, but my body is on auto pilot, without thinking, I drive my rented Jeep down onto the beach and watch the lazy sun stretch its warm rays as they glimmer down the surf.

I had taken the red eye after Anna's wedding, allowing me to sleep part of the way here.

The beach is nearly empty except for a couple of men with metal detectors and a jogger with her dog. It's usually quiet this early in the morning, but I always loved being out here when it's quiet out. It's usually too cold for vacationers to be out this early. Slipping my feet out of my sandals I step out onto the cool moist sand. Rolling my jeans to my knees, I grab my hoodie shrugging it over my head. Walking toward the lapping waves I take in the beauty that surrounds me. Mornings were always chilly; the summer was no exception.

I have to say, this is one of the only places I could clear my mind and think. Maybe that's the reason I needed to come home, even though my parents are no longer here, this is where I feel closest to them. Brushing away the tear that slips down my cheek, I think back to that horrible day. The visit that changed my life forever.

I've been walking for a while, when I hear the roar of an engine quickly approaching. Swiftly wiping back my tears, I just continue to walk.

"Unless you want a ticket for driving your Jeep..." Turning, my hoodie pulled up protecting my face and neck from the morning wind and hiding me from all the busybodies who would want to meddle in my business, my eyes lock on the beautiful blue gaze, of the boy—no, the man—who I left behind He. is shouting at me through the passenger's window of the patrol truck, his extremely angry eyes stare back at me. "Syd?" His voice is deeper than I remember but still floated over my skin like melted caramel. Smooth and rich, and when he said my name, goose bumps peppered my skin, and it wasn't from the cool morning air. I wanted to melt in his arms the way I did all those years ago. But things are different now, and I've changed, and by the furious look in his eyes, he hasn't forgiven me either. "Get in, I'll take you back to your car."

My tongue flicks to moisten my wind-chapped lips, shaking my head. I can't do this now. It's not that I didn't think I would see Kyler Wiley—my best friend, my high school sweetheart, my first love, first kiss, my first... everything, I just didn't think it would be on my first day back. And now he's a cop.

Just like Dad.

He looks good. Really good. His golden skin tells me he's still a sun worshiper. His hair is a little shorter, but still long enough that it curls at the ends and the stubble on his face has finally filled in. Smiling to myself, I remember when he tried for the stubble look in school, but the hair on his face wouldn't cooperate. Every time he tried to grow it out, he would have bald patches which would frustrate him, so he kept it shaved. God, that's not a problem now. The sun shone on his bronzed face. The golden red undertones of his beard glimmered in the morning rays. My stomach somersaulted, and girl parts begin to throb. *God, Sydney, what are you thinking. You left him.* I didn't leave him at the altar, but there was supposed to be one. He'd even talked to my dad.

But that all changed. I couldn't stay here anymore. I wasn't trying to be selfish; it was to protect everyone I loved. I'd already failed my parents. I wouldn't do that to my friends, to him.

Turning, I begin walking back to my Jeep. Kyler's engine revs as he spins his truck around. This time he is barking out orders through the driver's window. My pace quickens. "Get in the truck, Syd." His tone is hard.

"I'll walk back." My voice is defiant as if I were a petulant child.

"Damnit, Sydney. Stop being so pigheaded. The tide is coming in and by the time you walk back, your car will be under water. I don't think I have to tell you what kind of environmental damage that will do to our little piece of heaven."

Stopping, my head falls. Water washes over my feet as the sand melts away underneath them. I watch as little sand shrimp quickly bury themselves in the melting sand. I'm such a fucking mess. Why did I think I could come back here walk on this beach and think I wouldn't run into my past?

"This was a bad idea," I mumble to myself.

Kyler stops. "Get the fuck into the truck, or I'll physically put you in myself. Then I'll arrest you for resisting," his voice is more than tinged with anger, malice and spite. It wasn't the old Kyler, the one I loved and walked away from. This Kyler is mean and full of hatred.

Taking a deep breath, I exhale, dropping my shoulders, I give into his threat, walking around the hood of the truck. Kyler leans over pushing the door open. Slipping into his warm truck, I pull the door closed, my eyes stare out the side window, the hood of my sweatshirt still covering my head, trying to brush back the overwhelming emotion not only slipping down my face, but ripping at my guts.

Stupid, stupid, stupid idea.

We're not moving, and I don't understand why. Turning to see what the problem is. I can see he has the same emotions haunting his face as well. "Seatbelt." He barks out as he turns to me. His face lifeless of any emotion. "Seatbelt, put it on." Of course, even driving on the beach he would go by the book. Pulling the strap across my chest, I fasten it with a click. "Thank you." His words are a quiet whisper.

My attention returns to the view out the side window. "You became a cop." *Duh! That was only obvious. What gave it away? Maybe the police truck or maybe the uniform?* I didn't turn to him when I spoke.

"Your father was the dad I never had. Of course, I followed in his footsteps. I lost him that day too or did you forget? He also got me into the academy."

The tension in the truck is thick and I can't slow the pace of my thundering heart. We pull up to the Jeep. I can't get out of the truck fast enough. Jumping out, I turn back to him. "He would have been proud of you. He always thought of you as the son he never had. He loved you too." Swallowing the lump of emotion in my throat. "Thank you for the ride." Turning, I quickly shut the door.

"Sydney."

I hear him calling after me, but I ignored him.

"Sydney."

Again, all I can do is ignore him. I wasn't ready for this. I wasn't ready to go down memory lane with Kyler Wiley, the memory of his face when I told him I couldn't stay here any longer. I needed to experience the world, to see what I'd been missing in this tiny little town, and that I didn't' love him. What a lie. I just couldn't stay with the memories that were locked away in my heart. We were a family, and then they were gone.

And the notes. God, they were the real reason, I wouldn't risk it.

I climb into the Jeep, my hands gripping tight to the steering wheel. I start the engine, then slam the gears into drive and flip a uey, exiting the way I came in, leaving Kyler on the beach, just like I did all those years ago.

KYLER WATCHING SYD LEAVE BEACH

You may have been destroyed in a thousand ways. But now you
know a thousand ways to rebuild yourself.

~Vishwas ॐ

KYLER

Staring at the Jeep as it drives out of sight, my heart thunders in
my chest and I'm sure I'm having a heart attack.

Glancing at my watch, my mind spins with dates and numbers.
It's been four years, three weeks, two days and about two hours
since I'd last seen Sydney.

I don't think about her every day anymore. Although this is a
small quiet town, to function properly in a job that requires my
complete attention, I just can't allow such thoughts to occupy my
mind. So, I block them. Now what do I do now that's she's back?
What hurt the most was being so close and then watching her walk
away, as if ripping my heart out didn't faze her.

While a trickle of memories of her faded somewhat, other
memories of her are so vivid, so intense as if it were just yesterday.
Her scent, the way her thick auburn hair slipped through my

fingers, the spattering of freckles that danced across her cheeks and nose, her laughter, those emerald green eyes that could cut through me with a single glance, stealing my heart as they sparkle when she smiles, seeing everything I felt. It's the connection that I looked for in others but could never find. Her fiery temper, God, yes, I remembered everything from her.

I went out of my way not to ask Mac anything about her.

Mac is my best friend and now owns what used to be called The Tipsy Squid, which was promptly renames to Mac's Place when he bought it. It used to be an old rundown tavern that had been owned by his uncle. When his uncle Ben decided to retire, Mac bought it from him and remodeled it, turning it into a restaurant and bar, booking up and coming bands to come in and play on the weekend, Mac's Place is now the hottest place in town to go.

During high school, it was always the four of us; Mac, Becca, Sydney and me. And even though Mac and Becca never had a physical relationship, they still stayed in close contact with each other. Becca has been Sydney's best friend all her life, even moving across the country to be with Sydney when she left me. We were all concern about her after her parents were killed.

Even though I always said I didn't want to know how Sydney was doing, I was just lying to myself, and now after all these years, she's back, stirring up all the old emotions that I'd buried. Emotions that are now running rapid inside of me.

Hate.

Love.

Anger.

Friendship.

Resentment.

Passion.

Loathing.

Love... Love.

Love, God, I've missed her so much. She was my best friend, and when she told me she didn't love me and needed to leave, she shredded me, gutted me, leaving me clinging to life. I not only lost the two people that I considered my parents, but I lost the girl that I planned to grow old with, have a family with, our family, my family.

What brought her back. I never thought I would see her again. But, fuck... she looked... Amazing, so goddamn beautiful but also, so sad. Why was she sad? *Damnit Kyler, why do you care. She left you... Left you! Who does that to their best friend?*

Frustrated, I slam the truck into gear, hitting the gas as the back of the truck fishtails, sand spraying into a high rooster tail in the deep loose sand before the tires grips the asphalt jerking the truck straight. This day can't get over fast enough.

My truck has a mind of its own. Several times today, I've found myself driving past the old Carmichael place just to see if I could catch a glimpse of her. I needed to see her again.

CHARACTER PROFILES

ALEC TURNER
NATASHA'S BROTHER
HAIR: DARK BROWN
EYES: ICY BLUE
HEIGHT: 6 FEET 2 INCH

ALIAH JAN TURNER
HAIR: BLACK
EYES: CARAMEL
HEIGHT: 5 FEET 9 INCH

NEELAM JAN TURNER
ALIAH'S DAUGHTER
HAIR: DARK BROWN
EYES: BLUE
AGE: 5

AGENT CONNOR NASH
HAIR: SALT & PEPPER
EYES: CHOCOLATE BROWN WITH GOLD FLECKS
HEIGHT: 6 FEET
LIAM'S HANDLER

NATASHA TURNER NASH
OWNER OF ELEGANT DREAM EVENTS
HAIR: DARK BROWN
EYES: ICY BLUE WITH SILVER FLECKS
HEIGHT: 5 FEET 10 INCH

WHEREVER OUR JOURNEY LEADS US

Nash's wife

Louis Kingston III
Natasha's betrothed
Hair: Salt and Pepper
Eyes: faded blue
Height: 5 feet 9 inches

Susan and David Welch
Natasha's aunt and Uncle

Walker
Agent
Hair: Shaggy blond hair with manbun
Eyes: Caramel
Height: 6 feet 1 inch
Psychology, Criminal Justice & Linguistics

Jenkins
Agent
Hair: Dark Brown
Eyes: Icy blue almost grey
Height: 6 feet 4 inch

Grover
Marine — Battle Body
Hair: Golden blond
Eyes: Light Brown
Height: 6 feet

Liam Tate
AKA Maison Keller
AKA Matthew Cleary
AKA Scott
Co-Owner of Saber Elite
Hair: Dark Brown
Eyes: Brown

SM STRYKER

HEIGHT: 6 FEET
CROOKED SMILE WITH A SLIGHT CROOKED TOOTH THAT LOOKS
SEXY

STEFANI (FINN) BARNETT
HAIR: BLONDE
EYES: BLUE
HEIGHT: 5 FEET 8 INCH
FASHION DESIGNER
ROSE RED — HER CAR
LUCY — LC9 HER RUGER

MARK CLEARY
LIAM TATE'S IDENTICAL TWIN BROTHER
HAIR: DARK BROWN
EYES: BROWN
HEIGHT: 6 FEET

CALLIE BAILEY STERLING
CO-OWNER SABER ELITE
HAIR: LIGHT BROWN
EYES: CERULEAN BLUE
HEIGHT: 5 FEET 7 INCH

KAI STERLING
OWNER STERLING REALTY
CALLIE'S HUSBAND
HAIR: DARK, ALMOST BLACK
EYES: GREEN — EMERALD

KELLER STERLING
CALLIE AND LIAM'S SON
HAIR: DARK, ALMOST BLACK
EYES: BROWN
AGE: 8

LUKA STERLING

WHEREVER OUR JOURNEY LEADS US

CALLIE AND KAI'S SON
HAIR: DARK, ALMOST BLACK
EYES: GREEN — EMERALD
AGE: 5

STELLA ABELLA
MOM OF ALEC AND NATASHA TURNER
HAIR: DARK BROWN
EYES: BROWN

MARCO ROBINO
DAD OF ALEC AND NATASHA TURNER
HAIR: DARK BROWN
EYES: ICY BLUE

TITLES BY SM STRYKER

-----~"*°•.♡.♡.♡.•°*"~-----

SECOND CHANCE SERIES

-----~"*°•.♡.♡.♡.•°*"~-----

THEN THERE WAS YOU SERIES

-----~"*°•.♡.♡.♡.•°*"~-----

SM. STRYKER

If you enjoyed this book, you can help others enjoy it as well by recommending it to friends and family, or by mentioning it in reading and discussion groups and online forums. But whether you recommend it to anyone else or not, thank you so much for taking the time to read my book! Your support means the world to me!

You can also review it on the site from which you purchased it. Did you know leaving a review helps authors get seen more. If you enjoyed this book, I would love to hear from you.

I really appreciate you reading my book! Here are my social media coordinates:

https://www.facebook.com/Author.S.M.Stryker
https://www.facebook.com/groups/149790685660456/
www.smstryker.com
shelly@smstryker.com
https://www.tumblr.com/blog/shellystricker
https://twitter.com/smstryker
https://www.goodreads.com/author/show/8389427.S_M_Stryker
https://www.bookbub.com/authors/s-m-stryker
https://instagram.com/s.m.stryker/

ABOUT THE AUTHOR

As an Amazon Bestselling author, SM Stryker writes stories that are deeply emotional with subjects that lean toward the taboo; subjects she learned and lived as a child, then later as a teen and young adult. She has always believed that things happen for a reason. That is the message she often tries to portray. Her books are filled with raw emotion and grit, but also inspiration, showing the reader, they too, can survive all things.

Outside of writing... is there such a thing? I'm just a regular country girl from the Pacific Northwest. I've been married to the love of my life, for almost thirty-one years, have four beautiful daughters and four amazing grandbabies. I don't watch a lot of television other than football and softball. I'd like to say I love working out, but... Nah. I'm a huge creature of habit, most evenings, and weekends you can find me in front of my computer. I try to read every day or listen to books on audio when I can't. I'm quiet and shy by nature, which, if you don't know me, some would think I were a bitch but ask me about my books, and you will see me bloom and open like a rose. If I don't get the chance to write ... watch out. Writing is my solace. I love diverse types of music and when I get hooked on a group, I'll listen to them and only them for months at a time. Playing their CD incessantly.

I learned a few years back, that life is unpredictable and to not to take your loved ones for granted, you never know what each day will bring. So, hold tight to your loved ones, tell them you love them, while you have the chance.

I hope you enjoy my stories.

Made in the USA
Middletown, DE
24 November 2020